PRAISE FOR *S*

'Sweet and spicy, fun and witchy, and altogether delicious!' Sarah Beth Durst, *New York Times* bestselling author of *The Enchanted Greenhouse*

'A feel-good and atmospheric story of magic, second chances, and belonging.' Jessica Gadziala, *USA Today* bestselling author of *My Big Fat Vampire Wedding*

'A sexy, hexy second-chance witchy romance that will sweep you off your feet (or broom).' Hazel Graves, author of *Four Weddings and a Funeral Director*

'Agatha Willow has invoked romance at a coven-worthy level.' Sofia Shelley, author of *Dead Poets Sorority*

'Pure magic—a bewitching tale of romance and whimsy!' Carly Bloom, author of *Hot Hex Boyfriend*

'A sweet, witchy romance with cozy vibes and plenty of heat. If you love sapphic yearning, academic settings, and a dash of magic, this book is for you.' Susie Dumond, author of *Bed and Breakup*

READERS LOVE *SPELLFIRE*

'A great mix of lust and angst, combined
with a quirky cast of characters that you'll
really want to be friends with.'

'Sweet, spicy and funny romantasy. I love the
setting. I love the characters. Both FMCs are very
funny and witty. A lovely read!'

'I absolutely loved the cozy vibes, definitely a good
read for coat season. I absolutely loved the characters.
I can't wait to read more from this author.'

'A spicy second chance romance? Sign me UP.'

Agatha Willow lives with three mischievous cats and one witchy teenager. Ze firmly believes in science, magic, and love, and zir favorite type of story includes all three.

SPELLFIRE

AGATHA WILLOW

avon.

Published by AVON
A division of HarperCollins*Publishers* Ltd
1 London Bridge Street
London SE1 9GF

www.harpercollins.co.uk

HarperCollins*Publishers*
Macken House, 39/40 Mayor Street Upper
Dublin 1, D01 C9W8, Ireland

A Paperback Original 2025
2

First published in Great Britain by HarperCollins*Publishers* 2025

A catalogue record for this book is available from the British Library.

ISBN: 978-0-00-877943-6

This novel is entirely a work of fiction. The names, characters and incidents portrayed in it are the work of the author's imagination. Any resemblance to actual persons, living or dead, events or localities is entirely coincidental.

Set in Sabon LT Std by HarperCollins*Publishers* India

Printed and bound in the UK using 100% Renewable Electricity at CPI Group (UK) Ltd

MIX
Paper | Supporting responsible forestry
FSC™ C007454

This book contains FSC™ certified paper and other controlled sources to ensure responsible forest management.

For more information visit: www.harpercollins.co.uk/green

*For Amy and Courtney, without whom none
of this would have happened.*

1

The first thing Bryn Delmar noticed when she got out of her rental car at the gates to Grimoire Academy (*Providing excellence in the education of young witches since 1919*) was that absolutely nothing had changed since she'd graduated five years earlier. The same distant, looming Spanish Revival main building (a castle, naturally), all archways and columns and the telltale monument of two crossed broomsticks on the roof, which marked all witching schools; the same palm trees overhead (uplit by cleverly charmed lights), which were currently stained pink by the sunset.

The broad coastal view was also the same. The Pacific spooled out into the horizon, vast and endless, increasing Bryn's feelings of loneliness. She did, after all, come from a family of sirens; of course the ocean felt like home. But she resented it for making her feel that way, especially now, after she'd tried so hard to find a new home. She'd moved to the mountains, to a city with a far different skyline and a more contained view, without the sprawl of *forever*.

Yet, standing here in Grimoire again, the sensation was unavoidable: this was her home, even though she hated it a little bit. Sometimes *more* than a little bit.

The subtle hum of magic was also the same. Most individual witches weren't strong enough to make the air around them vibrate, but a magical institution, housing many of them (some of whom were quite strong), definitely altered the space it inhabited. A "magical planar field" was how the physicists referred to it in those books she'd bought when she still intended to study the subject. The ability to sense such things had marked her as different from her mother and sister, both sirens. It was also what had gained her early entrance to Grimoire Academy at the age of just thirteen.

"But you're a siren," her mother had said, with that familiar edge of *I don't know what to do with you* desperation that had been such a feature of Bryn's childhood.

"I . . . think I'm a witch, Mom." She remembered holding up the glossy Grimoire Academy pamphlet. "Like they are."

At the time, the look of resignation on her mom's face had been a victory sign—she was going to say yes! Only later did Bryn wonder how hard it had been for her mom, a proud siren, to raise an odd little witch she didn't understand, and then to send her off to a school, entrusting her to strangers she understood just as little.

Which reminded her that although she was back at the school, her favorite professor was not. Professor Herringbone had been the best thing about Grimoire Academy. She'd died suddenly the month before, leaving Bryn her beloved library. When Bryn had asked if the collection could be mailed, the unknown woman on the

2

other end of the phone line (whom she'd pictured as a permed-and-blue-tinted old lady with a furrowed brow and glasses the right shape to peer over in irritation) had coughed and said she didn't have the staff to take on "such a project" and that the rooms would need to be cleared, so if Bryn wanted the books, she'd have to come herself. It had seemed like such a dismissive way to treat the belongings of a professor who'd made Grimoire Academy her life, and who'd cared so much for the school and its students.

Raw emotion caught Bryn off guard and she steadied herself against the car, before turning back to the wrought-iron gates. The wind picked up, blowing hair across her face. She was jittery with nerves. The flight from Denver had been delayed, and she'd forgotten (or repressed?) the dire state of the traffic, which meant that not only was she late, but she also hadn't stopped to pick up boxes and packing tape. No doubt she could find shipping supplies on campus somewhere.

She could do this. She was an adult now. It had been five years. Sure, she'd suffered here, but didn't everyone in high school? Embarrassment, public humiliation. This was where she'd been betrayed by her first love—well, her first girlfriend, anyway. In retrospect, *love* was laying it on a bit thick. And who needed love? Good sex was easy enough to find without having to fling open the gates of your heart, just to have it ripped out. She'd always been a loner and she was happy that way.

Well, content at least. Right?

She shook her head, trying not to examine that claim too closely.

In an attempt at distraction from her thoughts, from the gate she really needed to walk through any minute now, she looked around more carefully. Only then did she notice the things about the school that had changed. The sandstone pavers that made up the driveway and entrance had been power-washed in the not-too-distant past. She hadn't paid attention as she'd parked on the side of the wide semicircle driveway, but now that she was standing, she could see the telltale marks of a high-pressure sprayer. She wondered if she could craft a spell for that; cleaning spells were all well and good, but didn't hold up to large expanses or uneven surfaces. There had to be a way to . . .

Before she could go down that rabbit hole, her eyes took in the plaza beyond the gate, lined on both sides by glittering fountains, with the school's ceremonial cauldron in the center. She remembered the awe she'd felt the first time she'd walked towards the looming castle, laid eyes on the cauldron and seen the bright residue of generations of graduating classes adding their own magic. The jittery thrill of thinking: *This is my new home* had filled her until all of her nerves were humming, and despite the ups and downs of adolescence, it had never fully gone away. Tonight, the sound of falling water and the scent of summer combined in some aching cocktail of nostalgia and regret that Bryn tried to push away as she approached the iron gate with the informational plaque about the school's founding.

Bryn didn't need to read it; Grimoire Academy's backstory had been instilled in its students from the first day they arrived. The struggle for magical education, the establishment of legal protection for witches, fights for

4

justice and equality and empowerment. It wasn't that she didn't engage with those issues, but the legislation codifying magic and its users had been signed into law over a hundred years ago, and she'd had other things on her mind at thirteen. Like trying to figure out her place in the social pecking order of boarding school, as well as working out how her relationship with her mom and little sister had changed since she was officially "Other". Trying to make friends . . . but it soon became clear that Bryn was terrible at that. She'd told herself that maybe it was the siren in her; maybe she didn't actually *need* friends. For that matter, her mother had left home in Baja as a teenager, then spent most of her life in Grimoire and still hadn't made any friends—magical or non-magical—so perhaps it was some sort of genetic thing and she may as well give up.

Sex, though, was different. Her mom (and, as far as Bryn knew, most sirens) had a sex drive that overcame her social distaste for others—or had at least a few times, judging by Bryn's and her sister Luna's existence. Bryn, at age fifteen or so, had decided maybe that was the solution. Maybe she needed to leap over "friendship" and go straight to "sex". At the time, it seemed like a reasonable theory. And so, somehow, she'd worked up the courage to ask a girl to the winter solstice dance and everything went so well that she almost couldn't believe it. Her first kiss was glorious. Holding hands on the way to class was even better. She finally felt like she belonged. But then her girlfriend found her diary and read about her silly crush on one of the older girls, the completely unattainable Amelia Hexford. Bryn hadn't even thought about Amelia (much) since she'd been kissing and holding hands with someone else. And anyway, Amelia wasn't a threat to their relationship. She was way out of Bryn's league—popular, cool, so beautiful that it almost hurt to look at her. But her girlfriend was furious and at dinner that night she'd stood up and read the whole embarrassing paragraph out loud. In front of everyone. In front of *Amelia*.

It had been, bar none, the worst moment in her life. She'd been humiliated, but more than that, she'd been ashamed. Why had she written that down? Why had she left her diary in her bag, and how had she ever trusted that girl, who'd not just read it, but read it in public?

They had all laughed at her. Some of them nervously, just glad it wasn't them—but all of them had laughed. For months.

Except, actually, Amelia, whose expression had gone stark and unsmiling—though her friends were laughing the loudest, as if the very idea that a little toad like Bryn would dare to have a crush on her was the most ludicrous thing they'd ever heard. Bryn, flushed bright tomato-red with humiliation, had dared to dart a glance towards Amelia, who was pretty red herself. Possibly because it was embarrassing just to imagine being crushed on by someone like Bryn. Even years later, Bryn wanted to cry when thinking about the look on Amelia's face.

Amelia Hexford, who was now the headmistress of the school, at age twenty-four, and a glowing example of Grimoire Academy's excellence.

Bryn cringed. *What am I doing here?* Except she knew. She was here because Professor Herringbone, the only person who'd made Grimoire Academy feel like home, had died. And left her incredible, enviable, rare-as-hell library to Bryn, out of all the students she'd ever taught. The fact that the news had been delivered by an icy-voiced stranger, who hadn't seemed to care about the professor's books (or at least wasn't going to bestir herself to make sure Bryn received them) had also contributed; it had felt so personal, like dismissing Professor Herringbone's entire life work. Maybe that's why Bryn had felt so compelled to come in person: to show that the professor had made a very real difference. That she honored that legacy. Or maybe she was trying to prove something to the girl she remembered being, the one who'd fled the refectory in tears after her diary had been read to the whole school. She hadn't really been an ugly little toad, though she had felt like one. She was just a girl who'd grown slightly too tall too fast, whose light brown skin and non-witching background set her apart from most of her classmates, and who wasn't skinny enough, or rich enough, or confident enough. The girl who'd kept her head down for the last two years of school until she could finally escape to *anywhere but here*.

Except now she was *here*, again.

She had to go in. It was just her old school. No monsters lurked here, only a few painful memories (and a *very* few good ones). All she had to do was enter the gates and ring the bell, which would magically alert whoever was currently on duty. Was it still Madame Thwaits, who served as majordomo at the castle? She'd been rule-oriented, but not mean with it.

Maybe Bryn could avoid Amelia altogether. She just

needed a few hours in Professor Herringbone's rooms, with some boxes and tape. A lot of boxes and tape. That would be best: get in, do the job, get out. Load everything she could fit into the rental, arrange with Madame Thwaits to ship the rest. No need to bother the headmistress at all.

I'm an adult, she admonished herself again. *Plus, Amelia probably doesn't even remember me. Hopefully. She was Amelia Hexford, and I was no one.*

On this reassuring note, she pushed open the gates—just as the doors of the castle swung open. A clear voice rang out, carrying to Bryn across the plaza: "That's all right, Mrs Mallory, I'll take care of this!" Then a figure in a flowing emerald dress, with a matching over-robe, practically flew down the main stairs right towards Bryn.

Amelia freaking Hexford was, right now, in real life, skipping right at her.

2

Bryn's mouth dried up utterly, obliterating any notion of speaking. *Amelia Hexford.* Hotter at twenty-four than she had been at eighteen—and oh boy, oh goodness . . . Bryn realized she was standing there with her mouth open and quickly shut it, but that was all she could do before Amelia reached her, grabbed her arm, and called back towards the castle, "We have a lot to catch up on! We'll just take a walk around the grounds!"

Then, to a still-stunned Bryn, Amelia said, voice strained and totally in contrast to her grin, "I'm so glad you're here, you have no idea. I desperately need your help."

She steered them towards the gardens and Bryn, shocked but also not about to resist the pull of her high-school crush, could only say, "You remember me?"

This time Amelia's smile was real. "How could I forget you?"

Umm, do I faint, die, or kiss her? But Bryn didn't do any of those things. Instead, she managed to ask, "How can I help?" And her voice hardly even trembled.

"Wait." The false smile returned, firmly (and unnaturally) in place. But Amelia's eyes—blue, but gone lilac in the pink reflection of dusk—were serious and intense.

A girl could swoon. Bryn felt herself flush with remembered humiliation and way-too-current arousal. *Down, girl.* She could feel Amelia's quick breaths, the heat from her body, the subtle pulse of magic radiating from her. Years of unrequited love (lust?) surged through Bryn, but she fought it back, and forced herself to focus on the humiliation instead, that feeling of being an ugly toad from nowhere amongst beautiful princesses from magical backgrounds. That was who they were, who they would always be.

Except, Amelia's hand on her arm was warm, tingling, and so, so immediate. Bryn wanted both to lean in and pull away, in almost equal measure.

Then they rounded the corner towards the pool and Amelia dropped her arm, pulling out a phone and a wand. She cast a quick, familiar spell above the phone—a spell Bryn knew because she'd created it herself and published it in her spell collection.

Amelia Hexford, cleverest witch of Bryn's entire time at Grimoire Academy, had read *her* book? Not just read it, but actually used a spell from it? She opened her mouth to ask, then thought again and went with, "Why do we need a sphere of silence spell?"

"I think someone's been spying on me. I know that sounds bananas, but . . ." Amelia gestured with her phone hand, but Bryn, now on alert, grasped her wrist and held the device between them, stepping in closer and accidentally inhaling a sudden burst of jasmine that seemed to be coming from Amelia's skin.

At Amelia's startled blink, she explained, "I designed the spell for phone calls, not in-person conversations—politeness more than privacy. So we need to be . . . close for it to work." She gulped, aware suddenly that she was taller than the other woman. Not by much, but this close together, Amelia had to tilt her face up a little.

Kissing distance, Bryn thought, feeling herself blush. *Oh gods, I'm standing in kissing distance with Amelia Hexford.*

Then Amelia spoiled this thought by saying, "Something strange is going on and I need your help. I had them make up a guest room for you."

"A guest room? But I can't stay, I—"

Amelia stepped in until her phone hand, where the spell was centered, was the only thing keeping their bodies from pressing together. "I'm aware we don't know each other, but I know you're smart, and I know you're *here*. Please say you'll help me."

The naked need—*No, don't even think the word NAKED this close to Amelia Hexford*—in her voice was hard to resist, but there was no way Bryn was spending the night in the castle. She wasn't a child. She'd left. She'd moved on. Hell, she'd moved hundreds of miles away. She didn't owe Amelia, or the school, or anyone in this town a damn thing.

"Professor Herringbone left you a note." Amelia's voice was just above a whisper, like she didn't quite trust the spell. Or like she was afraid. "I swear, she knew more than she told me, but maybe now that you're here we can figure it out."

"A note?" Bryn remembered the professor's scrawl with a pang of grief.

"It's in her rooms." Amelia grasped Bryn's wrist, so they were standing there entwined. "*Please*, Bryn."

Bryn, with the distinct sensation she was stepping off a cliff, said the only thing she could: "Uhhh . . ." Then, bracing herself, she nodded. "Fine. One night. That's it."

Amelia's relief was immediate and it manifested as an awkward one-armed hug. "Thank you. Thank you so much."

The hug was very nice, but Bryn's brain was mildly distracted by the alarm bells now ringing loudly. *What have I done?*

* * *

The strangest thing about walking at Amelia Hexford's side into the main castle was how much more three dimensional she made everything feel. No longer a memory: now Bryn was walking through this ghost of her past. The entrance hall seemed somehow brighter or lighter than it used to be, but it still smelled the same. The same mix of stone and chill, with a sweet undercurrent that she knew came up from the kitchens. It still smelled—again, to her irritation—something like home. She'd spent four years in and out of these corridors, these rooms, and while those years may not have always been happy, they were definitely impactful.

"This way," Amelia said softly.

Bryn, feeling unaccountably annoyed, snapped, "I know the way to her office." She immediately regretted it when Amelia murmured a low, "Sorry."

Amelia did seem sorry, and she was clearly very stressed out. Bryn bit her tongue. There was no need to be so sharp, especially after all this time. It wasn't Amelia's fault that she had been the epicenter of the most humiliating moment in Bryn's life.

And then there had been that much more recent moment when they stood so close together that she could feel Amelia's breaths . . .

No, stop it. Schoolgirl crushes were to be left at school, or at the chronological timing of school—or whatever. Bryn brushed off all these thoughts and determinedly kept up with Amelia as they walked the familiar corridors to Professor Herringbone's rooms. Most of the professors lived either in cottages on campus or in town, but Professor Herringbone was one of the few who'd resided in the castle proper. She hadn't been part of the residence staff tasked with looking after the students who occasionally boarded there, but her constant presence had been familiar and comforting to Bryn when she'd been at school. She frequently arrived early and stayed late, and the professor had always been there; her rooms had been a sanctuary.

Judging by the sight that greeted them once Amelia swung open the door to the classroom, the professor had continued this habit. A young witch was sitting in the professor's desk chair, feet not quite touching the floor. For a split second, Bryn was almost offended, until she recognized the behavior. Not this particular witch—a young girl with

13

dark skin and closely plaited hair—but her attitude. Hadn't that been Bryn not so long ago? Hiding in the professor's rooms as the only safe bastion? She wouldn't have sat in Professor Herringbone's chair, who back then would have been around to sit in her own chair; in a world deprived of the professor herself, maybe Bryn would have sought the comfort of that familiar seat and the sphere of calm that she associated with it.

"Circe," Amelia said in surprise. "What are you doing here?"

The girl's eyes darted up, then away, but she didn't speak.

"Are you doing an after-school program of some sort?" Amelia followed up, but the girl only gathered her things—a bulky backpack, a hoodie in aubergine with silver piping, the school's colors—and then held them in front of her like a shield.

"Get something to eat before you go back to the dorms," Amelia called after her, as she started to walk quickly down the corridor.

"What was that about?" Bryn asked.

Amelia shook her head. "One of my second-years. The transition to the school has been rather rough for her. She's not from a witching family." Amelia glanced sidelong and then away.

Bryn felt herself flush as if her own non-witching background was a source of some embarrassment or shame, which it wasn't. It could be complicated, especially at the big witching schools, which had only begun allowing those from non-magical families towards the end of the last century. In the time Bryn had been at Grimoire Academy, she'd been one of maybe ten witches from non-witching families. She glanced down the hall, wondering what else she shared with this young, silent girl, but Circe was gone.

"Should you go with her?" Bryn asked tentatively.

"I'll check on her later. She boards here in the dorms, so while she technically shouldn't still be in the castle, as long as she's checked in with the resident advisor, I won't be too concerned." After a self-conscious pause, Amelia said, "Anyway, that's not what you're here for."

"No." Bryn glanced back down the corridor, but this wasn't her business. This had nothing to do with her.

She was here for one reason and one reason only: to collect her inheritance from the professor. And definitely *not* to kiss Amelia Hexford, which wasn't even an item on her list, she assured herself.

The second she entered the rooms, scent memory seemed to impale her, and she knew she'd failed to prepare herself. The slight sweetness from the kitchens rising up from below had triggered feelings of home, but the smell of Professor Herringbone's office made her come to a complete stop. She caught her breath and closed her eyes.

This had been the true heart of her home here, the place where she'd felt okay. The place where, when other kids made fun of her, someone stepped in to tell them firmly, but not cruelly, to stop. Tears pricked her eyes, and for a moment she tried to fight them. *Not in front of Amelia, not at the school. Wait till you get home, get back to Denver . . . Get at least to the car.* But then, well, fuck it. She had loved Professor Herringbone, and she would never see her again. And that was worth crying for. That was worth mourning.

15

So what if Amelia saw? So what if anyone saw? She was allowed to be sad about this.

Decision made, she squared her shoulders, then felt the lightest touch on her arm.

"I think it was the hardest thing I ever had to do, standing up in front of the school and telling them that the professor had died," came Amelia's voice, also choked up. "I'm still so sad."

Bryn opened her own tear-filled eyes to find Amelia right in front of her, but Amelia had let the tears fall. Her cheeks were wet.

"Sorry," Bryn said, and Amelia shook her head.

"Don't be. It's really nice not having to pretend."

The idea that Amelia Hexford felt the need to perform around others was so foreign that Bryn had to take a moment just to let it sink in. "Do you have to pretend a lot? That sounds difficult."

"No. Well, sometimes." Amelia shook her head again. "It's— You're not here for this. I don't want to trouble you. Come on. Let's go look at the professor's books." She withdrew her hand and led the way through the classroom. "I'm so glad you came for them. There was talk of donating them, or putting them in the library and indexing them, and people offered to buy them, which—I don't know why that hit me so hard. The school could use the income and the collection's last valuation, which was twenty years ago, put them at a rather astronomical amount. But it feels like they should be with someone who really cares about them and the professor's memory."

"Yes." Bryn agreed, in principle, though it was strange

16

to imagine Grimoire Academy needing something so boring and mundane as *money*. But clearly Amelia didn't want to discuss the details, so Bryn didn't ask any questions.

The professorial suites had bedrooms, studies, and sitting rooms. Students were only permitted to go into the latter, but in Professor Herringbone's case, that sitting room was a library first, and a place to sit second. The space had clearly not changed in five years, because every available surface in the room was covered in books and papers.

"Oh my," Bryn said, feeling overwhelmed. How had she thought she would do this in an afternoon? "What about her papers?"

"That is a topic under some discussion right now. It's agreed that they should be cataloged. It is less clear who owns them."

"Not me?" Bryn asked, feeling the loss of all those many, many papers she hadn't even thought about until that moment.

"No, the professor's will was very specific." Amelia was also gazing around, taking it all in. "You are to receive all of her books and unfinished manuscripts, but otherwise her belongings go to the school to be distributed as we—or rather, the school governors—see fit."

"There's so much," Bryn said, looking around.

"So, so much," Amelia agreed. "And I'm out a world-renowned teacher. You know, she was considered something of a genius in her field."

"I know," Bryn said. "I mean, I didn't know when I was her student, but I know now. She's cited in so many books about spellcasting and the history of magical science, and all of these other things. Even podcasts and television programs will discuss her and her work."

"It's gratifying sometimes, but it makes me sad, too," Amelia said. "We never knew any of that when we studied here."

"Would it have impacted anything if we did? I mean, she was our teacher. We lucked out, I think."

"True. It just seems like—" her eyes cut to Bryn's, then away. "It just seems like the school should be harder hit by her passing. But perhaps I am projecting. In any case, what help can I offer? I need to go to my rooms to get the letter she left you. Can I bring you anything? A cup of tea or coffee? I could order some food sent up."

At the mention of food, Bryn's stomach, heretofore paralyzed with anxiety, decided it had relaxed enough to contemplate eating. "Oh, maybe," she said awkwardly. School food again, what on earth was she doing? "Whatever was for supper . . . It doesn't bother me."

"All right."

Still slightly thrown off by the change in tone from reminiscing about the professor to practical tasks, Bryn added, "And boxes and tape, if you have any?"

"I'm sure we have some somewhere. I'll find a minion or something." Amelia smiled weakly. "I'll be back. Don't go anywhere without talking to me, please. And I'll find out which guest room they've made up for you."

"Oh, right." How had she forgotten already? It seemed like an unnecessary waste of time and resources. Could they bring a cot and stick it in the professor's library? Or were her rooms still being used for classes? Bryn decided none of these questions were important right now, and Amelia was halfway through the classroom already. On impulse, she called out, "Amelia?"

Damn, the woman could swing those robes around her. Bryn's words choked in her throat. She cleared it, focusing on Amelia's face and not the striking, attractive figure she cut. "Congratulations about the headmistress thing and all."

Instead of the smile and thanks she'd expected, Amelia's face tightened. "Thank you," she said stiffly. She swung around again and left the room.

Bryn, heart pounding for no reason she could immediately discern (except having accidentally offended Amelia by congratulating her on an incredible promotion), stood for a moment amidst the piles of books that filled the bookshelves to the brim, and closed her eyes again. *Professor, if your spirit is still here, please let me not make a fool out of myself in front of Amelia Hexford.* It was petty, maybe. It was a cheap thing on which to use any kind of spirit communication, no matter how slapdash. But still, she thought it anyway.

And then she got to work.

3

By the time Bryn finally fell into bed in her guest room in the visitors' corridor of the main castle, she was exhausted. She'd worked later than she'd intended, after having mindlessly eaten the food Amelia had sent up and gone through an entire pot of tea. Enough tea that she was a little worried she wouldn't be able to sleep at all. But either someone had put decaffeinated tea in her pot, or she was just that tired. She barely even had time to think before she was fast asleep.

Still, she woke up, as she often did, right around two o'clock in the morning. The hallowed hour of second thoughts. Her younger sister Luna had been having some personal troubles, and their mother didn't think that Bryn was the best person to talk her through them—not that she'd heard that from their mom, but from Luna, with many sighs and eyerolls. Bryn suspected that her mom knew her advice would be: "Move away. You have nothing to lose." And that was a fair enough concern, since Bryn had embraced moving far away as a helpful life transition.

Though when she thought of Denver, her apartment there, her neighborhood, she didn't exactly feel longing. She felt something more like obligation. She really liked Denver, but she was no better now at making friends than she had been when she was in school. She was lonely, she realized belatedly. Which was not a topic she wanted to be thinking about at two in the morning, while nestled in the Grimoire Academy castle.

What she needed to consider was how to cope with the job ahead. She needed to sort the professor's books, decide what she wished to leave to the school (for the library or anything else; that would be a question for Amelia), then box everything else up to be carted away in her rental car or shipped out. She would keep everything with the professor's notes scribbled in the margins, any books that seemed obviously spelled, and certainly any collection of papers that could be argued to constitute an unfinished manuscript.

She waved her wand at a candle, which immediately sprung to life, and reached again for the piece of paper Amelia had handed her the night before. The one the professor had left with her final documents. It was legible, barely, and only because she knew the professor's handwriting. But every stroke of that pen felt like a direct line, a telegraph from the professor, who had sat at her desk, dipped her pen in ink, and written Bryn's name at the top of the page. Her warm, Welsh tones came through as clearly as if she'd spelled the page to read itself aloud.

Dearest Bryn,
   I am so very proud of you and your accomplishments.
Your determination has always amazed and awed me.

You are destined for such wonderful things. I only wish I could be there to see them.

I am leaving you my library, in trust, to do with as you choose. You may pass it on to the school if you wish. You may sell it off. Whatever it is, please feel free.

You owe me nothing. You only owe yourself. Your past self, your future self, but most of all, the you who is reading this note.

I had the great privilege of watching you go from stumbling, nervous adolescent to confident, bright, talented young woman. Of my few bequests, this is the second most important.

About the other, you may encourage Amelia to share it with you. It is her gift now, and her burden.

I leave you both the school. Not mine to give precisely, but I fancy I've been around long enough to have earned a bit of responsibility in that area. The students are as they have ever been: some are more obviously in need of support and some less obviously, but all of them are still children, as you both were. Seek allies. Don't burn your bridges. And try always to see the magic that ripples beneath the words.

Yours, as ever, Antigone Herringbone.

Bryn wiped her eyes, wary of her tears staining the page. She waved her wand again, setting the candle to flicker gently. It was a small atmospheric spell she'd designed for when there were no adequate drafts to really make a candle flicker, and she had imagined its use in romantic settings, though she'd never used it that way herself. For Bryn, the

23

spell was usually for these moments in the middle of the night, when she contemplated things that could not be still and needed that bit of visual movement to keep her from becoming mired in her thoughts.

She had already boxed up much of what she desired to take with her, though she hadn't gone through everything yet. But the volumes that had special significance to her—those she had borrowed in the past, or that the professor had shown her—were ready to go. Amelia had ordered more boxes and more tape to be brought up from town the following day.

Bryn's mind spun with thoughts, and the notion of falling back to sleep seemed increasingly distant, as if receding in the rear-view mirror of a speeding car. She sighed. There wasn't much point lying back down in this state. She might as well get back to work, the sooner to finish.

It seemed strange and almost surreal to walk the castle corridors in the dark, but not unwelcome. Despite the ghosts said to roam the halls, she'd never had a negative encounter herself. Only the tickle of a presence at the edge of sensation, a hint of something not-quite-seen lingering where perception intersected reality. Contrary to many representations, ghosts were rarely unintentional; most were the result of deep planning and foresight. The so-called "rough hauntings" tended to be either because the body had died before the complex ghost magics were complete, or because the person in question had been targeted from outside, their spirit trapped in the wrong realm. At least Bryn didn't have to worry about Professor Herringbone joining them. The professor considered intentional ghosts short-sighted, and she would have never been successfully caught by someone else's spell. She'd written an entire text about protective magic. In any case, none of the castle's ghosts felt the least malicious. Bryn fancied that if any were roaming the castle, they knew what she was about and only wished her well.

A little over an hour later, seated on the professor's rug surrounded by her papers, eyes crusted from dried tears and exhaustion, Bryn pulled a throw blanket over her shoulders and snuggled into an armchair. She needed to rest her eyes now that her mind had been lulled by the monotony of sorting books. Just for a minute or two. Or three . . .

* * *

The knocking startled her out of an uncomfortable sleep. *Where the hell— Wait—*

She blinked around, disoriented by her upright position and distantly familiar surroundings. Another knock. For a moment, she felt a stab of remembered fear. Had she slept in and missed the bus that would take her to the bottom of the hill? Was everyone else at school already? Was she in trouble?

Then she remembered that although her back brain was correct and this was the castle, she was no longer a student. She was a grown woman, and if she wished to sleep in, even at her old school, she could do so. Though, ideally—she rolled her neck and winced—not in an armchair.

Amelia's voice called, "Bryn? It's me. It's Amelia."

At which point Bryn scampered up with haste, tripping

over the blanket and nearly going sprawling. She had sweatpants on, and a tank top—but surely she'd been wearing— She grasped around, found her wand, and waved it at the nearest lamp. Light helped and she located her discarded hoodie between two piles of books, one of which seemed to be leaning precariously towards the other. "I'll be ready in a second!" she called frantically as she tried to pull on her hoodie, right the leaning pile, and tidy away the blanket simultaneously.

And oh gods, her hair was a tangled knot. She grabbed a scarf hanging from the professor's reading lamp and wrapped it around her head. She didn't think it was hiding much, but it was certainly better than showing off her bed head (armchair head?) in front of Amelia Hexford.

"Sorry," Amelia said, taking in her appearance once she opened the door. "I keep school hours now, and I figured when you weren't in the guest room that you were probably already at work. Oops." A grin seemed to be tugging relentlessly at the corners of her mouth.

"Are you laughing at me?" Bryn accused.

"I'm not, I swear I'm not. I mean, maybe a little, but only because you look so cute. I mean, adorable. I mean— I brought you some tea, and breakfast will be up soon, and I should definitely go so you can— So you—"

Bryn wanted to be offended that Amelia Hexford was laughing at her, when the woman had woken her up out of a dead sleep at 6.15 a.m., but it was hard to resist the playful amusement.

She sighed. Annoyed. Charmed. Something. "Don't go. Have some tea. Just give me another minute."

26

"I'll pour," Amelia said, discreetly backing out of the room. She may have giggled.

Bryn chose to ignore it. She finger-combed her hair, braided it back, and neatened her clothes. Damn, why hadn't she at least got dressed in her rooms before coming to the professor's office? And brushed her hair! That would have helped so much, but at least she was moderately presentable now. Ish.

"Tea is getting cold," Amelia called, still sounding amused.

"So spell it hot," she grumbled, then checked her reflection again and went out into the sitting room.

Amelia had not wasted her time. She had cleared two chairs and most of one side table so that they could sit. It hadn't even occurred to Bryn to do this the night before. She'd been so overwhelmed by the books and papers, and had eaten supper on the floor. She glanced guiltily at the debris of last night's various snacks and beverages. "I promise I'll clean up before I leave later," she said.

"About that." Amelia seemed to try to smile brightly and then gave up. "What exactly is your schedule right now? Out of curiosity, I mean. What do you, you know, do? Obviously, I know about your book. I own it. I use a few of the spells from it all the time. But I mean, day to day, what is it you do?"

"I work," Bryn said, unconvincingly, and was immediately annoyed with herself for sounding so unsure. "I really do. I'm always coming up with new spells, testing them, refining them. They didn't all make it into that one book, of course. I'm hoping to write more." Her gaze wandered along the professor's shelves. "That's all I ever wanted to do, even when I was here."

27

"I think I remember that," Amelia said. "Didn't Madame Schneider bring you up in front of the class once?"

Bryn sighed. "Yes. And told me it was highly unlikely that someone with my background would ever be considered a 'reliable' spell master." That kind of casual prejudice hadn't been uncommon, but it had certainly been discouraging.

"Shows what she knows. You've already published a book."

"Yes." The instant clapback at Schneider was nice, but Bryn had to be honest. Although she didn't want Amelia to think she was lazy, likewise she didn't want to sound *too* proud. "I'm still not where I want to be; there's just so much I don't know. When I got here, I was out front trying to think of how I could create a spell to power-wash the courtyard. Like, the power wash is doable—that's just an extended deep clean with some bits thrown in about force. But I can't work out how to tell it where to begin and end. I can't *scale* it."

"I did actually look in your book, but when I didn't find anything, I hired an actual power washer," Amelia said.

Bryn bit back another wave of insecurity. Was Amelia just saying that to flatter her? Except, Amelia was intently studying the papers on the table beside her. She refocused on Bryn and added, "Maybe that's for the next book?"

It didn't feel like flattery. Bryn decided to assume this interest was sincere, and anyway, Amelia was brilliant. There was likely no one else in their year at school who would also be intrigued by the spell-scaling issue. "Except, I can't figure out how to do it, how to set the physical parameters. Mostly because it's not something we talk about for small spells; it works so intuitively for something like a heating charm, or even my sphere of silence spell. But if I could work out the mechanics, I think they would have a much wider application. Writing books is a lot of fun at the wild ideas stage, and a lot more difficult once you're in the weeds with those ideas." She paused. "I guess it's not really that I lack material. I've got loads of it. It's just trying to publish more books that's been kind of a stumbling block. If your first book is a bestseller, it's no problem. If not . . . you just sit around hoping for the best."

"Oh." Amelia's eyes seemed to narrow slightly. "So you don't have another book to write right now?"

Bryn wasn't sure how to take this. Was Amelia implying that she didn't work hard? Because she did. She worked very hard. Was Amelia implying she was a washout at twenty-three because she'd only published *one* book? Well, that was one more than she herself had published. Was Amelia implying— Screw it. "What are you implying?" she demanded.

"I am not implying anything," Amelia said. "I'm hoping that you have some time, maybe five or so months, say, to fill Professor Herringbone's shoes this year at the school."

"Absolutely not— Are you— What?" Bryn sputtered. "I don't have any teaching credentials."

"I realize that, but I need a qualified spells teacher. And you are qualified in spells, if not in teaching. There are workarounds for temporary situations, such as this one. I've looked into it." The familiar Amelia Hexford self-assurance was out in full force. "I can hire you on the spot. I mean, the school can, obviously. Whether you would be able to continue next year would be up to—"

"Next year?" What the hell was going on? "Amelia, I'm not a teacher."

"No, but I think you could be a good one if you wanted to be."

Bryn realized she had sat forward in her seat and was clutching her teacup with the kind of grip that could do real damage. She imagined it splintering to bits and set the teacup down. "I can't stay here. I have a life in Denver, Colorado."

"Denver, Colorado?" Amelia asked dubiously. "Are there any witches in Denver, Colorado?"

"Some. Well, not as many as here. No."

"And there can't be any sirens. There's no sea."

Somehow Amelia remembered about her family. Despite the tension in the room, some part of Bryn's mind celebrated this little bit of apparent understanding. "That's what I like about it. I mean, not that I'm against sirens, but just, you know, my mom doesn't visit. She's never come to visit."

At this, Amelia's face changed. "Never?"

"No." Was that so strange? Did other people's parents visit them if they moved so far away, to such an alien landscape? She would have to think about that later.

"I see. Well. I can offer you wages at the regular rates of a first-year teacher for the amount of time that you will be officially instructing and, of course, accommodation, as well as meals on campus, which would be free of charge to you. So you wouldn't really have to pay for anything here. And-I-could-really-use-the-help." She added the last sentence in a single breath.

"Help? You're Amelia frigging Hexford. You've never

needed help." Except, as she was saying it, Bryn remembered the look on Amelia's face the night before, out in the garden. "Amelia, what's really going on here? And why don't you call one of your eight thousand friends?"

"I don't have eight thousand friends," Amelia said ruefully. "I had a lot of people who acted like my friends when doing so benefited them, like here at school. Maybe that's what friendship is, and I just didn't realize it. But now, I don't seem to have very many friends at all. And none of them are here. I don't—" She looked away before continuing, as if the prospect of meeting Bryn's eyes was too much for her. "I don't think that hiring me for this job was a universally supported measure, to be honest with you."

"Well, it must have been. They wouldn't have hired you otherwise, would they?"

Amelia hesitated. Then with the air of someone sharing a confession, she said, "I found some other papers in the professor's things. It seems like she basically blackmailed the school governors into giving me this job. So I didn't get it on merit, I didn't get it because I'd earned it. I got it because a professor once liked me. And that's— Well, it doesn't feel great. Actually."

Bryn blinked, staring at her. "Professor Herringbone got you this job? Why? I mean, not that I don't think you're capable of it. I just don't understand." And was that the tiniest twinge of jealousy she felt? Surely, if the professor had had a favorite . . . But no, that wasn't fair. The professor hadn't had favorites so much as she'd chosen to specially mentor some students, and both Bryn and Amelia had been amongst them. She'd sometimes envied Amelia's popularity and beauty, but only in passing. She had never felt less important in Professor Herringbone's eyes, she reminded herself.

"I don't think I understand either. But here we both are. And I did say yes."

That phrasing seemed intentional. "You regret it?"

"Oh, no, not at all. I love the kids. I believe in what we're doing." At last, Amelia's face regained its earlier animation. "We're making some changes, trying to modernize some things. The kids are allowed to have tablet computers now, and phones. They can google things. They can talk to witches all over the world. We have a pen-pal program with other witchy schools, and I'm hoping it will lead to more magical community-building. I'd like to establish some programs with other sorts of schools as well—even the siren school down in Grimoire. It can only help if our students interact more widely, whether they go on to magical universities or not."

"That's wonderful," Bryn said with feeling. What she wouldn't have given for some pen pals of any kind. And she had a special soft spot for building bridges between disparate magical communities.

"I think the changes have been positive, or have the potential to be so. But it hasn't been easy."

"I bet," Bryn said, laughing with something that wasn't quite like mirth. "I'm sure the governors had kittens over it."

"You could say that." Amelia actually smiled. "And Mr Wicks is not a fan."

"Mr Wicks." Bryn laughed out loud. "Gods, he's a grumpy old thing. He hasn't retired yet?"

"He shows no signs of retiring anytime soon. And he has resisted, I think, every single thing that I have done since I came back here."

That was all too easy to imagine. Bryn remembered Mr Wicks as the brand of stern and uncompromising that might have been fair, but wasn't friendly. "Yikes."

"Yes. He has a lot of sway. I think . . ." Amelia shook her head. "I shouldn't even talk about this. I have no evidence. I have no proof. I just have this feeling that they're trying to get rid of me. That the governors want Wicks in charge. And I can't even say they're wrong."

"I can," Bryn said. "That dinosaur?" She shuddered theatrically.

"Professor Herringbone was older and was here longer."

"Yeah, but she wasn't a dinosaur. Professor Herringbone kept growing and changing. Wicks is teaching the same lesson plans he has been teaching for literal decades, I would bet you unicorn tears."

"Oh, he is. I asked," Amelia said. "It was one of the first conversations we had after I got hired, and I literally asked."

Bryn covered her mouth. "You did not."

"I did. And he told me with total assurance that his lesson plans were good, and there was no reason to change them."

Bryn considered this for a moment before grudgingly acknowledging that Wicks, while not her favorite person, had been a good teacher in his own way. "I guess at least you always know where you stand with him," she said slowly. "Not that I think he would be a good headmistress—he would definitely not be."

33

"No, I know. But, here we are. It doesn't matter what I think as much as what the governors think. And Madame Schneider is the current sitting head."

"Oh." Bryn considered this. Schneider had been the sort of teacher she was afraid to make eye contact with, because it was seen as a threat to her authority. "Is that who you think is spying on you?"

Amelia waved a hand. "Maybe. I think both Schneider and Wicks are waiting for me to screw up. And I'm so afraid that this Herringbone thing— Sorry, *not* 'this Herringbone thing', but you know what I mean. I loved Professor Herringbone, who did try to get me to call her Antigone, though I absolutely could not."

"I cannot imagine calling her Antigone," Bryn agreed.

"Neither could I. But I think that with her gone, they have no reason to keep me here. So the governors are just waiting for the right moment to get rid of me."

"But we don't know this for sure," Bryn mused, and some part of her mind thought, *How am I suddenly a "we" with Amelia Hexford?*

"No, we don't. It's only a thought, a feeling that I have. And I don't know what I'll do if I lose this."

"Can't you do anything?" Bryn asked.

"Because I'm Amelia frigging Hexford?"

Bryn acknowledged the possible unfairness of this with a shrug.

"Not really," Amelia said. "I wanted to be a teacher. And I do get to do that sometimes. I take over for people if they need time off. But the rest of it is so exciting, Bryn. I don't even know how to describe it. My family have always

34

been in business in various forms. And they're all good at it. Super powerful, super skilled. Super magical. But I don't want to make money and be successful by those standards. It's not interesting to me. It doesn't feel like the right kind of challenge. But this school?" Her eyes lit up. "It could be so good. The things they're doing in other parts of the world, even other parts of the country, and we're just stagnating."

Bryn picked up her tea again and sipped it, even though it was now lukewarm. She thought about casting a heating charm. She needed to fine-tune her cup-heating charm, which sometimes didn't work at all and sometimes failed spectacularly, depending on the material the cup was made from. She'd gotten close a few times, but her spells needed more refinement. And it was one of many things she was working on in her real life. Because if she ever got the chance to publish another book, she wanted to be ready. She needed to be ready. That was her dream: more books, more respect, standing in her field. She wanted to earn her place in witching history, even though she hadn't come from one of the old traditional families.

She certainly didn't plan to return to her old school, haunted by all of her old demons, including Amelia Hexford.

Except, it was only five months. And Amelia looked so lost in a way Bryn didn't think she even knew Amelia could look. She'd known about the powerful, rich magical family, and the witchy background going back however many generations. But she hadn't really thought about the pressure that would put on someone. She'd mostly thought, *Wow, it must be nice to come from a family who understands what you are.* Maybe there were invisible downsides to that, too. Coming from a family that could project on to you what success looked like, based on their own experience, was clearly not as ideal.

Amelia sat forward. "I know what I'm asking is a lot. I get that. I really do. And obviously, I don't want to guilt-trip you into staying. I just . . . I'm so alone here, Bryn. I wasn't prepared for that. And I don't think I'm handling it well."

Bryn also sat forward, as if drawn there by the magnetic pull of Amelia's vulnerability. "I don't know how to teach, though. And I'm nowhere near as good as Professor Herringbone."

"No one is as good as Professor Herringbone. Teaching is a skill like any other. You can learn to teach if you want."

Bryn thought again about her apartment and the neighborhood brewery where she liked to write, and her open calendar where she had no appointments, no date nights, no meetings scheduled with friends. She would hit the apps if she wanted to have sex with someone. But she didn't ever tell herself that doing that was a route to anything else, anything deeper.

Sitting there with Amelia was the most intimate she'd felt with anyone in an awfully long time.

"I . . ."

Amelia's lips parted just slightly. *Stop staring at Amelia's lips.*

Bryn took a shaky breath and said, "Okay. I'll do it."

4

It all happened so fast. If Bryn was just a little more superstitious, she would have interpreted this as some kind of sign, some kind of preordaining that this was the correct path for her to take. But she wasn't that superstitious, and Amelia's words that first evening kept echoing back to her: *You're here.* That's why she was the one, because she just happened to be the person that Professor Herringbone had left her library to. If it had been some other witch in her year, or some other student they'd never met, that's who Amelia would have tagged to step in and take over the professor's classes. It wasn't that she was special; it was just that she was there, and Amelia needed *someone*.

The cottage Amelia had taken her to was tucked out of the way behind the kitchen garden, and by the entrance to the grotto, which was what everyone called the indoor pool. Students were not allowed to swim in it; she'd only ever peered through the windows, and even then, you had to squat down because it was sunken, although not quite underground. The usual rumors abounded—it was haunted;

it was off limits because someone died there, an untold number of years ago; and, once they were older, that it was used secretly by the professors for sex parties. Looking back, that last one was the least likely; the idea of Professor Herringbone and Mr Wicks and Madame Schneider all at the same sex party bent even Bryn's fantastic imagination.

In any case, at least her new borrowed cottage was not on the students' paths to any of their classes. The only time she'd been on the far side of the kitchen garden as a student was to round up escaped chickens and rabbits.

The cottage itself was tiny, but in a way that added to its quaintness instead of subtracting from its usefulness. Everything she needed was there: kitchenette, bathroom, bed . . . corner, and a little nook with a chair and table that she supposed was a sitting room of a sort. Amelia had apologized for how small it was but said this was the one in best repair, which reminded Bryn of something else Amelia had said, about the school needing money. It hadn't really occurred to her that Grimoire Academy would ever need money, but now that she was an adult and could only guess at how astronomical the costs were to run such a place, it seemed a very real and practical concern.

Still, the cottage was clean and warm, and the thickness of the stone walls on the outside definitely suggested a significant amount of mechanical insulation. All the same, she did a few charms: the usual ones that she would do in any living space—for privacy, barriers to air and moisture, things that she hadn't quite perfected but that still seemed to help. She could do an entire book on such intermediate household charms, if she ever got them completely right.

Hell, she could be one of those witches who went into business for herself doing such charms for people who had no magical abilities.

She'd wondered whether other races and groups could use spells. Was there a type of spellcasting that demons might need? She knew of many spells that would be helpful to sirens, though she'd never been able to test any of them because her mother did not allow magic in the house; Bryn didn't take it personally. She knew that was just one more thing outside her mother's control, and there was very little that her mother hated more.

For that matter, were there things sirens took for granted that might also be helpful for witches? What chances were all of them missing by failing to consider cooperative efforts between magical races? Was this something she would know if she'd gone to university? Magical universities, for practical reasons, were fully integrated; anyone magical could attend. Still, even if that was so, why did it seem like universities were the exception instead of the rule? She needed to think more about it all, and made a mental note to return to it later.

At that moment, she had enough to do, settling into her cottage and getting ready to teach. She'd hardly brought any luggage, not intending to stay, and now that she was here, she realized she didn't miss much either. She could pick up a few more clothes, but what else did she need? Certainly not reading material, not with all of the professor's books at her disposal. And while she knew she needed to leave the papers to the school, this would give her a chance to thoroughly go through them, index them, even create her own kind of taxonomy . . . perhaps take high-res pictures of anything that might be helpful to her. That wasn't cheating, right? She suspected Amelia would be in favor of it, especially if it took her five months to do.

She had all of Sunday to figure out what exactly she was supposed to be teaching, and she'd left the cottage only to gather up any potentially helpful papers from the professor's office, as well as relevant lesson plans she needed to familiarize herself with. Except, to her growing dismay, she hadn't *found* any lesson plans.

Around late morning, there was a knock at her cottage door, which she answered expecting Amelia, but it was, in fact, a man maybe a few years older than herself that she'd never met before.

"Hi there," he said, his accent nebulously East Coast, or at least not matching the relaxed tones that she was used to from California and Colorado. "Headmistress sent me down to update you on Professor Herringbone's classes."

"Oh, good, come in. Obviously, I just moved here, and it doesn't really feel like my place yet, but come in all the same," she said, smiling.

He nodded in a friendly way, but didn't move. "Sure. I'm Piper. Er, Professor Anderson . . . Piper Anderson, um." He cringed. "Sorry."

Someone more awkward than she was, what a relief. Bryn found herself smiling even more widely. "Please come in, Piper. I'm Bryn."

"Amelia told me— I can call her Amelia, right? You went to school with her. That's not some kind of breach of etiquette, is it?"

"No, no, it's fine," she said. He was really seriously awkward.

He reached out his hand more formally than seemed necessary and said, "Piper Anderson. My pronouns are they/them. I teach athletics, sort of, you know, witchy athletics." They did a funny little head bob as they said it.

"That's great. I'm Bryn Delmar, she/her." She mentally corrected Piper's pronouns, hoping she didn't screw it up. "But would you like to come in? Because it seems like we're losing heat just standing here in the doorway."

Piper nodded. "Yes, I would like to come in, thank you. I have my own cottage here on the grounds. I get the impression that Amelia would like some members of the team to be, you know, under fifty."

Bryn smiled at that and led the way inside, only then remembering her lack of seating. "You go ahead and take the chair, I'll take the bed. Would you like tea? I don't think I have coffee yet. I haven't been to the store."

"The kitchen will give you some instant if you ask nicely. They might give you ground coffee too; I don't drink it, so I've never asked."

"Good to know," she said. "I'll have to get used to that. When I was in school here, some of the students attempted to argue it was a human rights violation for the kitchen to withhold coffee."

Piper grinned. "Very dramatic."

"Right? I didn't get into coffee until after I left. Would you like tea, though?"

"No thanks." Piper looked around. "It is funny that none of the cottages are exactly the same. You'd expect them to be, but they were all built at different times for different reasons, I guess."

"Oh. Hmm." She searched her memory for what she knew about the outbuildings. "Yes, I think they were initially for the staff of the castle, and eventually became guest houses. There are rumors that they're all connected by some kind of tunnel system to the main building, but if that was ever true, the tunnels are most likely collapsed now."

Piper raised their eyebrows in appreciation. "Really? I hadn't heard that one."

She shrugged. "Hazard of going to school here—you hear all the true and made-up stories. Where did you go?" She immediately wished she hadn't said it. Not all witches went to school at witchy schools, and it could be a real social faux pas to imply they should have.

"Well, I went to USC, but that's probably not what you mean." Their expression was a little pained.

"Sorry, not my business. Should not have asked. Don't know what your situation is—"

Piper waved a hand. "No, no," they said. "You're right. I went to Academy New Amsterdam, obviously in Manhattan."

Which meant that—in terms of wealth—if Amelia's family could be considered very wealthy, then Piper Anderson's family was extraordinarily wealthy. Academy New Amsterdam was the poshest possible school on the East Coast. She checked the thought, scanned her mind, and amended that to *in the country*.

Some of Bryn's good cheer dried up in a momentary

42

internal flailing of class consciousness. "Oh," she said. "And how was that?"

"It was fine." After a moment of thought, they amended, "It was high pressure, I didn't get a good night's sleep for the four years I was there, and I escaped out here as quickly as I could. I never plan to return, but that's probably not the school's fault, if you know what I mean."

She realized she did know what they meant. Entirely. "Well, I understand that."

"Oh . . . but I thought you were from here."

"I am, and then as soon as I graduated, I left." She gestured to the cottage with a sense of oddness she wasn't sure how to explain. "And now I'm apparently back accidentally, or at least temporarily."

Piper seemed to wait for her to say more, and when she didn't, they took a deep breath. "Well, I have tried to take over some of Professor Herringbone's classes. I'm not bad at spells and spellcasting, but it isn't exactly my forte, and to be honest, I could not make head or tail of her lesson plans. I don't think she really made lesson plans? Or at least I couldn't find any."

"No, me neither."

They seemed relieved. "Oh good. I thought maybe I was just too dumb to figure it out. I mean not good-good, since it would be much easier if she did have a perfectly planned-out lesson for each day of the year, but to be honest, I think she was doing it all off the cuff, if you can imagine that."

"Well, having been in her classes, I guess maybe I can imagine that. At least, it didn't seem like she ever taught the same exact way twice in a row, though that seems rather daunting to me right now."

"Improv all the time." Piper crossed their legs, and tapped their knee with one thumb. "That terrifies me. Apparently, there hasn't really been an athletics program here until this year, and it's been a bit bumpy."

"I wasn't sure if I should ask. We didn't have athletics when I went to school. What exactly are you teaching? Like . . . sports?"

"Well, Amelia and I spoke a lot about it over the summer before term began, and she really just wants to encourage the students to find ways of discovering their own joy in movement, whatever that joy is. And that's led to a very relaxed, shall we say hard to grade, policy of physical education." Piper's awkwardness was somehow the most endearing thing Bryn had seen since returning to the school.

"So, it's miserable?" she asked.

"No, I didn't say that!" They hesitated. "It's just hard to know if I'm making a difference or doing it right, because there's nothing to do right. It's not like, 'Today we'll learn polo, here are the rules, here are the teams, here's the equipment, and here's how you use it.'"

"Polo? Isn't that played in a pool?"

"No, there's field polo too—with horses."

"Horses?"

Piper grinned. "I guess it's not really that big in California, but it doesn't matter. I'm just whining. This is supposed to be about me briefing you on your classes. So, do you have any questions?"

Did she have questions? She had nothing but questions.

How were the students? Was there anyone to look out for? Was there anyone to take care of? Were there sibling groups? Were there bullies? Did she need to worry about substance abuse, or depression, or family troubles? Were any of them actually good at spellcasting?

"Um. I guess I don't really have any questions at the moment. Can I take a rain check on that?"

"Definitely," Piper said. "I did my best, but I don't think they've learned anything since the professor passed. Honestly, it was a shock. Amelia brought in grief counselors, but I think people are still pretty upset." They paused. "*I'm* still upset, and I only knew the professor for a few months. Some of these kids have been her students for three and a half years. But there's a lot of pressure right now, and of course the second-years are taking their MSEs soon, so . . . Do let me help if I can be of help."

She shuddered. "How did I repress the MSEs?" The months of anxiety leading up to the annual Magical Scholarly Examinations, the spinning nausea of exam week, the stifled silence of the written tests and looming dread of the practicals.

"I know," Piper said. "At least we don't have to do them ourselves again."

"Thank the gods. Though I'm not really sure how to improve the experience. There is some science about physical activity and brain activity and correlations with test scores," she said thoughtfully.

Piper's eyes lit up. "Oh, there's loads of science. It's really fascinating. Even small amounts of consistent daily activity will increase exam scores, as well as grades, as well as quality of life—self-reported obviously, because that's not really a metric we can track scientifically. But there are so many implications."

This was why Amelia had hired them, Bryn realized: the excitement, the passion, the energy. All things she did not herself have for teaching. She set that aside. "Okay, maybe we can help each other. Maybe we can surprise the students, swap classes or something. I'm not sure, but I do think that one of the greatest gifts of Professor Herringbone's lectures was that you were always a little bit surprised in the middle of it. You were certainly never bored."

"Yes," they said, "that's good. I struggle with that, because I feel like I'm always saying the same thing, and they don't really need to hear it again. But it's all so interesting if I could just get them engaged."

"I definitely get that," Bryn said, while thinking, *This is so not a job I was cut out for*. She hadn't even been good at making and keeping friends when she was younger. How the heck was she expecting to motivate a bunch of teenagers to do or think anything?

They chatted for a while longer and Piper did accept a cup of tea. She liked them. They were excited and not that much older than her, and they didn't scare the hell out of her, which was nice because she didn't anticipate seeing Mr Wicks again going well. She should be able to dodge Schneider and any other old crone who might be around, but surely some metaphorical ghosts lingered still, even if the real ones were mostly inert.

By the time Piper left, she felt . . . not better about teaching, but a little bit better about being at the school.

Not everything was the same, and some of these changes were for the better.

* * *

That night, she dreamed that she was an excellent teacher. The dream was so vivid that for a moment, when she woke up, she felt the certainty of it lingering in her cells, like that future was at the edges of her fingertips, and all she needed to do was reach out and touch it.

In the dream, which was like many dreams—a sort of strange metaphorical playground of images and colors and emotions—she had stood on a rock in the middle of a roiling orange sea, and her students had surrounded her. And somehow, with all of them working together, they had cast a spell that transported them back to the school.

It had been a triumph. They'd celebrated. These strange, faceless shapes of people she knew were her students, along with another figure she knew to be Amelia. The kids hugged her and thanked her for her help, and dream-Amelia kissed her in victory, which sent her stomach tumbling.

When she realized, after a few seconds of basking in this newfound glory, that it was only a dream, the disappointment ran very, very deep.

Of course, that dream figure couldn't possibly be Bryn— dowdy, silly little Bryn, with her head in books, her mind doing anything to escape wherever she happened to be standing. She did not inspire people to new heights, like Professor Herringbone did.

She did not get kissed by Amelia Hexford.

After nearly an hour spent lying in the strange bed, she gave up and surrendered to the day. It was just past four o'clock in the morning, her first day of teaching. She put the kettle on and stared at her reflection in the window above the sink, wondering what she was doing with her life, and just how difficult today was going to be.

5

It only took her first class, with a group of second-years, to convince her that she was not cut out for teaching— just in case she'd wondered or even fantasized that she would discover her calling in this odd, surprising situation.

She didn't.

In fact, she was terrible at it. The kids (she supposed she should call them students but, en masse, they seemed more like a herd of young mischievous goats) clearly didn't care what she had to say. None of them even acknowledged her authority as their teacher, and the two who seemed at all inclined to listen to her were the sort of students who were always inclined to listen to adults in positions of authority—not to learn anything from them, but only to intuit what they wanted, how to deliver it, and how to succeed in that system. Which, granted, she hadn't noticed with the first one, who'd raised a hand to ask a far too specific question about lunar spell timing (not universally applicable, but still an important factor in certain types of spells). Only after Bryn had explained, at length, the factors involved in such decisions did she notice the poisonous looks that other students were shooting at the original questioner, whose head was bent to take copious notes. She'd felt slightly suckered, and a bit frustrated that her desire for engagement had briefly seduced her into seeing it where it likely didn't exist.

Bryn wondered if that's how she had looked at that age. Had she seemed like a goody-two-shoes, a teacher's pet? She hadn't intended to, but, well, things had been so hard, and her mother was always so detached and cold. Icy, even, no matter what Bryn tried to do to earn her affection. After arriving in a place where there were rules and grades, and she understood how to succeed, she could probably be forgiven for taking it all so seriously, for working so hard at her studies that she tended to eclipse other students by accident.

It wasn't that she'd wanted so much to be good at school. She just wanted people to approve of her. She wanted the adults to think she made sense, now that she'd finally landed somewhere her talents were taken seriously. She wondered if Piper had done the same thing in search of understanding, but with some sort of posh sport at their fancy witchy prep school. And then she scolded herself for being unkind, to Piper, to herself, and to everyone else.

Still, by the end of her first day, after teaching students for six separate periods, she wanted to quit. She wouldn't, if only because her pride wouldn't allow it, but it had become unavoidably clear that she was going to make a mess of everything. She couldn't decide if she should speak to Amelia about it. After all, Amelia should have the opportunity to unhire her and find someone better as quickly as possible. But when she knocked lightly on the headmistress's door, there was no answer, which made sense. Headmistresses were very busy; Amelia wouldn't have a lot of time to sit around and hold Bryn's hand through her first terrifying, frustrating day of teaching.

She briefly became lost in the notion of holding hands with Amelia, as she remembered those moments when their bodies had been pressed together that first night, and the delicious spark that had thrummed through her blood when Amelia looked up at her, within kissing distance. But it was all nonsense. She was making it up. This was the woman who years ago had stood by while all her friends laughed at Bryn's pathetic crush; the girl who'd seemed just as humiliated, despite the fact that no one had been trying to hurt *her*. There was no sexual tension there; Amelia needed a teacher. Bryn just needed a break. Maybe her creativity was stifled by having too much free time, too much time to think about the next book, which didn't exist, or other books in the series, or other publishers she should approach. Maybe she should go to university. There were some excellent choices, some of which had specialties she found intriguing. She could get a degree in magical healing or advanced spell craft, or she could pursue her studies in magical physics, which had always fascinated her. Grimoire Academy had only the most basic of science classes, with a mere glancing across magical sciences in the final year of study. It hadn't been nearly enough for Bryn.

When she'd once asked Professor Herringbone why that

was, the professor had only said, "Well, you see, it's not that witches don't believe in science. It's that they can't see it. And what you can't see, you do not necessarily value." Bryn had been shocked and pointed out that science was literally everywhere, that nothing happened without physics, and the professor had only smiled, patted her shoulder, and said kindly, "That's why I like you, Bryn. You see beneath the surface of things."

At the time, the compliment had made her feel warm. Now, sitting in the professor's chair, in her study, contemplating the coming months of daily lessons for which she felt completely unprepared, she wasn't so sure she saw much at all.

Amelia stopped in for a moment at the end of the next day, literally poking her head in and remaining in the doorway as Bryn informed her traitorous heart that it had no business racing, because there was nothing there. She got through the next two days—how, she didn't really know. By the time she went to bed each night, she was exhausted. She had prepped to the best of her abilities, which didn't seem very good, considering that each lesson she tried to plan for had to be abandoned within ninety seconds of the students arriving in her classroom. When Piper stopped by in the early evening on Wednesday to ask her how she was doing, she accidentally spilled all of her worries and fears right into their ear. Which she shouldn't have done for any number of reasons, not least because she hardly knew Piper. She couldn't even really call them a friend yet. And there she was, practically crying on their shoulder.

Instead of the sympathy she expected, or the pity she feared, they only gazed at her with something more like curiosity.

"What?" she finally snapped. "Why are you looking at me like that?"

"Umm. Have you—" They hesitated. "I really don't mean to offend you, but have you never done something that started out feeling impossible?"

"What? Why would I do something that felt impossible?"

They blinked. "Many of us don't have a choice? I mean, are you really just naturally that good at everything you do?"

This seemed like a foolish question. "I don't know what you're saying. Why would I pursue things I wasn't good at? How do you get successful doing that?"

"Interesting," Piper said. "It's just, well, none of us would be walking right now if we didn't, as small children, keep trying things we weren't good at. Or talking. Or writing. I hated learning to write. Didn't you?"

"No." Her turn to blink. "I loved it. I wanted to be able to write books."

"What about learning to read? That wasn't difficult for you?"

"I loved it," she said again.

"Huh. Interesting."

Growing ever more frustrated, Bryn said, "What point are you trying to make, Piper?"

They raised both hands in a defensive gesture that made her feel like a bully.

She softened her voice. "Sorry. Long week and we're

only halfway through. I just feel like I'm missing something in what you're saying."

"I apologize. I'm not really trying to make any big point. It's just . . . It sounds like you expected to be good at something in which you have no training, that you didn't even get time to prepare for, and that you're only doing because Amelia asked you to. And it sort of seems unrealistic to think you would immediately be good at it. It's only been three days."

Confronted with this unassailable, if rather annoying, logic, Bryn sat back. Her hands clenched and then released, and then curled around the wooden arms of the chair where she had seen Professor Herringbone rest her hands many, many times. "Okay, maybe it's possible that doing difficult things is not exactly—" Piper's word from their first meeting came back to her. "Maybe it's not my *forte*."

They smiled in acknowledgement. "I think very few teachers are naturally gifted at all aspects of teaching. Most of us are lucky if we're gifted at any of them."

"So it gets easier?" she asked hopefully.

They didn't answer right away. "Let's just say that finding any aspect of it that you're at all good at makes it easier to do the things you're not as good at."

"Okay," Bryn said with a sigh. "Right, so I just have to figure out what that is."

They shrugged. "I mean, it's theoretically possible you're not good at any of it."

She groaned. "That's not helping."

Piper stood, smiling. "I think my work here is done. But when are you going to start eating with the rest of us? It is a little weird you keep taking all your meals in your cottage or—" they glanced around "—in here."

"It's just I feel like an interloper. I'm not meant to be here. I'm just sort of Amelia's whim, not hired because I deserve this job."

"Well, yes. But it seems like everyone new feels like an interloper here, if I'm being honest. That's not about the teaching credentials."

"Fair enough." She suspected it had not been easy for Piper either, and it had only been six months or so for them.

"So. Dinner." And then they held out their arm, gallantly, like a gentleperson to a lady.

Bryn, wishing the one holding out an arm gallantly was Amelia, nonetheless acknowledged that this was far less nerve-wracking. "I don't mind if I do," she said, and allowed Piper to guide her to the refectory for dinner.

6

Amelia stopped by Bryn's classroom—Professor Herringbone's classroom—on three occasions in the following week. Just for a few minutes each time, to check in, to ask her how she was doing, how she was settling in. And Bryn appreciated it, though she couldn't help the part of her that wanted more. She *wanted* Amelia to stop by the cottage, to come in, to sit down, to share a pot of tea, to show any sign that she had felt the spark that Bryn fancied she'd felt herself.

Amelia, however, showed no evidence of having felt a spark of any kind. Whenever she checked in (Bryn's heart registering impending disaster), she made sure everything was going "all right" (Bryn had no idea what the definition of "all right" was in this context, but agreed that things were fine, mostly because she didn't want to add to Amelia's workload), and then nipped back out again with a sweeping swirl of her cape, fully in Headmistress Mode. Maybe she was always in Headmistress Mode and any hint of something else was a fabrication of Bryn's lonely mind, desperate for human connection and unexpectedly placed in close proximity to her old schoolgirl crush. That was likely all it was.

Just in case she wasn't making it up completely, though, she watched for those less guarded moments when Amelia seemed to briefly drop her professional force field. Never at meals or around students, but Bryn swore she wasn't *entirely* delusional. Which was not the same as believing Amelia Hexford actually wanted her, she reminded herself. Often.

Piper came by more frequently and sat next to her at every meal, which she was grateful for—and suspected they were too. Surprisingly, in the middle of her second week of teaching, Mr Wicks came around between the end of classes and dinner. She had to control the jump-scare part of her brain that immediately assumed she was doing something wrong and was about to get in trouble for it.

Of course, Mr Wicks was no longer her professor, or her teacher, or really any kind of authority figure at all. Still, her heart was pounding slightly when she said, "Oh, hello, Mr Wicks."

"Ms Delmar," he said with a smile. "You really can call me Robert, you know. You're not my student."

She felt herself flushing in some mixture of embarrassment and resistance, and just general flusterment. "Right. I did forget that for a second."

"It happens to everyone," he said, and for a moment it almost looked like he might smile. "Everyone who went to school here, anyway."

"Right, of course." She realized she'd stood up. A sign of

respect to an elder? More likely, a sign of thinking, *Please don't get me in trouble, Mr Wicks, I swear I didn't do it*, even though she had never been the one who did it and her guilt response made zero rational sense.

"How are you coming along?" he asked. "I know this job can be a bit overwhelming at times, and coming in during the middle of the year is harder still."

"I am overwhelmed a bit," she agreed, cursing herself for the unintentional word repetition. She suspected it was an old defense mechanism to appease her mother by echoing back things she'd said. Sirens did kind of like that sort of thing, but she thought she'd stopped doing it as an adult. Plus, this was Mr Wicks—she'd once seen him shouting at a first-year whose prank spell had misfired in the Great Hall, causing ice to form over the cobbles of the floor between the main doors and the stage at the far end. It had only been a dumb attempt to trip a friend, but the spell had more power than the kid expected and went haywire. The infirmary had filled up with bruises, bumps, scrapes, and two students who had hit their heads hard enough to qualify for overnight observation. Maybe Mr Wicks's apparent overreaction hadn't been as extreme as it had felt at the time.

"That's all right, it's very normal." Was he . . . trying to reassure her? "Even if you had gone through the entire university program to get your certificate, you would still likely be overwhelmed a week and a half in."

"That makes sense," she said, though it had not independently occurred to her. What was wrong with her brain right now? She knew these things. "I'm not used to feeling bad at stuff."

This time Mr Wicks laughed and it was so sincere, a sound she didn't think she'd ever heard in four years of being his student, that she inadvertently smiled in response. "No, I remember that about you as a student. Always good at things."

"I tried," she said, and then gestured him awkwardly to sit by her desk. Professor Herringbone's desk, really, still covered in her things. Bryn had cleared about half of the blotter in order to set down her own notebooks. Mr Wicks reached out and picked up a small snow globe, though it was actually a sand globe—some kind of touristy thing from somewhere the professor had traveled to. When you shook it, sand blew around, landing on cacti and Joshua trees.

"And I'm afraid we lost our best teacher mentor," he said softly, suddenly bleak. "When I arrived here, overwhelmed and doubting my ability to do the job, it was Professor Herringbone who talked me off the edge of the cliff more than once."

"Really?"

"Really." He set the sand globe down. "I cannot fill her shoes and you won't be able to either, so my advice is to not try. Find out who you are as a teacher, instead of trying to be anyone else." He hesitated. "Having said that, I do have some thoughts if you want to hear them."

It was so strange, interacting with Mr Wicks as a colleague. When she was a student, he had been stern and demanding, and full of the kinds of blustery semi-threats that had started by scaring her and, by graduation, inspired mostly eye-rolling. But some of that *I'm a white man in a position of authority* vibe seemed calming to her now, which she would probably have to think about at some later date.

"It's important to be clear with the kids where the boundaries are," he began. The fact that Mr Wicks knew the word *boundaries* was somewhat surprising.

"Okay," she said slowly. "What does that . . . look like?"

He spread his hands. "They're developmentally primed to take advantage whenever they can. I know you kids always thought I was being hard on you, but it's important to maintain structure with adolescents. I think it's vital to give them something they know they can count on at this stage in their development. I try very hard to be clear with my students what the lines are and what will happen if they cross them. Whether that's about homework or cursing or disrespecting other members of the class."

Bryn nodded thoughtfully. That Mr Wicks had this philosophy made a lot of sense. She could reconcile it with his behavior as a teacher. "Right," she said. "I can probably try that, though I don't really know what I'm doing."

"That's fair. And I suppose Antigone didn't exactly leave you good notes."

"She left . . . a lot of notes," Bryn said, not wanting to sound skeptical about the professor's tactics, but unable to help her unconvinced tone completely.

Again, Mr Wicks laughed, which sounded strangely natural to him, though she swore he'd never laughed when she was a student. "I'm sure she did. Notes in the margins, notes on little pieces of paper, notes on the walls, even. I would not be surprised, but notes about teaching?"

She shook her head. "Not a single one that I found, and Piper looked too."

"Well, I would encourage you to look up the MSE requirements and cram as many of them into your lessons as you can. It's not the most inspiring way to teach, but if this is a temporary measure, it's probably your best bet. And of course, let me know what I can do to help. I will never be Professor Herringbone, but we are all trying to work together here, and I'm invested in that."

The comment seemed almost edged. She wondered if that was somehow a critique of Amelia, but she didn't want to bring it up. What would she say if he launched into some kind of diatribe against the new headmistress? "Thanks," she said instead. "I appreciate it. At the moment, it would be great if I could just get them to pay attention to anything I was saying."

"It sometimes helps if you can demonstrate that you know what you're talking about," he said, and raised an eyebrow. "You have written a whole book. Have you mentioned that to your classes?"

She almost gasped aloud. "No. I mean, I didn't see why I would."

"Well, you don't have to. I won't insist, but it can be helpful to prove you have game." With that statement, he rose, nodded cordially, and left the classroom.

Prove she had game? Did Mr Wicks just say *game* to her? It was astonishing. Her sixteen-year-old self would never have believed that one day she would be in Professor Herringbone's classroom as a teacher instead of a student, and that Mr Wicks would come by to offer her support.

She couldn't help finding the entire scene completely surreal.

She pulled out her laptop, connected to the school's Wi-Fi, which was significantly stronger in the main building than it was in her cottage, and started looking through the Magical Scholarly Examinations website's teacher resources tab. That's what she was now: a teacher. She started downloading, googling, and taking notes. At least it gave her something to do that felt like it might be helpful, eventually.

* * *

The opportunity to prove she knew what she was doing arrived two days later. She had downloaded year-appropriate practice tests from the MSE website and decided they would be the best way to rip the Band-Aid off and evaluate where her students were with regard to what they were supposed to be learning. Her first class of the day was first-years, who wouldn't need to do their MSEs for another year yet and felt less pressure about them. Still, the pop quiz did not go over well.

She gritted her teeth and promised herself that this was a normal student response to any unplanned exam. She had hated pop quizzes herself. She couldn't believe she was delivering them. Of course, her students felt like she was trying to catch them out, rather than using these tests as a barometer to gauge their level of preparedness, which she did try to explain briefly before realizing they didn't care about her explanation. She could do what she wanted. She was the teacher. They weren't going to agree with her that it made sense.

Reassuring her wasn't their job and she couldn't reasonably expect it from them. Though she secretly planned to use this as an excuse to stop by Amelia's office later for external validation. (She shouldn't *need* validation . . . but she kind of did anyway.)

Right now, she just needed to get through this first period and the rest of the day. And grade all the tests. And figure out what the results of those tests meant for the rest of the year.

As she watched the students bend over their papers, scribbling furiously, she saw a couple of suspicious things. A few glances at cell phones. When she'd gone to school here, cell phones weren't even allowed. A few glances at smartwatches (ditto). Were they cheating somehow? Could they cheat on an unplanned test? But of course they could cheat on an unplanned test. She would have figured out how if she had been the kind of kid who had ever even thought about cheating. But she hadn't needed to; she'd liked being good at school and derived arguably too much of her self-esteem from that skill set. Add that to the list of things she'd need to examine in some nebulous later, when she wasn't super stressed out about pretty much everything.

She made a note of which students seemed to be accessing their electronic devices and shuffled those particular tests to the top of the pile to grade as she was waiting for the next class to complete their own.

Sure enough, those students got almost perfect scores. A few of them got *literally* perfect scores. On a pop quiz for which they hadn't prepared, and they weren't students who had in any other way distinguished themselves.

She glanced up in time to see another student in her second class sliding a cell phone out from under the desk, glancing at it, then writing something down.

Curiouser and curiouser. Or maybe not that curious after all.

She spent the rest of that period coming up with a spell to prevent potential cheating via electronic devices. It was fairly straightforward—she was good at spells that interacted with technology, and this one was a very basic disabling charm, which she could cast roughly on the room at large, affecting all nearby devices. No student in her class would be able to connect to either the Wi-Fi or the cellular network. In this case it would also affect her own phone and laptop, but she'd design exceptions later; this was a quick and dirty job just to hopefully disprove her suspicions.

She cast it discreetly before handing out the tests for her third-period class, which was indeed the MSE class. Second-years, fifteen- and sixteen-year-olds starting to think about their futures. Bryn remembered it as an exciting time, when the end of high school was just appearing in the distance and life afterwards held potential without being quite near enough to overwhelm.

This time, as she watched, she could see even more students pulling out phones and checking watches. One even tapped on what seemed to be an extra-thick pair of glasses, as if frustrated. AI glasses? Was that a thing? Actually, it was definitely a thing. She could probably program a pair of those glasses to look at a test and pop up the correct answers. Certainly the students were capable of doing so.

More restlessness. More shuffling. More frustrated looks around. Less test answering. Bryn's heart sank as she collected the papers at the end of the period.

This time the results were significantly lower. She considered this. It had now been six weeks since Professor Herringbone had died. Were these kids six weeks behind, or were they quite a bit more behind than that? Some of them had failed the exam entirely. The professor wouldn't have let people get away with cheating; surely that was just a thing they were doing to take advantage of the new teacher?

Except that Professor Herringbone had sat at her desk during exams, scribbling away, working on her own research. Probably writing some of those incredibly clever, incredibly hard-to-decipher books that had built her professional reputation. Nothing like Bryn's silly little spell books for merely average witches.

But then again, when had the school allowed the use of phones? Would Professor Herringbone have twigged to just how much they could do by opening their camera apps, pointing at the test, and waiting for the internet to supply an answer? Would she have known that they had the answers to any test question at their fingertips? Probably not.

Which opened up a lot more questions. Had they been doing this all year? In fact, were they doing this in all their classes?

She sighed and sat back in her chair, trying to remember what the format of the MSEs had been. When she was in school, the exams had been held at Grimoire Academy, but they'd been proctored by people from the Magical Scholarly Association, which was a national body that monitored all such exams in the country, and which worked in concert with similar bodies all over the world to ensure that wherever someone came from, their education was supplying essentially the same material. She clearly remembered there being anti-cheating spells enacted, though back then that was to keep anyone from bringing in outside notes or carefully writing answers on their forearms. What was the likelihood that those spells would also include the use of technology?

High, she decided. Very high. Grimoire Academy might be a bit behind times with regard to cell phones, but she suspected the MSA folks were not. They likely had quite clever anti-cheating spells, much more sophisticated than what she'd managed on the fly between periods.

This probably did not bode well. What even were the consequences for attempting to cheat on the MSEs? Not good, for sure. Possibly even negatively affecting the school's reputation. She performed the same charm for her next three classes, and all three also did worse than the control groups.

Rats. She was going to have to tell Amelia. This was really not the excuse to have a casual, maybe even slightly flirtatious, conversation with the headmistress that she had so been hoping for.

7

The headmistress's office had not changed location in the last five years. Amelia was now residing in the same rooms where the headmistress had resided when Bryn was in school. A four-room suite located in the non-ostentatious far end of the third level of the main castle. She wondered if Amelia wouldn't rather have her own little cottage somewhere instead, but presumably she'd had a choice in the matter and, as far as Bryn could tell, Amelia was fully residing in the official chambers.

Feeling a spark of trepidation, even though she was now a teacher and she had good reason to be here, she knocked on Amelia's door.

The woman who opened it was not Amelia.

"Ms Delmar."

Oh gods. "Madame Schneider. Hello."

Schneider looked her up and down with the usual sense of disapproval. It seemed to be her only mode. She had taught the science courses when Bryn had been in school, and it was kind of a miracle she hadn't gone off the sciences altogether afterwards. Madame Schneider had made it clear that hardly any of her students were smart enough or magical enough to benefit from her teaching.

Well, Bryn thought as she stood there paralyzed in terror. *At least I have a good model for the kind of teacher I don't* want *to be.* Not that she could imagine ever being like Madame Schneider.

"Ah, Bryn," Amelia said. Her relief was clear not just to Bryn but also, judging by the tightening of her lips, to Madame Schneider. "How good of you to come. Make yourself at home." She turned to the professor and said, with finality, "Governor."

That was a dismissal. It might not have been the strongest dismissal Bryn had ever heard, but it was clearly a dismissal, and Schneider just as clearly knew it, which was satisfying in its own way.

"Mind what we spoke about," she said to Amelia.

"I always do," Amelia replied cooly.

Well, that seemed tense as hell.

The professor—or, Bryn supposed, the governor now—stalked off down the corridor. Amelia pulled her inside.

Oh, her touch— *No, focus, you're here for school reasons.* But Amelia didn't immediately withdraw her hand, so Bryn thought it was fair she should enjoy the moment while it lasted.

Then Amelia shut the door and leaned against it, as if she had to hold it closed against another onslaught from Madame Schneider. For a long moment she stood there, eyes shut, just breathing. Bryn felt as if she was watching a transformation; Headmistress Hexford was morphing

70

back into Amelia, who was a complicated woman, but not a superhero. It was too bad she wasn't wearing her cape, so she could symbolically hang it up to mark the difference.

"What was *that*?" Bryn asked after a moment, when Amelia's breathing seemed to be settling into a slower rhythm. *Maybe stop looking at Amelia's . . . breaths . . .* She drew her gaze up to Amelia's face, where her eyes were just fluttering open, looking strangely vulnerable.

"My ongoing nightmare. Sorry, I don't mean to be dramatic. It's just, it's a lot sometimes, this job. I'm grateful for it. I'm really not taking it for granted, but . . ." Amelia took a long breath through her nose, then exhaled, blowing the air through pursed lips, the way Bryn breathed when she did Pilates.

"It's a lot," Bryn echoed, feeling helpless, but also a bit honored by the fact that Amelia had allowed her to see this moment, when she transformed back into herself.

"Yes, but come in, um, let me make tea," Amelia said. She glanced at her watch. "Or . . . I guess it's probably still too early for a glass of wine?"

"Probably," Bryn said. "And I don't drink. Something about the siren side of my genetics and alcohol not really mixing well."

"Oh, of course, sorry, I didn't even think. Actually, I don't know much about siren genetics."

"Nor do I, though I've always thought I should really study it. That's just what my mother tells me, and my few experiments have borne it out. But I would love a cup of tea."

"Wonderful. I would love to *make* you a cup of tea."
Amelia paused, cheeks flushing just slightly pinker. "That
sounds kind of weird. I do not have a tea-making fetish, I
swear. Not that I judge. I would happily engage someone's
tea-making fetish. It's just been a long few days and it
would be nice to do a task with a clear beginning, middle,
and end, and share that task with another person."

"I'm not too worried about your tea-making fetish,"
Bryn said, smiling, and noticing that the pink tinge to
Amelia's skin had, if anything, deepened during her talk
about fetishes. Internally, she was rejoicing. A long few
days! So Amelia hadn't been avoiding her or not interested
in her—she'd just been busy. Which was exactly what
Bryn had kept telling herself. But it was still nice to have it
confirmed.

She should launch directly into the reason she'd come.
She needed to tell Amelia exactly what she'd discovered
and then ask for help dealing with it. What she *wanted*
to do was sit in an armchair and share a table with this
beautiful, incredibly smart witch and chat. *Oh gods, stop
this. She isn't really your boss, but she's definitely someone
you work with. So be chill.* Chill had never exactly been
Bryn's default position, which seemed to vacillate between
completely stone-faced and completely jubilant.

"Busy?" she asked in an attempt to bring things around
to, well, anything that wasn't her current lovesick crush on
a woman she kept reminding herself she didn't really know,
even though they had gone to the same school with each
other for four years.

"Oh, the governors. They have it out for me. I know I

keep saying that and I know it sounds paranoid, but they really don't want me here."

"Why?" Bryn asked. "I mean, that doesn't make sense, does it? The professors seem okay with you." Though she wasn't sure she'd know if that wasn't the case. Everyone seemed to assume they'd been friends in school and that's how she'd gotten the job, which probably should be more hurtful, except it kind of felt like an excuse to be bad at it. Maybe there was less pressure if it was nepotism? That seemed backwards.

Amelia poured tea into two mugs, then led the way back through to her sitting room, where she gestured Bryn into a seat and sat down herself. Her eyes were bright and intent, but there was a betraying puffiness beneath them. She looked like someone who needed a cuddle, and boy did Bryn want to be the person who could give her that cuddle. She momentarily wondered if she could pull off the line, *Hey, you look like you could use a hug* . . . But no. Amelia could probably deliver that without sounding either awkward or like she was inappropriately propositioning someone. Bryn definitely could not pretend that her interest in hugging Amelia was merely to provide comfort.

"You know, I really was so excited to be here, even after I discovered that the only reason was because Professor Herringbone essentially blackmailed the governors into giving me the job. I still thought I could make a difference."

"You are making a difference," Bryn said, with a confidence that wasn't exactly earned because, to be honest, she didn't know—but it was impossible to imagine Amelia Hexford not making a difference.

"I hope so, but in reality, I've just made changes that most people weren't really on board for, and even the people who were willing to give them a chance won't be surprised when I'm proved wrong. Like Mr Wicks, who has made it very clear that when my technology initiative fails, he will not say *I told you so*, or at least not to my face."

Bryn felt an immediate rush of disloyalty for having actually sort of enjoyed Mr Wicks's company when he stopped by her classroom. He seemed to have changed so much in the intervening years, but surely if one of them had changed, it was Bryn herself. Was her perspective so different than it had been as a student? And everything Amelia was saying now completely jibed with both versions of him: the version that thought he knew everything and was kind of a jerk about it, and the version that thought he knew everything and was compassionate to someone who admittedly knew less.

"And the athletics program," Amelia continued. "Which, despite my best efforts, I can't figure out how to explain in a way that makes sense to anyone but me and Piper. Even the kitchen staff think it's a joke."

"The kitchen staff?" Bryn asked. "What do you mean?"

"It's so silly. I went in the other day just to pick up a snack because I hadn't eaten breakfast, and I heard them talking about the kids playing—I don't even know what they were playing, and how it wasn't proper to witches."

"Proper to witches?" Bryn paused, then decided to risk a little bit of teasing. "I mean, was it baseball, though? Because baseball is not proper to anyone, and yet so many people seem to irrationally enjoy it."

This got a slightly startled laugh out of Amelia. "Right? Hit ball with stick. How many sports come down to *hit ball with stick*? It's funny how much people build around these things. Hit ball with stick. Or put ball through hoop, or goal, or basket, or hole."

"We may not be sporty people," Bryn said after a second. "Piper would probably have some other ideas here."

"That's another thing! When I put that program together, I guess I thought it would be successful and that within the first year the professors would start noticing, I don't know, more teamwork in their classes, better test scores after PE, more focus. Which are all things that my reading suggested would result from a properly run athletics program. I wasn't thinking that if it's not successful, I can't keep employing Piper. What will they do? They have so much potential." She sighed heavily. "They're so good with the kids, but I can't keep them here full-time to teach stickball games to the ten kids who come from non-magical families and think they're fun."

"Is that a problem for today?" Bryn asked.

"No. No, it's not. Anyway, I'm so sorry that I haven't been to check in with you more often. How are things going? How are your classes? I really apologize. I meant to come by every day, I swear, and it's just gotten away from me. Now you've been here two weeks? Are things a mess?" Amelia added.

"Things have been touch and go," Bryn said after a moment. "More touch than go, if I'm, you know . . ."

"Not lying?" Amelia suggested.

"Well, I wouldn't lie, but I'm not good at this. I'm

afraid you picked a dud. Amelia, I'm so sorry. I'm really completely at a loss with how to do this job."

Amelia, far from daunted, actually smiled. "That's exactly where you're supposed to be two weeks in."

"That's what Mr Wicks said." So why wasn't it actually reassuring?

"You talked to Mr Wicks about teaching?"

"Well, he talked to me." Bryn looked down at her hands, then glanced up through her eyelashes, not quite sure how Amelia would handle that, if Mr Wicks was some kind of professional rival. "Sorry, I know that you don't necessarily get along with him—"

But Amelia only waved this off. "No, no, I think it's wonderful. That's what I hoped my senior teachers would do with a new teacher, especially one in these kinds of circumstances. I think it's great, and I don't have a problem with Mr Wicks. I really don't, personally. I'm just worried that he's going to take my job." She slumped. "I guess I'm more worried that he would be right to take my job. That he would do this job so much better than I am."

"I'm sure that's not true," Bryn said, wondering if she should be in *listening mode*, or *problem-solving mode*.

"Anyway, so you're struggling with teaching." Maybe Amelia was the one going into *problem-solving mode*. Or rather, *Headmistress Mode: activated*.

Bryn blew out a long breath. "It's so hard. I don't know why I didn't expect that, but apparently, I didn't. Not that I thought it was easy, but . . ."

"I think it happens to everyone. I definitely struggled when teaching."

"You were a teacher?"

"Oh, yeah. I mean, Professor Herringbone didn't just pluck me out of the ether."

"Where were you teaching?"

Amelia sat back, suddenly looking more relaxed. "Well, I went for my training at Wyndemere University, and I met some really awesome people there, and one of my professors happened to be a demon and got me an internship—which became a job later—at a demon elementary school. So that's where I got started." She smiled in recollection. "It was fantastic. I mean, very, very different, and the kids constantly made fun of me for having no idea about demon culture, but it was great. I'm so glad I learned there. Not that here isn't also good, but it gave me a really different perspective. Demons have zero rules against technology. Nobody thinks that tradition means a failure of progress. It was, well, really refreshing."

"Wow," Bryn said. "That's awesome. So that's why the professor thought you'd be good for this job?"

"Maybe . . . not exactly? I reached out to her about two days into my first semester of teaching to say I was doing everything wrong. We hadn't kept consistently in touch after graduation, but you know how much she liked to teach people, and I became her student again, in a way. And she was absolutely fascinated by how demons do things, so she loved hearing about all that." Amelia paused, her smile growing slightly melancholy. "There's so much more I wanted to learn from her. Oh well. Anyway, I think the professor thought Grimoire Academy needed an influx of new energy and new ideas, that we're falling behind. You've probably noticed that enrollment is lower than it used to be, and we need a significant amount of infrastructure work on some of the buildings." She cast her eyes up at the ceiling. "Our broomsticks sculpture required some magical and engineering work last year, which the professor had done, but I'm not sure we could really afford it."

Bryn blinked. The crossed broomsticks on the roof of the castle, magically lit at night in different colors depending on the time of year, were a landmark so well known that even non-magical tourist guides pointed to it as a must-see in the area. (Often with a proviso that unauthorized persons entering school grounds would be faced with "consequences of untold discomfort", which just about covered being told off by a seriously annoyed witch.) "What was wrong with the broomsticks? I mean, it's not like we could have them taken down." The castle would look unnatural without its trademark sculpture.

"Professor Herringbone looked into that too, quietly, but in fact it would have cost more." Amelia's lovely face creased in a frown. "You should investigate that yourself. She said the spell work was magnificent and nearly indestructible. Tied into the school's roots, or something."

"Roots," Bryn repeated. "I wonder what that means. And how they did it."

"I don't know. But I do know we're still paying off the magical engineering firm that worked on it last year."

"Yikes." There didn't seem to be much else she could say, though this felt inadequate.

The frown softened and Amelia sipped her tea before

saying, "Sorry, I didn't mean to drop all this on you. It's not your responsibility. I just wish the professor were here."

It made sense that Amelia had lost so much more than a colleague in Professor Herringbone, but Bryn had really only considered her own loss, which seemed shortsighted now. She wished she could reach out, take the other woman's hand. But she didn't. She settled on saying, "I'm so sorry for your loss. She meant so many different things to everyone."

"She really did. We're still getting emails and letters from people. I keep thinking, I don't know, maybe we should put up a memorial somewhere. Online, or here in person." Amelia's expression turned pensive.

Tempting as it was to get sidetracked, Bryn braced herself to deliver more bad news. "I'm also really sorry I'm not measuring up. Not to add to your burdens at the moment."

"What? What do you mean?"

Bryn took another breath. "I gave my classes MSE pretests today for their year levels."

Amelia went tense. More tense than she'd been with Madame Schneider in the room. "What happened? How'd they do?"

"Well, I made a discovery." Oh, this was so hard. How could she break it to Amelia that her really inspiring technology program was having a disastrous effect? At least on the students in Professor Herringbone's classes. "It turns out some of the kids have been cheating a little bit."

"Okay." Her voice was deceptively mild, the kind of

mild that meant she was practically holding her breath, waiting for the ax to fall.

And I'm the one with the ax. "They seem to be using their phones and their smartwatches, and I'm pretty sure at least one of them was using some kind of fancy glasses."

"What do you mean?"

Bryn didn't think Amelia was having trouble understanding. She thought Amelia was in denial and she didn't really blame her. So she explained about the first two classes, and how she used them as control groups, and then her new spell that disabled the use of electronic devices during the class.

"I'll refine it later. It really only disabled connections to networks outside the school, but I'm afraid the grades plummeted. I don't know how long it's been going on, but it doesn't seem like it's all my fault. I mean, I wish it was and then you could just get a new teacher, but—"

"I'm not getting a new teacher," Amelia snapped. "Damn it." She set down her mug with a thud, got up, and began to pace. "Fuck. Oh shit, what am I gonna do? I need these MSEs to go well. This is not— I can't let this—"

Bryn watched with growing concern. Amelia wasn't finishing sentences, and she looked very, very upset, but what else could Bryn have done? She had to tell her. Maybe she should have gone to Mr Wicks, but he was already anti-technology, so that wouldn't have been good either.

Finally, when the pacing seemed to be speeding up, Bryn stood and set herself right in front of Amelia, who stopped just in time to avoid a collision.

"Can you undo the charm? Maybe if we can just squeak

by this year, then next year I'll figure something else out. Next year we'll start afresh. They can keep their phones, we'll put charms on them, everything will be fine." Amelia frowned. "I know it's not really ethical, but maybe this once—"

"Amelia, the MSEs are proctored by an outside organization. There's no way they'll be able to cheat. Plus, half of them are practicals. I don't see how you could use your phone to cheat on a practical."

Amelia's shoulders slumped, her head lowered, her eyes closed. She looked like she was about to cry. Bryn reached out impulsively, her hands on Amelia's shoulders.

"Why is this a crisis? I know it's inconvenient, but even if it's more than one class, it's just a blip. New program, new policies. Maybe we can argue the MSE class has had, I don't know, too much disruption this year and get them a delayed test. That happens sometimes." Bryn wanted so much to pull Amelia into a hug, but it was too soon. Or too abrupt. Or just not the right moment. "It doesn't seem like this is a crisis," she said softly.

Amelia looked up, tears in her eyes. "They're going to fire me. That's what Governor Schneider was here to tell me. They had a meeting and if the MSEs do not maintain or exceed an average grade of B, they're going to remove me from my position."

"Oh shit," Bryn said.

Amelia started to cry.

8

Amelia's composure only broke for maybe a minute or two at most. Then, as if some invisible person was telling her to straighten up, she wiped her eyes, pressed her shoulders back, and took two deep breaths. Bryn watched this with some remaining concern.

"The news you might get fired over things you don't have any direct impact on is legitimately stressful, and crying about it for longer than a minute and a half seems reasonable," Bryn suggested.

But Amelia clearly didn't wish to stay in her emotions. "Sorry," she said. "Sorry, this is not on you. I'm just . . . I don't even know what I am."

"Pretty logically upset?"

Amelia offered a weak smile. "I take your point, but I shouldn't be crying on you, and I don't see how it'll help."

Feeling a little daring, Bryn gently steered Amelia towards her chair. "Another cup of tea?"

Amelia took out her phone, looked at the time, then set it aside. "Oh, I shouldn't. Too late for caffeine, too early for alcohol." She then covered her mouth as if scandalized. "I can't believe I just said that out loud."

"You're a grown-up."

"Yes, but would I want any of our students to think that way? To count down the minutes until they can numb their work woes with booze?"

Bryn laughed. "Okay, this is getting a little dramatic now. You're allowed to have a glass of wine on a stressful day, without it, you know, being anything more than that."

"What do you do on a stressful day?" Amelia asked, raising an eyebrow.

Bryn blinked. "I'm not sure. Work harder?"

"Oh, very healthy," Amelia said.

"Thank you very much," Bryn replied primly. "But for real? I'm not sure I have healthy coping mechanisms. When I was here, I did work harder, like if I got good enough grades I could believe I deserved to be at this school. And after . . . Well, I worked on my book while doing some pretty mind-numbing day jobs. That was a lot. And the book deal made me enough money to at least quit the day job, after which I guess I'd work on the book during the day and then work on the book at night as well." She'd taken long walks, and spent a lot of time at coffee shops and breweries and in parks. "I take a lot of walks. Not in a healthy 'getting my steps' way, so much as a 'if I walk far enough maybe I can outrun my thoughts' way. But drinking and vaping don't seem to work with my body, so I guess it's not a bad alternative."

"Maybe we should take a walk together," Amelia said. "Around the grounds."

Don't act like a lovesick baby. "Oh, um, that would be

nice." *Okay, maybe there's a middle ground between lovesick baby and "my mom is making me say this"*. "I mean really, I'd like that." Before she could embarrass herself further, she continued, "The governors can't seriously hold you responsible for grades on an exam taking place less than a year after you were hired? That doesn't make any sense."

Amelia shrugged. "And it's totally contributing to my intense paranoia they've been trying to get rid of me the whole time."

Which might actually be justified (Bryn couldn't get the image of the retreating and somehow aggressive back of Madame Schneider out of her mind), but there was no obvious way to address it regardless. "Okay, let's set that aside for the moment. What do you want me to do about the cheating?"

Amelia sat back with a sigh. "You're right. I think we tell the students that we have new spells to prevent it, and then we enact those spells." She glanced up. "I'm sorry that I momentarily considered just cheating on the MSEs. You know, I would not normally want anyone to cheat on tests."

"Standardized testing is a terrible metric for how well people have absorbed knowledge, and we've known that for a hundred years, but we keep doing it. I guess it's better than nothing, but I don't really take it that seriously. I mean, outside of the current situation, in which case your job is dependent on it." *Stop talking*, she told herself.

"That is not a system I'm prepared to overhaul quite yet," Amelia said. "Not that I disagree." She grimaced. "Do you think it's worth us running more practice tests in every class to see where the students are? I'm afraid to find out, but also I feel like I need to know."

"Maybe that's where we start." What if the students were bunk at all levels, in all subjects? The MSEs were a little more than three months away. Was that enough time to bring an entire class up to snuff? "Do you want an excuse for it?" She stopped to think. "We could say that you're considering a new curriculum, and in order to best select one, you want to know the standing of all current students."

"The professors would love that," Amelia mumbled.

"I don't think we have to lie to the professors, do we?" Realizing she'd said *we* way too many times, she added, "I mean *you*, obviously, I'm not really involved, since I'm only here for a few months, but I wonder if you can tell the truth to the professors?"

Amelia nodded reluctantly. "I agree. Mr Wicks is gonna be so smug. Students are using their phones to cheat. Am I foolish for not having thought about that? It didn't occur to me."

"Well, you and I never really needed to cheat. At least, I didn't really need to. School was something I was good at."

"That's true, yet I still feel dumb for not considering it."

"Well, let me take care of some of that. I can at least handle the professors. I'll just tell them I uncovered something and give them the spell for it, and only offer more information if people ask. And then once we have the test results, that's when we should strategize." That pesky *we* had crept in again.

"Yes, let's not reason ahead of our data." Amelia paused. "I can't remember if that's Sherlock Holmes or every prime-time crime show."

"I'm pretty sure it's Sherlock Holmes." Honesty

compelled Bryn to add, "I think it's actually *theorize*, but same idea."

Amelia blew out a long breath and met her eyes. "How bad were the results, really, in your pre-tests?"

Bryn momentarily pressed her lips together, as if trying to find a way not to answer. Then she said, "Not great. I mean, really not great. But I don't think this can only have started this year, can it? You're sure they didn't have their phones before?"

"They weren't allowed to have their phones before, but that doesn't mean they didn't have them. I guess that's probably true in a lot of places. I'll look into it. I wish Professor Herringbone were here. I just want to talk to her. Not only about this . . . I want to know if I'm screwing everything up."

Struck by this, Bryn said, "So, basically, you need Professor Herringbone to be to you what you are to me?"

Amelia, looking shocked, blinked. "No! I mean, not exactly what I am to you, I hope. I mean . . ." She bit her lip. Then she unbit and said, "This is me trying not to dig the hole any deeper." And she bit her lip again, looking repressed.

Did this mean . . .? What did this mean? It meant something, surely. "Ummm," Bryn said. And then, "If it's any consolation, I definitely don't think of you the way I did the professor."

Amelia's lips slid up into a smile. "Oh good, that actually does help. I mean, not that I was really worried, but yeah. I don't want to be your, um, professional mentor."

Bryn fluttered her eyelashes. "What if I had a thing for mentors?"

Amelia laughed out loud. "Stop it. We're strategizing, remember?"

"Right, strategy." But Bryn didn't feel at all like her tentative flirting had gone badly. "I'll refine my spell tonight and give it to the other teachers tomorrow."

"Good, thank you. And I will explain the situation, and make the testing announcement at lunch."

Both of them nodded. Having a plan felt so much better than not having one. Bryn thought about it, then said, "Is there anything I can do to help? Aside from, you know, delivering bad news, freaking you out, and giving you a sleepless night?"

"Well, you're saving me from the students all trying to cheat on their MSEs, and the humiliation of being the only school where that happens, so I think you've already done a lot." Amelia's clear gaze locked on hers, eyes narrowing slightly in a way that made Bryn's insides fizz like a predictable and controlled chemical reaction. "But there is one thing you can do for me. If you're offering."

Bryn had a moment to think *I would low-key do anything, but preferably sexy things*. In fact, there were contexts in which it would be very hot indeed to say the words: *I'd do anything for you* and then wait to see what Amelia did with that. Sexy mentor, indeed.

Obviously, that was *not* what Amelia was thinking in the moment. Still, in the spirit of discovery, Bryn said lightly, "I'll do anything."

Amelia's smile widened.

9

On the following Monday at three p.m., Bryn found herself sitting in the lower library in a little grouping of chairs arranged in front of wide windows with a backdrop of books, books, books, and a mezzanine filled with more books. It was not her favorite of the libraries, but it was the brightest, most open, most airy, and, Amelia thought, least threatening. She was here to meet the after-school club.

In itself, this was kind of a mindfuck. She'd been part of the after-school club when she was a student, and she'd hated it, but also relied upon it. Maybe she was relying upon hating it as a sort of stable throughline for her otherwise higgledy-piggledy social life. If you took *higgledy-piggledy* to mean a few times when people seemed to like her and many more times when she seemed socially invisible. In Bryn's time at the school, the after-school club was considered a catch-all for weird kids, the ones who didn't fit in. Membership in it had been mostly grudging, and Bryn had only joined because Professor Herringbone had told her it would be good for her—something she'd taken quite personally at the time. She vividly remembered the sudden flush of shame, the desire to say, *Am I really that bad? Can everyone tell I don't belong here?* The sensation of being exposed had lingered, coloring even the relatively mundane aspects of the club, which had been more of a support group than anything else, and one in which Bryn still never truly felt included. She hadn't realized then that her challenges with adjustment applied across all mediums and formats of socialization. She missed the illusion that it was simply because she came from a siren background, instead of really understanding that she was just kind of odd. No matter what context she happened to be standing in.

Though after she agreed to be the faculty facilitator, she realized that it had never been explained to her (or, as far as she knew, anyone else) what the club was supposed to accomplish.

Perhaps things had changed, or perhaps the club seemed less alienating with the clarity of age; in any case, it was clear that the new after-school club had a focus on academic support for witches from non-magical backgrounds. According to Amelia, these were the three second-year students who were struggling the most with both adjusting to Grimoire Academy and their impending MSEs, which was supported by Bryn's recent pre-tests and the reports of other professors.

"I've been meaning to set this up all year," Amelia had confessed. "But time got away from me, and Professor Herringbone had always played club sponsor until she became headmistress shortly after we graduated. No one picked it up and . . ." Amelia had looked at Bryn as if, of all people, she was the one who was truly best suited to help her. And that sensation went directly into Bryn's bones.

Now, actually waiting for the club to begin, it was hard to recapture that feeling of competence. Mostly, Bryn just worried she'd do or say something that would make it obvious how out of her depth she was. The first student to arrive was Circe, the girl who'd been in the professor's classroom the first time Bryn and Amelia had walked in. Having now known her for a few more weeks, Bryn had heard her say exactly as many words, which was none. Circe didn't seem to talk. Not, Bryn thought, in a *some kind of physical or mental or behavioral issue with talking* way, though of course she wasn't an expert. More in a *this is all impossible and I will not participate* way. And to be honest, Bryn respected that.

Still, it could well be a sign of failure to adjust to the witching world. And so here she was.

The other two names on the list were Violet and Luke. Violet, she/they; Luke, he/him. No additional details. Both of them arrived five minutes late. But not as if they'd been traveling together, merely as if neither of them had cared particularly to arrive on time. In those five minutes Bryn had spoken to Circe a few times, and Circe had only looked up through eyelashes and then away again. It did not feel rude or standoffish. It simply felt like she didn't wish to speak.

"I don't know why I'm here," Violet said, hands on their hips. "My grades are fine." Which was both true and not true. Violet had been one of the kids who'd taken out their phone and been frustrated to discover that it could no longer help with exams after Bryn's network-dampening charm. Bryn had no idea how much of their current grades were a product of previous cheating.

"Please have a seat," she said, gesturing to a chair.

"Please tell me why I'm here."

"I was hoping you could tell me why you were here." That got a spark of interest from the defensive teenager. Bryn sensed a possible in, and went on, "I'm new here, but this is the list of names I was given. So I guess, from my perspective, you're here because your name was on a list. I assumed you three would be able to tell me more."

Luke dropped heavily into an armchair. Far more heavily than his skinny, bony frame seemed to warrant. "I'm here because I'm a dunce."

Bryn raised her eyebrows. "A dunce? What, with the cap?"

Luke's face split into a grin. "Yes, pointy cap in the corner. 'Stay there until you can focus.' Or, 'Luke you haven't even started on your work.' Or, 'What are you doing there? That's not where you're meant to be at all.'"

"Is that what being a dunce is?" Bryn asked.

He shrugged. "I don't know, but it's better than being called stupid, I think. It feels like being a dunce is sort of a choice, and being stupid is a thing that you were born as and you can't escape from. So I'd rather be a dunce."

"You're not a dunce," Violet said, enunciating carefully. "You have ADHD. Calling yourself a dunce is actually quite ableist."

He frowned. "It is? Even if it's what I am?"

"Yeah, that's *internally* ableist," they said in an exhausted tone. "Ugh, why don't you know this?"

Another shrug. "Well, anyway, whatever I am, I know

why I'm here. I'm here because I don't do my homework. And I often don't do my schoolwork either, which really annoys the professors. And I get that, but also, I just can't make it important in my brain? I want to. I try to make it important. But I just . . . don't care. Is that wrong?" He shook his head. "I don't want them to think that it's personal. It's really not. I just—"

"Have ADHD," Violet said again.

"Maybe," he agreed. "I mean, I don't know. I'm not diagnosed, so I'm not sure you should really be saying that. But it does kind of make sense. I've done like 7,000 internet quizzes, and they all come up ADHD."

"Okay," Bryn said. "Thanks, Luke. Why don't you tell me a little about yourself, Violet?"

They sighed and finally took a seat in a chair. She didn't settle into it with the same gravity that Luke had, but sat instead towards the front, their back ramrod straight, hands clasped loosely on their lap. "I'm Violet Peltier. I turn sixteen in three weeks. I've been here at Grimoire Academy since my first year. And before that, I went to a regular public school with non-magical people. I come from a non-magical family. And even though I displayed magical abilities from a very young age, they still didn't put me in a magical school until high school. So any problems that I have with culture shock are definitely my parents' fault."

This was delivered with a straight face and serious tone, leaving Bryn to wonder if she was on one of those hidden-camera shows, and these kids had been called in from Central Casting. She glanced up at the crown molding, but no small black lenses looked back. "Okay, thank you, Violet."

Amelia had said that these three seemed to be academically struggling and unengaged with any other micro-communities on campus. *Micro-communities* had been the term she'd actually used, which Bryn hadn't asked her to define, but she assumed it meant all of those cliques and groups and clubs to which she, as a student, had also never belonged.

"And Circe? What about you?"

"Circe doesn't speak," Violet said.

Circe, glancing up again from beneath her bangs, shrugged. Just slightly. Just enough so that Bryn knew she was paying attention.

"You don't speak ever?"

Slight head shake.

"Are you physically capable of speech? I mean, is there something wrong with your vocal cords, or something else?"

Slight head shake.

Violet piped in with, "I don't think you should really ask things like that. It might imply that different abilities are less deserving of respect."

"Well, I definitely don't mean to imply that. I guess I'm just curious." Bryn paused, checking her instinctive defensiveness. How much did it matter why Circe didn't speak? Was she going to insist? Surely not. She nodded, her initial irritation melting away. "Okay, Violet, I take your point. My curiosity is probably also not applicable to this situation." Bryn ducked her head to look at Circe. "As your teacher, though, do you need medical help of any kind?"

Head shake.

"All right, then. I think the headmistress just wanted to offer the three of you any additional support you might need to make your time here easier."

They stared back at her. Or rather, two of them stared back at her, and one of them stared up at her from beneath her hair. Great. *This is going well.* "So, does anyone need any additional schoolwork help? We could do homework if that would meet your needs." *Meet your needs?* Had she really just said that? What was she, a group therapist? She had to stop channeling the ghosts of schooling past.

"I shouldn't be here," Violet said, tossing their hair. "There's nothing wrong with the way that I do school or anything else. I usually excel."

"Wonderful. Maybe you're here to help your classmates."

This seemed to sink in. They turned to Luke and said, "Well, do you need help?"

"I did get slightly stuck on the math assignment."

Violet sighed. "What part?"

"It's just I never learned fractions, which I didn't think would matter, and then they keep coming up again."

"That's how math *is*. They just cycle through the same four concepts over and over and over again."

Bryn, slightly delighted by this answer, had to keep her smile under wraps. "Circe, did you need help with anything?"

Circe shook her head, then opened her backpack, pulled out a notebook, and began writing in it. Her hair was fully in her face now, long enough to drag along the page.

"All right," Bryn said, feeling that she was completely

adrift and had no idea how to make this club work. Or how she'd even know if it *was* working.

* * *

Later, at dinner, Amelia asked how it had gone. It wasn't exactly a private conversation, but Bryn, seated in between Amelia and Piper, couldn't resist the chance to get another read on the situation.

"I think maybe . . . terribly?"

"Can't have gone that badly," Piper assured her, still chewing on a mouthful of salad. "Circe doesn't say boo to a ghost and the other two aren't exactly troublemakers."

"Circe wrote in a notebook the entire time. For forty-five minutes."

Piper nodded. "Sounds about right."

"What about the others?" Amelia asked.

"Which others?" Mr Wicks asked from across the table.

"Violet and Luke, both second-years."

He nodded. "Violet has a lot of potential. Luke, I despair of ever getting to complete any of his assignments."

"I think they all have a lot of potential," Amelia said. Tension seemed to flare between them, but Bryn wasn't sure if she was imagining it, because she knew how Amelia felt.

Mr Wicks only nodded. "I don't disagree. But I do find Luke's continued misbehavior troubling."

"I'm intrigued by all three of them," Bryn said, hoping to defuse the possible conflict, even as she acknowledged internally that it had nothing at all to do with her. "But I don't have any idea how I can possibly help them."

"Being consistently available is a good start," Amelia said.

Mr Wicks cleared his throat. "I would caution against being *too* available. We best serve our students by inspiring them towards independence."

Gulping, Bryn shot a sideways look at Piper, who was studiously eating salad and pretending not to hear any of this.

"Be that as it may," Amelia said after a moment, "all I'm asking is for you to reach out to these three specific students." She offered Bryn a smile. "You don't have to work miracles."

Reflecting upon the possibility that a portion of the students were literally going to fail their MSEs, Bryn thought Amelia really did need miracles to be performed. Though, clearly, not by her.

"You should get them moving," Piper suggested. "Get out of the library. Take a walk around. Go feed the ponies or something."

The idea of Violet, with their long sparkling golden hair, feeding ponies did bring a smile to Bryn's face. "You think?"

Piper shrugged. "Can't hurt, really."

"No, that's true." She thought of something else and turned to Amelia. "What's the school policy on field trips?"

10

Whether due to exhaustion or overwhelm, Bryn was at least sleeping through the night more frequently than usual, and not consistently waking up to obsess at two a.m. Still, when she did happen to be up in the middle of the night, her thoughts frequently turned not to the stress of teaching, but to Amelia.

Or, okay, to both. It would start with something distinctly school-related—had she explained too much about how wands were useful tools, but eventually one could cast common spells without them, due to the way witches innately interacted with magical fields? At what point had the kids' eyes started to glaze over? Somewhere around the first five words, she feared. She could talk to Amelia about it. Was that just an excuse? But Amelia was so helpful. And anyway, she always assured Bryn that she was available any time.

She'd think about seeing Amelia in the hall and finding a way to invite herself to Amelia's rooms. Or Amelia to hers. She'd dwell on the way she'd phrase her question. About

Amelia leaning in to reassure her, maybe touching her arm, or even her hand. She would lean towards Amelia, smell that intoxicating scent of jasmine, breathe her thanks, look into the other woman's eyes, and . . .

At which point she'd snap out of it (most of the time) and attempt to wrench her thoughts back in a not-kissing-the-headmistress direction. Maybe her fourth-years needed more of a challenge. Should she be talking to them more about what they planned to do next year? She wasn't even sure how many of them planned to go to university. Should she have gone to university? What if she and Amelia had both gone to university, and spent their young-adult years together? They might have dated. Might have shared walks back to the dormitories late at night, held hands, kissed on squeaky dorm beds . . .

Bryn's nights were not unpleasant, but they were also not necessarily restful.

The field trip idea wasn't firm in Bryn's mind until the next after-school club meeting. She'd asked the kids more about their backgrounds, their families. What was their experience with magic? How familiar were they with witchy culture? At first, all three of them had clammed up— if Circe could be said to clam up when she actually didn't speak in the first place. She did, though. Bryn was getting much better at reading her body language. Circe clamming up looked like hiding behind her bangs and doodling in her notebook, as though she could pretend she wasn't in the room if only she didn't acknowledge anyone else.

Luke, somewhat surprisingly, was the one who had started talking. He'd confessed that while being a witch was awesome and learning about his witchiness really helped him understand his life and his identity, in other ways, it had been less helpful.

"My sisters either make fun of me or are jealous, or both—like, at the same time. But mostly it's just weird with my dad. He raised us on his own. He did a really good job. But then there's this thing that I can't really share with him, even if I want to. How do you explain that your brain can do magic even without really knowing how?"

Bryn nodded sympathetically. "My mom's a siren," she said. "My sister too."

"Is that easier?" Luke asked. "I mean, with them being— *Are* sirens magical? Sorry, I don't really know."

Bryn sighed. Sirens were rare, and most of them were clustered around the equator. They didn't settle into family groups, and it was uncommon for a siren to have more than one child. They were mostly on their own. The only other sirens she knew were vague relatives who lived far away, though her mom had said that there was a siren community down south somewhere.

"Sirens are magical, at least in the context of how we use that phrase to denote everyone who isn't non-magical, like sirens, demons, and shifters. That doesn't mean they understand being a witch," she said. "Or at least the sirens in my family don't understand it. I'm not sure how much it helps that they're also magical, because it's so different." It had been a shock to everyone and not necessarily a welcome one. Her mom, she reflected, had cried in her bedroom by herself late at night after they found out what Bryn was, and for years she'd assumed the tears were for the failure of her eldest daughter to be a good siren. Only as an adult did she wonder if her mother was weeping in recognition that her eldest daughter needed things that she herself could not provide. That would be enough to make any parent cry.

Luke nodded. "Yeah, it was hard for my dad too. He doesn't really get it. He doesn't understand why I have to go to a special school. He thinks that everything you need to be a witch can be found online."

Violet snorted. "A lot of things can be found online, but a lot of nonsense is also online." Then, with a glance at Bryn, they added, "I know, because I checked. I really liked my old school. I liked my friends."

"But you decided to come here?" Bryn asked.

"Well, yes, it's not every day you find out you're special and that there's a place where you can go to meet people who are special in that same way."

"Uhh." Luke frowned. "Isn't everyone special?"

Violet only waved this off. "Yes, but you know what I mean. I always knew I was different, and then suddenly someone didn't just recognize that, but could explain it. Finding out I wasn't just randomly weird, but actually a witch . . ." She paused. "It meant a lot to me."

"And your family?" Bryn asked.

"They're fine." With a violent hair-flip, Violet continued, "The weirdest thing is that even regular stuff like going to the shops is different for witches. They go to different shops. They buy different things." Violet set their chin down on their hands. "There's this whole . . . context I don't understand. I'm not sure I'll ever understand it."

Different shops. Bryn's question to Amelia had been

102

playful. Field trips? Wouldn't that be fun? Maybe after they petted the ponies. But in that moment her ideas coalesced into something more specific.

What if there was a program at the school for kids who didn't have witching backgrounds? A program to give them the context that Violet despaired of ever having? And what if it started here, with these kids? There were only three of them, and out of everyone, on staff or otherwise, Bryn was probably the best person to take them on a field trip into Grimoire town.

With some effort, she controlled her wilder imaginings—a pilot program, one that other types of schools later took on (because surely there were sirens born into witching families and maybe even demons growing up amongst shifters or something)—and suddenly she understood why Amelia wanted to make so many changes. Once you began to see a vision of how to make things better, where did you stop?

After the club ended that day, she stopped by Amelia's office and when no one answered the door, she left a note. Just a couple of lines. *What about we take a field trip into town? Bring the kids to a witchy shop or two. Let them pick out something to charm or something to—* At this, her invention failed her. They could, of course, get potions and ingredients, but getting Mr Wicks on board to advise about potions seemed fraught, given his resistance to new teaching tactics. She'd never been quite sure if he agreed with the inclusion of non-witchy families into the school, though now she was back as an adult and a teacher, he had been nothing but kind to her, so maybe the perception of

103

his bias was unfounded. She admitted to herself that as Mr Wicks was kind of a grumpy old straight white guy, she might have misjudged him. Maybe. She admitted to herself that her own ideas about Mr Wicks had been informed not just by his stern demeanor, but also by her experiences with other grumpy middle-aged men. Perhaps she'd misjudged him all along. Either way, she didn't feel the need to get him involved with her field trip for the after-school club.

Once she'd tucked the note under Amelia's door, she went to her cottage with a sense of relief that almost didn't seem justified after so little time in her new place, but returning to it at the end of the day was more like coming home than going to her apartment in Denver had ever been. Part of that, of course, was working outside. When she worked mostly in her apartment, it felt a lot less like a relief to end the day. Surely that explained it.

Teaching was nothing like writing a book, or working on research, or testing out new spells. After her school day, Bryn was exhausted mentally and physically, though she didn't really understand how she could be so physically tired. Mentally made sense; she'd implemented a five-question quiz at the start of every period—easy stuff she was certain her students would know, but which would aim their thoughts towards the most high-priority topics. After her disastrous pre-tests, she felt the need to rebuild their confidence, even if that meant she wasn't exactly testing their knowledge, but she hadn't realized how challenging the preparation for all these daily quizzes would be. She was already repeating questions, and it had only been a couple of weeks.

Physically, though, she'd barely done anything except walk to and from the castle each day. She hadn't done her Pilates once since returning to Grimoire, and back in Denver she'd done some kind of workout five days a week. She knew it helped not only her body, but also her mind, *especially* when she was stressed out.

Once she'd thought about it, she couldn't unthink it. She didn't feel like working out but then again, she *loved* how she felt after Pilates, all tingly and strong and kick-ass. And the sore muscles the day after, when she got to feel good about her workout.

Plus, there were the mood benefits. She needed Pilates, arguably way more than she'd needed it for the last few years. How many times had she wondered if her time as a student might have been easier if she'd had this physical de-pressurization valve? Well, now she did have it so she may as well use it.

She rolled her mat out, already feeling like this was absolutely the correct move, and cued up one of her favorite thirty-minute videos. She loved Pilates. It was something she could do even though her shape was not skinny or lithe or particularly graceful. Pilates was about core and coordination, and she could manage those things. At least now, after five years of doing it, she barely had to open her eyes; the words of the instructor flowed through her ears and seemed to go straight to her limbs. She'd started going to classes in her neighborhood, and then branched out to classes in other neighborhoods and online; she'd even paid for a service so she could stream her workouts wherever she was. Twenty-five minutes in, when she was trembling with intensity and so, *so* ready for a well-earned cool-down, there was a knock on the cottage door.

Bryn, drenched with sweat, her leggings and sports bra clinging to her, jumped off her mat in alarm. Who was that? Piper? *Oh gods, don't let it be Piper*. She didn't really want them to see her like this, though of course they would be delighted she was doing something physical. Still, being interrupted mid-workout when you were really sweaty and gross was not ideal for any new friendship, or any old friendship—or any witnesses at all.

Panting, both from exertion and now nerves, she clicked pause on the workout and waved her wand in the direction of the door where she'd set a spell to magnify her voice. "Who is it?"

"Just me," Amelia called back, louder than was necessary with the spell enacted, though she had no way of knowing it was there. Bryn's voice would have sounded just like it was coming from the other side of the door to her.

"Oh." Bryn glanced around, but her perfectly neatened cottage showed no obvious things that she could pull over herself. "Just a minute," she called, and almost dived into her laundry basket. What could she put on? A shirt—surely a shirt—but she didn't really want to pull one of her button-downs over her drenched sports bra. She was still sweating; it would stick to her. She ended up with an eye-wateringly pink Hello Kitty pajama top, which was at least looser, but still clinging to her in every place there was sweat.

She swung open the door, pretending everything was normal—except, of course, she was standing in the doorway in front of Amelia Hexford, in a pair of black leggings

106

pasted to her body and a Hello Kitty pajama top. She'd tied her hair in a messy topknot, but it had come loose everywhere and strands were now sticking to her skin.

"Hi," she said, and playfully leaned against the doorjamb, as if flirting. Then she realized how ridiculous she looked and straightened up again, cheeks going red. (She didn't have to see them to know they were going red. She could feel it.) "Um, Amelia. Oh, um, hello, what . . . What are you doing here? Not that you shouldn't be here, you're welcome here, obviously, just . . . I wasn't expecting you."

Amelia, taking in her appearance with something that looked suspiciously like a smile, held up the note that Bryn had left under her door. "Thought I would stop by to talk about your idea."

Which was now so obvious—and indeed 2 a.m.-Bryn, who specialized in just this sort of scenario, would have been absolutely thrilled. She cursed herself for spontaneously doing Pilates instead of stopping by the kitchen for a pretty appetizer plate and a bottle of something fizzy. (The school kitchen did not provide alcohol, but it did a great run on lightly fizzy water flavored with fruits harvested from the gardens.) "My idea, right," she attempted, but immediately gave up the pretense. "Oh, my gods. Sorry. Please hold."

Bryn squeezed her eyes shut, took a deep breath, and then opened them, meeting Amelia's with a vague plea for understanding. Or mercy. Or something. "I was doing Pilates."

"Why should you be sorry for that?" Amelia reached out a hand and tucked a stray lock of hair behind her ear, making her shiver, which in turn caused Amelia to snatch her hand back. "Sorry, I didn't mean to touch, *really* didn't mean to touch."

"No, no, you can touch me! I mean, if you want— I mean, I would love that! No, I mean . . ." Bryn's fragmented sentences ran down. Her face was now on fire. She lined up a mental spell to put out flames, just in case. "I am officially giving up on this conversation now. Please come in. I'm going to have some water, would you like some?"

Amelia laughed, and the sound was so welcome to Bryn's ears that she turned away quickly so that Amelia wouldn't see how wide her grin went.

Once she'd retrieved two glasses of water and sat down on her bed, gesturing Amelia to the chair, Bryn felt a little more relaxed. Maybe not completely at ease, but as relaxed as she was likely to be in leggings and a Hello Kitty top, low-key worried she probably stank of anxiety and workout. "I didn't expect you to come by, but I'm glad you're here. I had an idea for the field trip."

"Okay?" Amelia said slowly, the hint of a smile still lingering on her lips, which Bryn should probably stop staring at.

"I think we take them to a normal witchy place."

"Interesting. Define *normal*."

"I mean a regular store where if they had grown up in witchy families they would have been going their whole lives." Bryn waved a hand to conjure specific examples, but before she could, Amelia was interrupting.

"Maybe a spell shop?"

"That's perfect, yes!" Bryn tried to calm her excitement,

but she heard her voice rising. "Exactly. Every time I'm in a spell shop, not even a fancy one but just your average spell supplies shop, there's someone with a four-year-old who is trying to touch everything—only, everything's charmed so they can't, but they don't know it yet. But that's normal to you, right?"

Amelia sat back, nodding. "Sure. I definitely don't remember the first time I was ever in a spell shop."

"Right? Because your family is full of witches, so that was your normal. But I'd never gone to one until I was in school, and it felt so weird to be the only kid who had no clue what was going on." She set her water glass down to better gesture. "It's disorienting when it feels like everyone else understands things that you don't even know you don't understand. I think that's part of the issue with kids who don't come from witchy families."

"That makes sense," Amelia said. "And you think taking a field trip will eliminate that feeling?"

"Not eliminate, but alleviate, sure."

Amelia nodded again, more slowly this time. "All right, I'm definitely here for the experiment. But I don't think you should take them by yourself."

Bryn deflated. Right, she wasn't a real teacher. She wasn't even a *good* teacher. She was just a lowly commoner who happened to be standing there when Amelia needed someone to take over the esteemed professor's classes. "Oh, okay." She didn't want to turn her club over to someone who wouldn't understand. Maybe she could get Piper to do it. Or one of the younger teachers who'd arrived since she graduated. Not some old dragon traditionalist who—

"I think I should go with you," Amelia said. "I have teaching experience. I've taken kids on field trips before, and I think it'll be fun." Her tone was so intentionally light-hearted that Bryn looked up again.

"Wait, really?" She trembled on the edge of excitement, afraid to commit in case she'd misunderstood.

"You, me, and three recalcitrant students in a spell shop. How could it not be fun? It might also be chaos, but fun for sure." Amelia shrugged. "Don't you think?"

"Oh," Bryn said, thinking: *Amelia wants to field trip with me!* Then, realizing that she hadn't agreed, she said quickly, "Right, yes, definitely. So, when do you think we can go?"

Amelia blew out a breath. "To run it by the governors or not to run it by the governors? They don't really have any grounds to say no, since it's educational, but that doesn't mean they won't."

"Isn't that bad?" Bryn asked.

"It doesn't feel good, to be sure. But all the same, I think we'll just go," Amelia said with finality. "I'm the headmistress. I ought to be able to authorize a field trip for three students on my own, right?"

Bryn gulped, hoping that this wasn't going to get Amelia in even more trouble with the governors. "Right."

"Next week?" Amelia asked, with a conspiratorial gleam in her eye.

"Next week," she agreed, wishing like hell she could lean over and kiss Amelia to seal the deal.

"That sounds great. I will secure the necessary permissions from their guardians." Amelia smiled so warmly that Bryn thought she might melt into her bed. Then Amelia stood, and all melting ceased. "I'm really sorry I interrupted your Pilates."

Reminded, Bryn straightened her Hello Kitty top as she also rose to her feet. "That was so embarrassing. I didn't even think—" She made herself stop talking.

"Nothing to be embarrassed about." Amelia walked to the door, then turned to smirk over her shoulder. "Physical exertion is a very healthy thing, I've read."

Is Amelia Hexford coming on to me right now? "So many benefits," Bryn agreed, nodding with mock seriousness. "The mood lift, the cardio boost." She did a little spin in her ridiculous pink pajama top and leggings. "The hot outfits."

Amelia laughed out loud, and for a second—the tiniest fraction of a fraction of a second—Bryn swore they were about to kiss. The air practically crackled with humor and desire, and something Bryn swore was even brighter, shimmering between them.

Then Amelia covered her mouth with one hand and mumbled, "I should go. See you tomorrow."

She was out the door before Bryn could protest, and what would she have even said? *No, stay, I like flirting with you.* Or: *Would you like to join me for Pilates? Sorry there's only room for one yoga mat, but we can take turns . . .* Ridiculous.

Still, the cottage felt empty now that Amelia had gone. Thirty minutes later—yoga mat put away, sweaty clothes peeled off, shower taken—Bryn's phone dinged with a message. When she saw Amelia's name, her breath stopped.

111

It was almost certainly about work. Of course it was. They worked together. That would be perfectly normal.

But it wasn't.

You do look good in your Pilates clothes. 😊

Bryn made herself breathe, then texted back a GIF of an animated mouse in a pink tutu, taking a bow. Then she tossed her phone on her bed and pressed her fingers to her lips, as if that would stop her from grinning like a lovesick girl. *But that's what I am.*

No. She wasn't. She could not be. Even if she *did* look good in her Pilates clothes.

The thought made her smile all night.

11

The week seemed eternal. Bryn gave up on her five-question quizzes; the stress of creating them was undermining her ability to focus and the kids hated them so much that she feared any of the evidence-based advantages would be lost. It felt like a defeat, though when she confessed that to Piper, they sagely inquired as to what she wanted her students to learn: stick with something that isn't working because you can't bear to change it, or realize that adapting plans is a natural part of life?

She had stuck her tongue out at them right before saying thanks and breathing a huge sigh of relief that she didn't need to come up with twenty more quiz questions for the following day. She had found no good excuse to go visit Amelia, and Amelia had not visited the cottage again, even though Bryn had done Pilates every single day just to tempt the universe to mess with her. (Upside: she was already seeing the benefits of actually getting her workouts in.) They saw each other at meals, which was better than not seeing each other at all, even if there were times when Bryn thought it was an unhelpful tease.

But Amelia really had said she looked good in leggings and a bright pink top. She had the text to prove it. She wasn't making the whole thing up. Not that it had been explicit, obviously. Merely . . . No, not suggestive either. Complimentary? Was she reading too much into a flirty smile and a silly text? Perhaps that was the downside of seeing Amelia only at meals; she was always in Headmistress Mode in the refectory, never in . . . in her other mode. Intimacy Mode. The mode Bryn wanted to see more. The mode that made her feel a little bit giddy (and a little bit tingly in all the areas she did not want to be thinking about when sitting across from Mr Wicks at the lunch table—shudder).

On the following Saturday morning, Bryn met up with Amelia in front of the castle, where Circe was waiting for them. Both Luke and Violet had host families in town and would be picked up on their way to the store, but Circe boarded at the school with about thirty other kids who were from far enough away to make it necessary, and whose parents could afford that option.

Bryn had always thought if she ever moved back to Grimoire town, she would herself happily host a student, especially one from a non-magical background. In fact, she thought (optimism at spending an entire day with Amelia tinging her outlook), today might be the first step in that direction.

Grimoire hadn't exactly started out as a big settlement for witches. It had started out as yet another of the many

Spanish colonial settlements taken over by white colonial settlers who came from the east. The town had not been named for its witchy citizens, but by an enterprising woman of Irish descent who thought *Grimoire* sounded foreign and exotic and would attract people, which it did. Early on, the township had boasted two general stores, which doubled as bars; two saloons, which doubled as brothels; and a number of livery stables so that people could rent or purchase their horses before heading to the gold mines.

As far as Bryn knew, no actual gold strikes could be traced back to Grimoire or any of its citizens. The fanciful name, chosen by a woman who didn't speak any form of French and delighted in correcting people's pronunciations through her thick Irish brogue, ended up being a sort of signpost for either the right or wrong sorts of people, depending on your perspective. Witches had already begun to settle in the area when an agrobaron, with dreams of a central coast vineyard dancing in his head, had bought the hillside and hundreds of acres around it to build his castle. When the agrobaron's aspiring empire had been felled by a series of bad harvests and worse investments, he'd finally sold the property in 1919 to a wealthy witching family. They'd begun turning it into the academy almost immediately.

"Do you know much about Grimoire town?" she asked Amelia, who was driving her incredibly practical dark green Volvo. Bryn wondered if she'd used any of the "traveling convenience" spells from Bryn's book on her car.

"I don't think so. At this point, I've lived here for a lot of

115

my life, but I'm ashamed to say I've never even looked into the background or the history of the town." She glanced in the rear-view mirror. "What about you, Circe?"

Bryn craned around in time to catch Circe's head shake. "Hmm," she said.

"Maybe we should do a walking tour, at the beginning of fall term," Amelia offered. "For the first-years. Something about the town itself or about witches here. Or both?"

"I don't know how much you can separate them." Bryn thought about what she'd learned in her non-magical elementary school about the local area. "I'm not even sure the town would still be here if there hadn't been a significant settlement of witches to sustain it."

"What about sirens?" Amelia asked, eyes twinkling.

Bryn laughed. "Oh, sirens go wherever they want, as long as it's connected to water." The history of siren migration patterns was also fascinating, or at least what she'd gleaned through talking to her sister seemed to be.

"I'm definitely intrigued by the idea," Amelia said. "Aside from the only quasi-historical sketch we get in our history classes with Professor Flowers, I don't feel like I know much about witchcraft in the Americas at all. We focused so much on the ancient stuff, and the European witch trials, and King James of dubious memory."

Bryn thought Amelia might have kept going, but then they pulled up in front of Luke's house, and once he was in the mix, conversation did not return to distant history. He greeted Circe cheerfully, then immediately launched into at least a dozen questions about where they were going, what they would see, and how long they'd be there. He didn't pause long enough for any of his questions to be answered, until Circe reached out and touched his arm.

"I don't know why I'm nervous. Are you nervous?" he asked.

She smiled slightly and shook her head.

Luke took a deep breath. "Okay. I'll try to stop being nervous. Thanks, Circ."

In the front seat, Bryn couldn't help but feel warm and fuzzy. Circe didn't need to speak to communicate, and Bryn was so glad she had at least a few friends who *got* her. After collecting Violet, they drove to Old Town Grimoire, where they parked on a side street.

"You can parallel park," Bryn said, impressed. She *hated* parallel parking.

"I have many skills," Amelia replied, glancing over. Her gaze was playful, but Bryn, distracted by just what Amelia's other skills might be, couldn't stop her face from flushing. They both looked away at the same time.

Noted, Bryn thought, smiling at her reflection in the car window and making a mental note to ponder various skill sets that did not involve parking later.

Of the kids, only Violet had been to the spell shop before, and only briefly with a friend from school. Though they didn't say it outright, Bryn had the distinct impression that she was delighted to be able to roam to her heart's content. There was so much to look at, and Bryn remembered feeling like she could spend an entire day in the store.

She held the door for Amelia and the kids, then stepped in herself, only to be pulled up short, staring at the girl behind the counter, who was in turn staring at her. "Luna?"

"Bryn?"

They both said: "What are you doing here?" at the same time, then laughed.

"I work here," Luna explained, her tone only slightly tinged with the insufferable unspoken *obviously* tagged on. She'd just turned eighteen, an occasion Bryn had marked by sending her a coffee mug with the Denver skyline on it. She couldn't remember the last time they'd actually talked to each other, though they texted on most days.

Still, her sister hadn't mentioned the new job. "You work in the spell shop?"

Luna's eyes darted over, to where Luke was tinkering with something on a shelf.

"He'll probably be fine," Bryn said, at least seventy per cent sure. "These are some students from the school."

"Oh," Luna said, her expression clearing. And this time, it was impossible to miss the way she looked at Amelia. "So this is like a colleague?"

What had she thought? That Bryn had secretly gotten married and adopted three teenagers?

"I'm the headmistress," Amelia said. "Amelia Hexford, so good to meet you."

"Wait, this is—" Luna broke off, seeing Bryn's stricken face.

"Yes, this is the headmistress," Bryn said quickly. "I'm sure I've mentioned her." Meaning: *If I've mentioned her in any other context, shut up right now.*

Luna thankfully caught on. "Oh right, your friend from school. Well, make yourselves at home." She leaned over the counter. "They're not going to break anything, are

118

they? I've only just started working here and I really don't want to get in trouble."

"If they do," Amelia said, "I'm sure we can compensate you, but I don't expect it will be necessary."

Bryn added, "These are the kids who are from non-witching families, like me. I thought it would be cool if they could look around."

"Oh, yeah, definitely." Luna craned her neck, watching Circe drag her fingers along the spines of all the books on a lower shelf. She straightened back up, seemingly reassured that no one was going to wreak havoc. "And feel free to ask me if you need any more information on stuff, though to be honest, I don't always know, but I can definitely look things up on the computer." She glanced between Amelia and Bryn. "And you guys probably know more than I do anyway, so we'll be great."

"Thanks so much," Amelia said, and walked farther into the store, leaving Bryn and Luna to chat awkwardly.

"That's Amelia Hexford," Luna whispered, and despite knowing that it was almost impossible anyone had heard, Bryn still felt like the question was written in neon print above her head in a huge dialogue bubble that everyone in the universe could read.

"The headmistress, yes."

"Oh, my gosh." Luna eyed Amelia's retreating back. "I get it, though. She is hot."

Bryn smacked her arm. "Stop it. Don't talk about that."

Luna, eyes glittering in sisterly malice, pretended to zip her lips, then immediately spoiled the effect by saying, "Really, though, you're going to make a move on her, right?

You sorta have to. You missed your chance in school, and now here you are, together again, so . . ."

Noticing Circe lingering a little too close to the front desk, Bryn smacked her sister's arm again and said, "I'm going to help my students."

"Very responsible of you," Luna called after her.

Bryn hadn't known how long to plan for the store trip. Twenty minutes? Two hours? How long did three witchy kids want in a spell shop for their first proper visit? They were still browsing with considerable fascination at the end of the first hour. It helped that Luna was walking around with them and genuinely seemed to be learning from their relatively limited knowledge of what all the things were for.

"I'm not a witch," Bryn heard her explaining to Luke and Violet, "but my sister is, so that's kind of how I got the job. They needed someone, and I kind of had some idea what I was doing a little bit, or at least I could fake it." She glanced up, as if to make sure Bryn wasn't listening, then accidentally caught Bryn's eye instead. She froze as if she'd just confessed to a crime, but Bryn only smiled.

It was a little bit heartwarming that her witchiness, which had seemed to only inconvenience her family, had finally come in handy. It was genuinely nice to see Luna out in the world, not under their mother's watchful eye. No one knew better than she did how overbearing Mom could be, and Luna was still living at home.

They'd given each kid a budget of twenty dollars to spend on something. Bryn suggested it would be good to pick up something they could cast a spell on or with.

"Cast a spell on?" Luke had said dubiously. "What does that mean?"

Bryn had pointed her wand at a carved dolphin nearby, and it had immediately sprung to life and dived off the counter. She'd caught it before it hit the floor. Even Luna, who must have seen her do magic before, had gone all eyes wide and mouth agape.

"Whoa." Luke, unabashed with his admiration, had taken it from her hands and then turned it over in his own, as if trying to feel where the spell had landed.

She'd lowered her voice confidentially. "Now, if the headmistress had done that spell, you could probably see a fading shimmer on the surface of the wood. That's how powerful she is."

He had immediately looked to Amelia to confirm this. "I don't know about that," she said, though she did not seem upset at the insinuation.

"You're saying we can do that?" Luke asked.

Violet shook their head. "Absolutely not. We haven't learned how yet."

"We've learned some stuff," he protested, still turning over the dolphin and searching for clues. Beside him, Circe also leaned in, so he held it out between them. Neither looked illuminated by their examination.

"You've learned plenty of things," Amelia said.

"But how do you learn things like that?" Violet asked. "Unless you're going to teach us how to turn wooden dolphins into toys that move. Is that in the curriculum somewhere?"

"Not exactly," Bryn said. "Spellcasting is a language.

121

You learn certain parts of it, and then you can piece those parts together in new ways. Roots, prefixes, suffixes, verbs and nouns and prepositions—this is similar. It's not quite like you have to memorize every single spell."

Circe looked up with such intensity that Bryn almost thought she might speak. Her eyes were narrowed in contemplation, then turned downward to the dolphin again, which she took from Luke's unprotesting fingers.

He had already moved on, expression frustrated. "Wouldn't that take forever, though? Learning a whole language just to make a thing do a thing?"

"It does take time. Maybe not forever."

"But are *we* allowed to do that?" Violet demanded. "Would I get in trouble if I was sitting at lunch and like—" she mimed waving a wand "—summoned the salt?"

Summoning in a chaotic field was deceptively complex magic. Bryn decided not to go into the details, though she suspected Amelia could tell she wanted to, because the woman was fairly *twinkling* at her. She cleared her throat. "I don't think you'd get in trouble, but all the same, the social skills you'd learn by saying, 'Circe, please pass the salt' would probably be more helpful to you than learning how to summon the salt."

Violet sighed. "That is a *supremely* dissatisfying answer, Professor."

In the background, at the edge of her peripheral vision, Bryn saw her sister mouth *Professor* with a big grin, which totally derailed her train of thought. She was sure she was about to say something smart and to the point. Almost certainly.

"Not all witches care to invent spells," Amelia said, picking up the conversation. "But if you do, it's all there to learn. Now, what are you thinking about for your spell object, Violet?"

The three of them finally decided on their new witchy treasures, and Amelia paid. Bryn hoped the money came from the school's accounts, though she suspected the headmistress was probably using her own money.

They then sprung for desserts from the local ice-cream parlor and dropped Luke and Violet back at their homes before returning Circe to the dorms. Since Amelia and Bryn had walked her up to her building, they walked on to Bryn's cottage together.

They were united in a strange mix of friendship and camaraderie, and then something else—some thread of desire that Bryn definitely felt running through her, and suspected Amelia felt as well.

"So, what do you think of my field trip idea?" she said, as they walked through the gardens.

"I think it went very well, good instinct."

Bryn tried not to flush with the compliment. Was she pleased because it was praise from the headmistress or because it came from Amelia Hexford?

"And I think you were right in general. This is why we need a broad and diverse teaching staff. It never would have occurred to me that our witchy kids from non-magical families have never been to a spell shop before. It's obvious now, but I didn't think about it. I really want to lower those barriers." She sighed. "If they let me keep being headmistress." After a moment of contemplation, she brightened again. "It was so cool that we got to see your sister."

"That was so weird, but also great," Bryn said. "I can't believe I didn't even know she was working there."

"It does seem like a strange thing for her not to tell you."

Bryn shrugged. "When I thought about it, I realized it wasn't that strange. It's kind of how we were raised; we weren't supposed to be close. Sirens are super independent, like any kind of interdependence is a weakness, which we definitely both internalized. But now that we're adults and I'm back in town, however temporarily, I would like to see Luna more than I have."

"Then our outing was useful in more than one way," Amelia said, lips curving.

Their hands brushed against each other and Bryn realized that, maybe subconsciously—maybe a little more consciously than that—she was holding her arm in such a way that would ensure they'd brush against each other again. Amelia, if she noticed, did not step away.

They had, by mutual silent agreement, taken the longest way through the gardens, but the walk could only last so long, and they were rounding the final corner now.

"Have you gone swimming in the grotto since you got back?" Amelia asked, her voice teasing.

"Am I allowed to?" It immediately sounded ridiculous, but Bryn couldn't help feeling shocked by the idea. The grotto was so off limits to students that she couldn't even remember tall tales of people having found a way inside.

Amelia laughed. "Of course you are, silly. You're staff."

"Ugh, but what if I go down there and Mr Wicks is there or something? Ew, what if he was wearing Speedos?"

Amelia held up a hand. "Okay, first of all, no. And second of all, we will respect whatever bathing uniform any of our teachers would like to wear."

"But third of all, also no?" Bryn prompted.

"Also no." Amelia relented, with a little shake of her head. "I don't think anyone uses it. I've been down there maybe twice, but it's always empty."

The idea of Amelia alone in the grotto, fairy lights playing along the bottom of the pool, the sound of water, the darkness . . . "Is it as strange as everyone used to say?" Bryn asked to distract herself from the mental image, slowing her steps as they approached the cottage.

"It's actually lovely. Humid, because it's warm and wet, but the pool itself is painted this very dark blue, and the tiles are all blues and grays so the lights twinkle, throwing these beautiful reflections everywhere. And whoever charmed the lights in the water did something I don't understand, keeping them forever at the edges of your vision." She glanced over, her hand grazing Bryn's again. "You should probably see it one of these days, for research purposes. Could be interesting spell applications in there."

"Indeed," Bryn said with mock seriousness. "Research is very important." They were nearly at the cottage now and she couldn't think of anything to prolong the walk more than they already had.

"Very, very important," Amelia agreed.

Impulsively, not fully aware she was going to say it, Bryn blurted out, "Do you remember me from school? I mean—

I mean do you remember when my, uh, friend told the whole refectory that I-had-a-crush-on-you?" She focused on her practical going-out shoes, and the weeds coming up through the pavers, glad they were still walking so she didn't have to look at Amelia.

"If she was your friend, you needed better friends." After a pause, and more softly, Amelia added, "I remember."

"Girlfriend. Technically." Oh gods. Now that she'd opened this door, Bryn had no idea what she wanted from what was behind it. She'd needed to know if that memory still lingered for Amelia as well, if both of them were still seeing Bryn as that mortified girl.

"Oh, Bryn, your *girlfriend*?" Amelia reached for her hand, grabbing it, squeezing, letting it swing for a brief moment, before pulling her own hand away. "I'm so sorry. I wasn't sure how to bring it up, but I have always felt bad about that. I should have . . . said something. Defended you."

This was officially the worst. Bryn regretted saying anything. The last thing she wanted was Amelia's pity. "It wasn't your fault. You didn't even laugh."

"It *wasn't* funny. At all. And I could have at least said that." Their steps slowed; it didn't seem like Amelia wanted to get to the cottage quickly either. "The thing is, I didn't understand how popular I was at the time. Which sounds ridiculous, but I don't think I really figured out what popularity was until I was teaching and saw it from the outside. I *could* have told them to quit it, and they would have. I didn't know that back then, and I'm really sorry, Bryn. You deserved so much better."

"It's fine." This conversation needed to be over now or she was going to—

"I liked you," Amelia said softly. "It's why I froze. Even if I'd wanted to say something, I was so completely flabbergasted. I didn't realize you knew who I was."

Bryn turned at her door, her eyes lingering on Amelia's lips for a moment before she managed to drag them higher, momentarily distracted from her bewildered surprise. "Amelia. You're *Amelia Hexford*. You're gorgeous and talented and brilliant. *Everyone* knew who you were."

Amelia bit her lip. "I'm sorry."

"No, I mean—" For a long second, Bryn stood there awkwardly, watching the other woman's face for any sign that she wasn't being wholly truthful. But Amelia looked earnest and regretful and somehow a little ashamed. It was the last one, so recognizable, that made Bryn reach out, taking both of Amelia's hands. "I thought you were embarrassed that a nobody like me had a crush on you, because you were so . . . so *you*, and I was nothing."

"You were *not* nothing! You were the cleverest witch at school. You were so good at thinking all the way around things in class, you'd ask these questions and the professors would just light up, which I appreciate way more now that I'm a teacher than I did back then." She smiled a bit ruefully. "That was your girlfriend, though? Bryn, that's so . . . so . . . shitty." The word sounded vaguely odd in Amelia's usually cultured voice.

Bryn fought a smile. "It was shitty." She shook her head, because that didn't even cover it. "It was honestly mortifying and I had actual nightmares about it." Before

Amelia could interject, Bryn went on, "But here we are now. And— Well, I'm glad we talked about it. Because it was just kind of haunting me."

"I'm glad we talked about it too." Amelia squeezed her hands. "And I'm sorry it happened, and that I didn't do anything at the time. Maybe that's another thing to add to my endless list of curriculum ideas: emotional intelligence. How to respond to awful situations."

"Not a bad idea." Abruptly, Bryn realized they were still holding hands, and looking at each other in the bright glow of the late afternoon, surrounded by blooming wildflowers, with a few bees droning as soundtrack. "So I'm allowed in the grotto, then? I'm not going to get hauled up in front of the discipline board if I'm caught?"

"Certainly not." Amelia raised an eyebrow. "Of course, if you want additional insurance against perceived rule-breaking, I could come with you? Just to ensure you don't have to . . . worry. About anything."

"That would definitely improve my experience," Bryn said, nodding slowly, schooling her face to be bland and not some variation on the same pink as her Hello Kitty pajamas. "I'll let you know when I'm free."

"I look forward to it."

Suddenly, in the fading light, Bryn couldn't stand it anymore. Impulse had always been a thunderclap for her, a thing that even when she knew it was coming, still surprised her when she gave into it. She'd wanted to kiss Amelia Hexford since she had been thirteen years old. And now, a decade later, she did.

It was quick, too quick, their lips hardly touching—a

static charge that only hinted at the fireworks in store—before she pulled away and said, "Sorry, oh gods, sorry." She grappled behind her for the doorknob.

"Don't be," Amelia said, but she also took a step back.

"I'm so sorry." Bryn, face burning, lips tingling from that way-too-brief touch, nearly stumbled backwards into her cottage. "I won't do it again!" she called before shutting the door and banging her forehead into it a few times. Not too hard, but hard enough so she felt it.

Outside, she almost swore she heard Amelia say, "But I want you to . . ." except when she looked out the peephole, Amelia was gone.

That was your imagination, she told herself. *Your naughty, naughty imagination, which is making stuff up, because she did not say that, because this is Amelia Hexford we're talking about*, the *Amelia Hexford, and maybe she did see your most humiliating moment, but at least you've got it all out in the open now*. It did, genuinely, feel like a relief. That image, which had loomed so large for so long, had been reduced. Not to nothing (probably never to nothing), but it had been altered by context and perspective to life-size once more. It had been shitty, yes; and Bryn had survived it, not been conquered by it.

And also, oh gods, had she just kissed Amelia Hexford? Why had she done that? No, she knew why, it was the *how* she couldn't reconcile.

But it had felt like a date in a movie, like Amelia was walking her to her door, and they were talking about the grotto and swimming in the dark with fairy lights, holding hands, and she'd just done it. She hadn't thought about it, hadn't considered her actions, just done it.

She pressed her palms to her face and waited for the blush to subside. Then she texted: *I deeply apologize for my inappropriate behavior*, because she was so sorry she'd screwed that up; she'd put Amelia in a bad position and hadn't even asked permission.

But the reply, which had come back immediately, said, *No apology necessary. Today was fun. See you at breakfast. xx*

Xx. Amelia Hexford, whom she'd just kissed, had sent her *kiss kiss* in text form.

It could just be how she ended texts to . . . people. Teachers. Bryn tried to imagine Amelia sending *kiss kiss* to Mr Wicks and almost giggled out loud.

It wasn't a rejection.

Bryn had just kissed Amelia Hexford. Once she'd stopped blushing, and staring at those two Xs on her phone screen, she decided that this was an impulse she was glad she'd given into.

12

In the next two weeks, Bryn began to feel a little bit more assured in class—so assured, she even brought her youngest students out to the stables to pet the ponies. The school boasted a grove somewhere deep in the acreage, with a semi-feral herd that included both unicorns and wild ponies. Bryn had never seen the unicorns and wasn't entirely convinced they existed, though Piper said a specialty vet service came out once a year to check on the group. There was also an elephant somewhere on the grounds, but he didn't like company, apparently.

"He had a partner, but the partner died," Piper explained in a low voice as their mingled classes petted the animals. They'd planned this class period with a couple of school goals in mind, but for the moment, they were mostly letting the kids do what they liked. Some had backgrounds in horseback riding or gymkhana, or even the horse polo—a thing Bryn still couldn't quite picture.

Then, when they were starting to get restless, Piper clapped their hands together and called all the students back over. "Professor Delmar is going to talk about a few conventional uses for spells."

This actually seemed to get the students' attention, so Bryn delivered the lesson plan she'd come up with after she'd bewitched the dolphin figurine in the store to dive. "Have any of you ever written a spell?" she asked.

They all looked around at each other. "Are we allowed to do that?" one of the students asked.

"Nothing in the rules specifically forbids the—" she readied the most posh and snooty voice she could muster "—'origination and experimentation of students as regards to spell crafting, providing no living creatures of any kind are the subjects or objects of such spells.'"

Scattered laughter at her accent. Piper said, "Wait, really?"

"I did some research," she explained in an aside. Then, to the students, she said, "I wish I'd known that when I was in school here. I was desperate to make up spells at your age. I saw places all around me that required magic. None of you do that?"

A few nods, a few tentative hands in the air, which lowered immediately when no one else joined in.

"So, you've met some of our animals here at the school, and you've seen the stables. Now I want all of you to spread out, working together if you like, and think of some spells that might make life easier for the animals or for the people who take care of them."

"Like what?" somebody asked.

"Like a muzzle for you," the kid next to him said and was elbowed to the side. A few laughs, a few calculating glances around.

"No living creatures," Bryn reminded them, smiling.

Piper clapped their hands again. "Go on. Come back when you have ideas."

Since these two groups of first-years were going to swap at next period, they could essentially take both time slots, so that's what they did. It was a rousing success. When Bryn had first brought up this idea with Piper, the two of them hadn't been sure the kids would be able to come up with anything, but in fact, they were imaginative. Some of their ideas weren't technically feasible by any means Bryn knew—you couldn't bewitch a brush to brush a horse as well as a human caretaker could, for instance—but some of the others had potential. She would have to reach out to magical folks with equestrian leanings about the spells and charms they used in their work. Even if such things already existed, she suspected the students would find it validating to hear that their brilliant ideas were so smart they'd already been invented and were in use.

Maybe the school should be putting out books of its own—*101 Spells and Charms for Your Livestock Stable.* She laughed to herself at the idea.

When the older kids found out that the younger kids had gotten to go into the stables and play with spell ideas, they demanded to do so as well.

"We're much smarter than they are," Violet informed Bryn at the next after-school club meeting.

"I'll try to work something out," Bryn promised, wondering if her bright new idea could be put to use on more practical things. She still wanted to come up with a good spellcasting way to clean all those pavers at the front.

Or the gardens? Were there spells to keep out aphids? Enchantments one could do around berries to keep the birds from pecking them? She was sure there must be, but it was odd that she didn't know. Maybe Grimoire Academy needed a student project website where they could post the things they came up with, though intellectual property laws were iffy when it came to under-age magic. She would need to send some emails.

She brought the fourth-years to the gardens, where they concocted, with surprising efficiency, a number of pest-prevention spells, including a rather clever way of keeping coyotes away from the chickens without harming them. "It's basically a car alarm, but for the garden," the student, who was non-magically raised, explained with a grin.

The only class that Bryn was reticent to take out for an on-the-grounds field trip was the MSE class. They were already so far behind and the tests were looming ever closer. But, on the other hand, in terms of practical application, this kind of work was good for their brains. And anything that was good for their brains would eventually be good for their test scores as well. Probably. She was less certain about that than she wanted to be. Still, she'd done it for all the other classes, and no one wanted to miss out on a treat.

She hadn't failed to notice the way some of the older professors eyed her classes disapprovingly as they made their way outside. Yes, it was unconventional, certainly, but it was hardly against the rules to take the students out onto their own campus. Still, she felt awkward about it. Clearly Mr Wicks didn't approve, though all he said to her was, "I know how tempting it can be to reinvent the wheel, but remember that our traditional ways of doing things have successfully produced witches for over a century."

This was both undeniably true and also a vast oversimplification. Producing witches from witch families, emerging from long lines of witchy tutors and with generations of wealth in their pasts wasn't exactly the same as running an egalitarian school that provided witchy excellence to children from a variety of backgrounds.

Still, she thanked her old teacher because she found she was sincerely grateful for his continued interest, and his advice hadn't seemed aggressive, only perhaps misdirected. Maybe Mr Wicks's idea of success for their students wasn't exactly the same as Bryn's.

Despite her conviction that her methods were sound, by the time she'd taken the third- and fourth-year classes outside for a bit of practical magical troubleshooting, she was beginning to feel self-conscious about it. Trooping them through the halls, even quietly, still made a ruckus, which had not gone unnoticed. She reminded herself that even if the periods had been entirely without educational merit, it was only one period for each class. Surely they hadn't lost more learning potential through this than they had for the entire month when they'd barely had a professor at all.

All the same, she thought she'd run it by Amelia just to make certain. *Or,* piped up some peppy unwelcome voice in the back of her head, *maybe this is an elaborate excuse to go see Amelia. Maybe you'd prefer to kiss her again and this is just the way you're justifying it.* She told that voice to go away and tried not to blush.

After her final class of the day, she straightened up, stacked the day's grading to be done later at the cottage, squared her shoulders, and went to Amelia's office. Maybe she wouldn't be there. If she wasn't, Bryn would leave a note, a long explanatory note—or, no, a quick note, because she was standing in the hallway. Or she could return to her classroom and write a longer note. Would any note be acting as an invitation back to her cottage? She didn't mean that, not that she was opposed to it . . . Would a short note give enough information? Should she just text?

At this point in her mental debate, she reached Amelia's office, neatly cutting off any further thought spirals. And when she knocked, Amelia opened the door.

"Oh! Bryn! Hi!" Were those chirps? They sounded suspiciously like chirps. *Oh! Bryn! Hi!*

Bryn felt the need to apologize again for the kiss, but then Amelia was swinging the door open and inviting her inside, and she was stepping inside because of course she wasn't going to stand in the hallway. And then they were standing too close again and she was looking at Amelia's lips and completely forgot why she had ostensibly come to her office in the first place. And then, realizing she was probably standing way too close, she stepped back. But just as she did so, Amelia leaned forward and both of them laughed, and Amelia gestured to the chairs where they'd sat before.

"I'm really sorry, again," Bryn said. "I promised myself I wouldn't keep apologizing, but I'm so sorry. I don't have any desire to make you uncomfortable, and if I did, or even if I didn't, I'm really sorry."

"I'm not," Amelia said, eyes clear. "I'm not uncomfortable with you, Bryn."

"Okay, good. And obviously if you want me to resign—"

"I don't want you to resign. If I did, I would have asked you already."

"Okay." Bryn took a steadying breath. It was good, she told herself. Amelia didn't want her to resign. That was excellent news. Amelia didn't want to kiss her again or to be kissed again. That was also very okay. Maybe a little disappointing, but she'd deal with her feelings later. Professional Mode, totally fine, Bryn could do that.

She cleared her throat. "So, building on some of the ideas we talked about with regards to applied magic, I have been taking my classes outside."

"I heard," Amelia said with a smile that didn't look disapproving at all. "Actually, Piper came and talked to me about it."

"Oh, that was such a good idea. I didn't think about it, but I'm glad Piper did. We've been working together on some plans. It's obviously in the early stages, but I have felt very positive about it and I hope Piper has too." Why was she talking so formally, like she was giving a presentation? Did Amelia notice she was being weird?

"They've told me as much. I think this collaboration has been very effective so far."

"Great." Bryn let out a sigh of relief. She hadn't realized she needed a release, but the second she had, she felt lighter. "Just, I know that some of the other teachers . . . don't seem supportive, and I wanted to give you the option to shut it all down now."

Amelia was still smiling, but the tiny muscles around her eyes tightened. "It isn't my intention to shut down innovation, as I'm sure you know."

"Is it innovation, or am I just screwing things up more?"

Amelia reached out, resting her fingers lightly on Bryn's arm, where her skin smoldered with the touch. "It's innovation. You're bringing in new ideas, you're experimenting, and I really appreciate that, Bryn. Not only because it makes me feel a little less like I'm mad to think change is vital, but also because it's good for the kids to see us trying things."

"Even if we fail?" Bryn asked dubiously.

"*Especially* if we fail, yes. How else do we build resilience except by demonstrating that it's better to try and fail than not to try in the first place?"

Which actually made a lot of sense. "All right," Bryn said. "I just wanted to make sure it was okay. I didn't want to do it without permission, or inadvertently bring any more negativity down on you because of some idea that I'd had."

"You're not. I am not worried about that. I promise."

"How can you not be worried about that? I'm worried about it all the time, and it's not even my job at risk."

Amelia sat back and nodded in acknowledgement. "Well, maybe it's more accurate to say I'm *trying* not to worry about that, and intellectually I understand that if this school does not want to embrace change and innovation and experimentation, then this school is not the right place for me." Even as she said it, she winced, like it was physically painful to contemplate.

"That sounds . . ." Bryn didn't want to be dramatic, but after a second she said the word that came to mind, dramatic or not. "Amelia, that sounds heartbreaking. You care so much."

"I do, and if they don't want me, that's their loss," she said with a confidence she clearly wasn't feeling.

Bryn took both of her hands. "It seems like I've just made things worse."

"No, not at all." Amelia gripped them back. "Not at all. You never make anything worse, Bryn. Everything is better with you here. I just want you to know that."

"Thanks."

The pressure on her hands increased. Amelia leaned forward as she had by the door and kissed her.

Bryn kept her eyes open, watching as Amelia's fluttered closed, the press on her lips so perfect—not too light, not too hard, just present. Unflinching.

And then Amelia's eyes opened and they were looking at each other, and it was glorious. It was wonderful.

When they pulled away, there was no sense of urgency or fear. If Bryn was being honest, what she felt was a sense of excitement, the thrill of the unknown.

"Should I apologize?" Amelia asked softly.

Bryn grinned. "No, definitely not."

"Good." Then Amelia kissed her again.

13

Bryn felt like she was gliding on clouds, like her feet weren't even touching the ground, and it was so lovely to feel this way. She wasn't even sure how *this way* was, or what it meant. They didn't have a future. She was only at the school temporarily.

They had not discussed *anything* practical. Amelia had kissed her and then kissed her again, and then they'd laughed and squeezed each other's hands. Bryn had said she needed to get back to grading, and Amelia replied that she needed to prep for a meeting, and they'd hugged at the door, and then Bryn had left and gone home to her cottage, and Amelia had stayed; they'd seen each other at dinner, traded looks, talked normally. Bryn felt sure no one had noticed anything different about them, but she knew, and Amelia knew, and that was more than enough. It wasn't some stupid unrequited girlhood crush anymore. It was *real*. Even if it was brief.

After some additional lobbying by her after-school club kids, she did manage to arrange for second-years to go out to the courtyard and front drive. This would be their area, the place where they could come up with spells or charms, enchantments, whatever they liked.

"First-years got ponies!" someone complained.

Bryn was growing much better at ignoring what she took to be the habitual grumbling that was developmentally appropriate for their age group, but also quite annoying. She ignored this one easily. "I look forward to hearing whatever you all come up with. It can be decorative, like the lights."

"Lights?" another student asked.

Bryn waved her wand to strengthen the lighting charms in the courtyard, even though she might have done the same thing without her wand. Role-modeling wand use was an unspoken policy amongst the faculty and staff. The spell wouldn't have worked in full sun, but it was early in the day and the fog hadn't yet cleared, so it was just dark enough to see the enhanced uplighting beaming up at the palm trees.

"Ooh, pretty!" A few of the kids expressed delight, which made her smile.

"Decorative is fine. Practical is fine. Think of things that meet a stated need, or no need at all besides entertainment. Please feel free to use your initiative and your imagination. But keep away from the Grimoire cauldron!" she called as she let the kids go. The cauldron was bespelled every which way and while Bryn had the sight enough to tune into its magic, she didn't think she had the experience, nor the skills, to fix it if something went wrong.

Only five or so minutes passed before her eye was

caught by the sight of Amelia trailing two older people in her wake, walking down the front steps. One of them was Madame—or Governor now—Schneider, the other was also a governor, but not someone she knew well. Blood rushed in her ears, sudden panic hitting. Was she doing something wrong? Were they there to fire her? Was she being escorted off the premises?

But, of course, she wasn't doing anything wrong. They were not going to fire her, and if they were planning to escort her off the premises, they would not have the school governors doing it—a body famous for skillful delegation. She moved forward, her eyes locked on Amelia's. She did not look happy, but she did not look panicked, which Bryn tried to take as an encouraging sign. It was the first time they had seen each other and Bryn hadn't immediately wanted to abandon herself to kissing. She couldn't imagine kissing anyone right now, let alone the headmistress in front of the governors and the students.

"Hi there!" Amelia called, her voice all too obviously full of forced lightness. "We're just doing some observations around the school."

"Right! Great!" Bryn said. Then as an afterthought, "Welcome to the second-year spellcasting class." She reached out a hand to shake Madame Schneider's and then turned towards the man she didn't know.

"Ms Delmar," said *Governor* Schneider. "This is Governor Blake."

"Good to meet you," Bryn said, shaking his hand as well. "Is there anything I can do for you?"

"You can start by explaining what's happening here,"

said Governor Blake, face set in the kind of wrinkled, disapproving mask that immediately made Bryn want to roll her eyes in irritation. He was older than Mr Wicks, but probably by no more than ten or fifteen years, making him around the average (i.e. retirement) age for the governors.

"Oh." She glanced at Amelia, who nodded almost imperceptibly, though Bryn thought that Schneider had seen it. "Well, we're trying an experiment with the spellcasting classes where we leave the classroom and think about new spells that we can make."

"New spells?" Schneider asked. "Is there something wrong with the old spells?"

"Not at all. Just encouraging the students to think outside the box a little." The two governors looked at each other. Amelia's jaw tightened, and Bryn fought not to grimace, wondering if she'd said something wrong. But the headmistress *liked* outside the box. The governors, of course, did not.

"I see," said Governor Blake. "And what is it they're supposed to be learning from this?"

Bryn felt her heart begin to race. She was surely too old to worry about getting in trouble, but every authority-avoidant instinct in her body was now on red alert.

"We're trying experiments this year at the Academy," Amelia said brightly. "This is one of those experience experiments."

"I'm told," said Blake, "that you took students off campus for such an experiment."

"Three students, yes, who attend one of our clubs."

144

Amelia was still smiling, though Bryn didn't think anyone was fooled by it. She was pissed.

"And what was the purpose of that?"

This time, feeling on much more stable ground because they'd had permission from the students' guardians—and even the governors couldn't override that—Bryn said, "When I was first here as a student, coming from a non-witching family, I wasn't as familiar with some of the customs that the rest of my peers took for granted. We thought that allowing some of our students who come from similar backgrounds to see what it's like to experience a spell shop for the first time might be fruitful."

"The first time? At their age?" Blake seemed shocked by this, as if Bryn had just explained that kids from non-witching families had never seen the sky before. This time it was Schneider who shook her head, as if telling him to shut his mouth.

"Many students come from less privileged backgrounds," Schneider explained, and Bryn couldn't help but take that a little bit personally. Less privileged? Was it really less privileged to grow up amongst non-magical people? Surely it was just different.

She bit her tongue. It was a worthy argument and one she wanted to have, but this was clearly not the time, when too many of her students were lingering close by to eavesdrop on the adults.

Speaking of which, Violet approached: confident, head up, shoulders back. They flipped their hair to the other side and said, "It was very informative. I don't know anything about magical culture, and it was the first time I'd ever been able to explore an actual magical shop. You may not have that experience, but a lot of us do."

Bless Violet. Bless their absolute confidence and somewhat obnoxious unwillingness to be silent. Bryn hid her own genuine smile in a cough.

"Is that right, young lady?" Blake said, not quite sneering.

"I'm not a young lady, and yes, it is."

She waited for another second to see if there would be an additional challenge, and when there wasn't, she turned and stalked away. Bryn didn't miss the fact that Circe, waiting nearby, almost immediately got into step with them. Not, of course, speaking; merely expressing solidarity.

"Impertinent," Schneider said.

"Yes," Amelia said, tone icy. "Violet is one of our most promising students."

"Well, we've seen what happens to our promising students, haven't we?" Schneider sniped. When she shot a sidelong glance at Bryn, it became clear she meant both of them.

What was the undercurrent there? Bryn couldn't work it out in the moment, wasn't even sure she wanted to.

"So, is this the new style of teaching, then?" Blake demanded with a huff. "You just allow them to roam the grounds freely?"

Bryn swallowed her apprehension, told herself she could afford to be as confident as sixteen-year-old Violet, and said, "They know where the boundaries are. If it helps them make magic their own, then I think it's a lesson worth learning." She could feel herself moving closer to insubordination and swallowed her temper. "Sorry, you'll have to excuse me, I should get back to my class." And with that, she turned and walked away, feeling a bit like she was leaving Amelia to the wolves, but, well, if she didn't walk away, she would just say something completely inappropriate, and that would be worse.

Still, she felt sweat gathering between her breasts, down her spine, under her arms. She might be sick. She could not be sick. Not in front of the governors, and not in front of her students, even though right now it would be tempting to pass out. Could she faint on command? No, she shouldn't faint. That would not help matters.

She glanced at the time, pulling out her phone with more obviousness than she normally would, knowing that phones were another one of the governors' objections, and then she waved her wand over it, setting a timer, and called out, "Last ten minutes!" When the timer went off, it would blare an alarm loud enough that her whole class could hear. When she turned again, Amelia and the governors were gone. Thank the gods.

She had planned to check in with Amelia after classes were over, but Piper was standing in her doorway while her students were still streaming out.

"What happened?" they said. "It's all over school. You had a showdown with Schneider and Blake?"

"It wasn't a showdown," Bryn said, aware that students were still close enough to overhear them.

Piper smiled benignly down at all of them as they passed, then closed the door. "What was it, then? It sounded like a showdown."

Bryn waved a privacy charm at the doorway before saying, "That's only because they're complete—" She faltered on what word to use for them. *Luddites. Neanderthals.* That was probably rude to Neanderthals. "They're unnecessary," she settled on.

Piper gasped. "That is the coldest insult, and also . . . Yes, exactly, they're so unnecessary, and the worst thing is they think they're the ones running the show."

"Well, they aren't. We are." Bryn, shocked at her own words, put a hand over her lips. "I can't believe I just said that. I mean, you guys are, not me."

"You are, though. You're here right now. You're running the place with us. How was it really, though?"

So she told Piper about it over a cup of tea in the back study. They were sympathetic but had no words of wisdom to share. "Needless to say," she said at last, "the governors do not want me here. I guess being a 'good witch' means not trying anything new. I think maybe, to people like that, being a good witch means not questioning them."

Piper sighed. "Just what we want to teach our students. 'Quick, whatever you do, don't question authority or think about making any changes.'"

"Exactly."

"'*What's wrong with the old spells?*'" Piper quoted, grinning a little. "Like every spell that anyone's ever needed was just poofed into existence a thousand years ago, and now that's it, we're done."

Bryn giggled. "A thousand years ago? Your grasp on witchy history is not the strongest." When Piper flushed, Bryn felt immediately bad for joking. "Just teasing, sorry."

"No, you're right. Is it longer than a thousand years ago? I understand that those things are really obvious to most people, but timelines don't really make sense to me. I know magic's always been around. I'm just less clear on what that 'always' encompasses."

"Did you have good history lessons at your school?" Bryn asked. "Because we had—and still have—Professor Flowers, whom I love, but she's not exactly accessible."

"More and more I think cutting everything up into subjects doesn't make sense at all," Piper confided. "I mean, what's the point? That's not how the real world is. You don't just cut math out until you're in a math mood, and not read unless you're in a reading mood. You don't go days without—" they gestured "—science existing, or geography. You're doing those things all the time, you're moving around all the time. Setting aside one period for physical education doesn't make sense. Shouldn't we be doing this stuff in a more integrated way?"

As the two of them playfully redesigned the entire education system for witches, Bryn had to admit that what Piper said made sense although she hadn't really thought about it before, and she'd liked breaking things up into subjects. They only got up when it was time for dinner and, except for the time she'd spent with Amelia and kissing had been involved, it had been the most enjoyable time she'd spent at the school so far.

She did stop by Amelia's rooms before going back to the cottage and left a note that only said, *I'm sorry, again. I didn't mean to leave you to the lions. Please feel free to stop by the cottage if you need anything.* Then, before she could think too much about it, she added *xx*, slipped the note under the door, and ran home, hoping she'd see Amelia later.

This time, instead of Pilates, she took a shower . . . and put on clean underwear. Just in case.

14

The knock at the cottage door came just as Bryn was beginning to resign herself to an Amelia-less evening. It was getting late. It was getting dark. She had already put on her pajamas (but they were her nicest blue pinstriped ones, because you never knew). When the knock came, she almost didn't believe that it was real. Was she just hearing that because she so desperately wanted a knock? And even if she did hear a knock, maybe it was Piper—or maybe Amelia was just stopping in for a moment, Headmistress Mode activated.

There was absolutely no guarantee that this knock, even if it was Amelia, indicated that she was as—well, *desperate* wasn't a very chill word, but Bryn could feel herself getting a little bit desperate to kiss her crush again. The kissing had gone well, she thought, but maybe this was Amelia saying it was all a mistake and they needed to call it off. Not that there was anything to call off—

At which point the knock came again and she realized she was standing there dithering, instead of answering her door.

When Amelia saw what she was wearing, she blanched. "Oh, my gods, I'm so late. I'm sorry. I've been meaning to get up here. I got super distracted. I did eight thousand things and now I'm too late. I'm sorry. We can talk tomorrow."

But Bryn ushered her in with a grin that she feared was about to split her face. Could your lips actually split open because you were smiling so hard? Probably not, right? That would be a design flaw. "No, come in," she said quickly. "Come in." She waved her hand and three candles sprung to life at the edge of the kitchen counter. The cottage was neat, tidy, clean, and it honestly looked adorable in the candlelight—much less like a place she'd only occupied for a few weeks.

"I'm really sorry it's so late," Amelia said again, standing awkwardly, not quite committing.

"I'm not," Bryn told her, taking one hand and, after a moment of indecision, leading her to the bed. "Sit."

It was definitely forward to lead her to the bed instead of the chair, but really it came down to the fact that they were holding hands and she didn't want to let go just yet. The bed was the place where they could sit next to each other. Perfectly innocent.

"I've been thinking about you all day," Bryn said, meaning this to be a romantic statement.

Amelia immediately shot up to her feet. "I'm really sorry about the governors. If I'd known they were coming, I would have warned you, obviously, and then when I suggested we go see someone else's classroom, they said they wanted to see yours. I really didn't mean that to be a trap. I'm sure it felt like it was."

"Only by the governors," Bryn said. "Not by you."

"Oh, good." Amelia still didn't sit down.

"Is everything okay?" Bryn asked, heart sinking. So this wasn't going to be about kissing. This was going to be about never kissing again. She steadied her nerves. It was okay. She had lived for this long, thinking that Amelia didn't want her. Even though it had been a nice few days, she could still go back to thinking Amelia didn't want her. It would take a bit of mental adjustment, but she could manage it.

"Violet did great, though, didn't they?" Amelia said.

Bryn smiled. Back on work. That was good. Much more neutral. "Violet was brilliant. I told them that they should be very proud. They rolled their eyes."

Amelia smiled. "That sounds like Violet."

Bryn had already sat down. Amelia was still awkwardly standing. It was the first time Bryn had ever looked up at her, probably in the entire time they'd known each other. At this angle, Amelia's profile was softer somehow. Less angular. She knew she was staring, but what the hell. There were only so many moments in her life when she would get to look at Amelia Hexford like this, before they'd go their separate ways and probably only see each other periodically at school reunions. So she looked.

Amelia, catching her glance, blushed. "I shouldn't have kissed you," she said. "Like, ever, at all. And I'm really sorry I did. And I hope, I really hope, sincerely, that it didn't make you uncomfortable, because I would be mortified. Not that it would be about *me*. It would be about you, obviously, but that was never my intention." The words came out with the rush of an unblocked dam, the force of them as if they'd been building all day or maybe for a period of days.

"Will you sit?" Bryn asked.

"I'm really, really sorry," Amelia said.

Bryn sighed. "I wasn't sorry. I thought it was nice."

Amelia sank slowly onto the bed beside her, not close enough to touch, even casually. "You did? I mean . . ." She looked away. "Just, I started thinking about it and, you know, I had no business doing that. And you kind of work for me. And what if you didn't think that you could say no, or you thought that it might make things awkward because I gave you this job, even though that has nothing to do with it. I promise. I swear. It's just, you kissed me first. And obviously that doesn't mean anything. I know that intellectually. I really do. I promise. You were probably just having a moment and I took it way too seriously and overthought it, which, to be honest, is kind of what I do."

"You too?" Bryn asked, feeling the barest spark of something that might be hope. Maybe this wasn't Amelia being disinterested, but Amelia worried that *she* was disinterested.

"But I'm in a position of power, or at least . . ." She paused. "Quote-unquote-power." She paused again.

"I was hoping we could do it again," Bryn said into the silence that followed. "The kissing, I mean, both of us kissing each other."

"You were?" Amelia's eyebrows went up, eyes wide, looking younger somehow, more vulnerable.

"Definitely," Bryn said. "Yeah, for days now. I mean, you should have come by earlier." She laughed a bit ruefully. "I

154

even made desserts. I mean, not made-made. I cadged them from the kitchen. But I got enough for both of us, just in case you showed up and wanted dessert. And I had the best casual *I definitely wasn't waiting for you, but I still look really cute* outfit on. Not the kind of thing I would wear to class, but you know."

Amelia laughed. "I want to see it."

Which was certainly possible. Bryn could get changed again. There was a bathroom. It would be proper. But she decided she didn't want to. She assumed a very prim expression and said, "You can't. It's my only cute outfit and I'm saving it for next time." She plucked at the blue pinstriped pajama set. "These are my cutest PJs, though."

"Very cute," Amelia agreed, with mock formality. "But are you sure you're not mad I kissed you?"

"Not at all," Bryn said. "Are you mad *I* kissed *you*?"

"No. No, I'm far from mad you kissed me, actually. It's probably . . . Well, I don't even think I should explain how not-mad I am about that."

"Oh, please do," Bryn teased. "Please tell me all about it."

"You're so naughty," Amelia said.

Bryn batted her eyelashes. "Have I been naughty, Headmistress?"

Amelia let out the most surprised snort of amusement. "Oh gods, don't say that." The amusement faded. "There is a power imbalance and I'm worried about it."

Bryn nodded, because this was serious and because, honestly, it was reassuring. Amelia cared about people and about the different levels of power and privilege that existed

155

between them. Bryn cared about those things too. "I hear that. And I appreciate you bringing it up. But as much as you gave me this job, it doesn't really feel like you're my boss. When you and I talk about things, it's collaborative. And maybe you could fire me at this point, but I'm not so sure." She shrugged. "No offense, obviously. The way the governors acted this morning made it feel a lot more like they are the ones in charge."

"Welcome to my world." Amelia sighed.

"I guess what I'm saying is that this doesn't feel like a power imbalance. It feels like an opportunity. To me, anyway."

"To me too," Amelia said. "But I don't want to screw it up."

"I'm not that worried about you screwing it up," Bryn said. "If anyone screws it up, it will probably be me."

"Um, excuse me, I have screwed up plenty of things," Amelia proclaimed.

"Okay, name five."

"All right. Well." Amelia considered this. "I once did very poorly on a geography lesson at university."

Bryn giggled. "That's your best example of you screwing something up? You did badly one time in one class?"

"It was quite irritating at the time."

"I'm sure it was." She struggled to keep a straight face. "But listen, I don't feel like there is any reason, ethically speaking, that we can't kiss more. If you don't want to, that's fine. I totally accept that. But if both of us want to . . ." She swallowed. She could do this, she could say this. It was true. "And I *definitely* want us to kiss again. So I think we should. Shouldn't we? Plus," she added, "I've always kind of thought the naughty headmistress thing was hot. I mean, to be clear, you *do* want to kiss your new teacher, making you a very naughty headmistress indeed."

Amelia blushed again. "Hush, don't even say that."

"Why?" Bryn asked, leaning closer. "Amelia Hexford, are you a bit into the naughty headmistress thing? Is this a kink we should explore?"

"Oh *my*." The blush deepened. "Bryn, I . . ."

There were many areas in which Bryn had painfully limited experience, and less than no confidence. Like teaching. But this was an arena in which she considered herself if not an expert, then at least an experienced amateur. She reached out slowly and let her fingers come into contact with Amelia's neck, gently sliding around the back, only resting there. "How does that feel?" she asked softly.

Amelia's breath released in one long exhalation that stirred the tiny hairs on Bryn's skin. "Incredible."

"If I do anything that doesn't feel good, tell me. Right?"

"Yes." Amelia leaned in, eyes on Bryn's. "Is it okay if you take the lead for a while?"

"More than okay. So, so much more than okay." The stirrings of an intensity Bryn didn't think she'd ever felt before seemed to sizzle at her fingertips and she closed the distance between them by pulling Amelia forward. "My safe word is pineapple."

The tension around Amelia's eyes seemed to relax just a little. "Mine is furnace."

"Furnace?" Bryn allowed her thumb to brush against

157

Amelia's throat in what she hoped was a super sexy way. "How very . . . hot."

It only took a split second for Amelia to process the silly joke. Then she laughed, leaned in, and pressed her lips to Bryn's. They kissed through laughter, and instead of lightening the mood, the laughter took it further.

Bryn had time to think, *This bodes well . . .* And then they were kissing again and thinking far less.

15

Sirens used sexuality for specific ends, some of which had to do with intimacy, while others had to do with procreation, and very few had to do with romance. Bryn had always suspected this was why she wasn't super inclined towards any romance that took a different form than schoolgirl crush, but since sex was fun anyway, she hadn't thought much about it.

Amelia had shaken up all the thoughts she'd ever had about sex and those thoughts had resettled in a very different order. Instead of shying away from kissing because it might lead to eye contact and (gods forbid) feelings, Bryn felt she could kiss Amelia forever. Instead of trying to avoid the implications of physical engagement— the way that touching someone and being touched by them almost inevitably made her reflect on how she saw that person and was seen by them—in this moment, with this woman, she wanted to bask in every second of connection.

Bryn drew Amelia to her feet, dropped both hands to

her hips, and then stepped in closer, her feet bracketing Amelia's. "Look at me," she murmured.

It took a moment, and when Amelia shifted her gaze, Bryn caught a flash of something almost burning within it, like this was as intense for Amelia as it was to her.

"What do you like? How do you want to be touched?" The questions, which seemed ordinary to her, seemed to strike Amelia in some indefinable way, and she dropped her eyes again. Red spots flared in her cheeks.

This was interesting. Bryn used the gentlest of pressure on Amelia's hips to pull her closer. Making her voice as light as she currently could, with this much arousal coursing through her system, Bryn said teasingly, "I can't do anything unless you enthusiastically consent."

"I do! I do consent. Enthusiastically." Amelia swallowed. "I *passionately* consent."

"Ooo, I like the sound of that." Bryn kissed her flaming cheeks, first one, then the other. "What kinds of things do you enjoy?"

Amelia pressed her face against Bryn's, breathing a little raggedly. "Being told what to do. I've never said that out loud before, oh gods." She shifted, this time pushing her eyes into Bryn's body as if to hide from her own words.

"Oh boy." Bryn slid her thigh between Amelia's and allowed one hand to drift down her back, putting the slightest pressure at the base of her spine, thankful that the dress Amelia was wearing had enough give so it could ride up instead of awkwardly catching. "You've never told anyone what gets you off?"

"Not that. I've said other things. Mmm."

Pleased with the effect their current position was having on Amelia, Bryn leaned down to whisper directly in her ear. "Spread your legs. I want you to feel me."

"Ohh, I feel you." Amelia shuffled her feet apart and moaned as Bryn's thigh came into more direct contact with highly sensitive parts of her anatomy. "Bryn, gods, that feels . . ."

"Naughty?" Bryn teased.

"*Hush*."

"You know what would be fun?" Bryn continued, as if musing. "Me telling you to rut against me like this until you—"

"*Bryn*." The pressure of Amelia's face against her shoulder increased, as if she was attempting to put out the fire on her skin by smothering it.

"Hey. Look at me. Please."

Amelia took a breath, then raised her head. The blush was deep and beautiful, and her eyes were clear. "I would, if you told me to."

"Would you enjoy it?"

"I . . ." Lips parted, Amelia hesitated. "Yes. It would be a little embarrassing."

"Does that turn you on?" Bryn asked, watching for all the clues and cues. Candlelight played across Amelia's features, and while Bryn didn't have decades of experience with this sort of thing, she'd had enough partners who enjoyed dancing with humiliation to feel a growing sense that she and Amelia might be very compatible indeed.

"Yes," Amelia said finally. "Actually, this is . . . really turning me on."

Bryn took her own deep breath, and the glorious buzz of sex was taking hold now, her body already opening, her cunt wet and her clit hard. Her nipples poked out of the light top as if aimed directly at the object of her desire.

She hadn't prepared for this exact dynamic, but damn, what a lovely surprise.

"Stand here," she said firmly, and stepped back, smiling too widely at Amelia's murmur of protest. But there was no need to be careless about the details, and anyway, Bryn was beginning to suspect that Amelia would thrive on delayed gratification. She wondered if that was common amongst teachers, for whom few triumphs were instant.

Think about that later; right now, you're busy.

She locked the door and double-checked all of her curtains, which were tightly closed, but it never hurt to make sure. She relocated two of the candles to the bedside tables, before returning to where Amelia obediently stood, watching all this with her hands clasped in front of her.

"Gods, you are so . . ." She searched for a word that someone as spectacularly gorgeous as Amelia hadn't heard a hundred times before. Then, almost without thinking, she traced an index finger over the other woman's eyebrows, her nose, her lips. "I can't believe you want to do this with me," Bryn whispered, the words far more raw than she intended.

Amelia's hands came up to cup her face. "So, so much. Kiss me again?"

Bryn couldn't deny such a delightful request.

A few minutes later, when her hands were roaming over Amelia's dress-covered back (though under her long

162

knit coat), Bryn made herself stop kissing long enough to say, "I want access to your body. Your skin. May I undress you?"

Amelia bit down on her lower lip, though she still managed to obviously smile. "Why, yes, I would enjoy that very much."

"Gasp! Are you making fun of me, Headmistress?"

"I would never." The smile escaped the confines of her teeth. "Well, maybe only a little, and in good fun."

"Don't make me gag you," Bryn said, grinning. "Actually, I probably wouldn't gag you unless you were really into it. It's not a particular kink of mine and I like demanding you talk, I think."

"Oh, do you?" Amelia arched an eyebrow.

"For instance . . ." Bryn settled both hands on Amelia's waist again and looked down at her. "Are you aroused right now, Ms Hexford?"

"Very aroused, Ms Delmar." After a moment, Amelia looped her arms around Bryn's neck, stepping in closer. In kissing distance.

"Are you wet, Ms Hexford?" Bryn asked, trying to keep her voice steady, though with Amelia this close, it was a challenge.

"Yes," Amelia breathed.

"Say it."

"I'm . . . very wet. For you. Oh gods." Amelia laughed. "I don't know why this is so hot to me, but it is. Talk dirty to me more, Bryn."

"With pleasure. But first." Bryn kissed her, moving in so their bodies moved against each other, so she could feel

163

Amelia's breasts against her own. "I'm taking off your clothes now," she whispered against Amelia's lips.

"Only mine?"

"I haven't decided yet."

It was so easy to fall into this dynamic. Seductively easy. Bryn stepped apart, then removed Amelia's coat, hanging it by the door. She then trailed her fingers along Amelia's shoulder, her collarbone, her other shoulder. So far so good. Now she just needed to seductively get a hot woman out of a dress, something she'd done any number of times before. She slowly rounded Amelia's body, letting her fingertips trail, building anticipation.

It was a charged, sexy moment, full of so much promise—which Bryn immediately spoiled by saying, "How the hell do you zip this thing up without help?"

"I'm *very* flexible," Amelia replied lightly.

Bryn pulled Amelia back against her, hands slipping down to loosely grip each wrist. "Is that right?"

"Yes. Oh gods. Bryn." Amelia trembled.

"Shall I continue?"

"Fuck. Yes. Please."

Bryn pressed a kiss to the side of Amelia's neck, then her teeth, gently biting down. Amelia's breath caught so she did it again, holding her in place at each wrist, the gentlest of restraints. No visible marks, of course—that did not need to be said. But perhaps elsewhere . . .

"Hands behind your back," Bryn whispered. When Amelia complied, Bryn pressed forward again, rubbing herself for a second over those welcome sources of friction and running her own hands up Amelia's body.

164

"I . . . I . . ." Amelia took a breath, then said, "I want to be naked. I want you to . . . touch me like this, but naked. Like I'm yours."

"Aren't you?" Bryn asked, the words leaving her mouth before she could call them back. "Sorry, that sounded creepy-possessive, which I totally didn't mean—" She gasped as Amelia's fingers seemed to come alive and slide against the soft cotton of her pajama bottoms.

"Tonight I'm yours," Amelia whispered.

"You keep this up, I'm not sure—" *I can let you go.* No, that was an absurd thing to say out loud. "—I'll let you out of here that easily," Bryn finished instead, hoping it came off more playfully: *you're my sex toy* instead of *I'm still too creepy-possessive.*

"Maybe that's my goal." Even at the awkward angle, Amelia's fingers betrayed some skill at their task.

Bryn went up on her toes and pulled Amelia's body back against hers so she could get a better angle—then she came to her senses. "Naughty. You're trying to distract me."

"I *am* distracting you. But only because I thought we were both enjoying it." Amelia withdrew her questing hand. "I'll be good, I promise."

Bryn nuzzled her neck again. "You know that only makes me want to tempt you to be bad, right?"

Amelia giggled, which seemed like a very good time to finally, *finally*, draw down the zipper of her dress, which had the knock-on effect of Bryn's hand coming into contact with Amelia's hands, which she grasped briefly, as if in greeting.

"Mmm," Bryn murmured, and lowered her head to kiss

the revealed triangle of Amelia's back. She dragged her lips down, the fabric parting for them.

Amelia made a delicious, strangled sort of sound. "Oh gods, Bryn, that feels so good."

"I'm glad. Though to be clear—" She nipped at the skin of Amelia's lower back. "—I'm primarily doing it because it makes me feel good."

Another giggle. "Noted."

Then Bryn rose and pushed the dress off Amelia's shoulders. It fell with a satisfying *whoosh* of fabric, leaving Amelia only in socks and underwear. She shivered.

Bryn immediately moved in. "Gotta share my body heat with you," she explained.

"Thank you." Amelia's hands shifted, reaching further until she could grip Bryn and hold on. "Touch me."

"With pleasure." Bryn's hands glided from Amelia's hips upward, trailing paths along her skin, reaching her small breasts and cupping them. "Is that good?"

"Mmm," Amelia said, leaning her head back against Bryn's shoulder.

Bryn tsked. "I said . . ." She pinched both nipples at once. "Is that good?"

"Yes." Amelia swayed in her arms. "Fuck. Please."

Rolling Amelia's nipples, Bryn leaned in. "How do you feel about begging?" she asked, lips brushing Amelia's earlobe.

"I want to beg right now," came the breathy reply. Amelia arched her back, pushing into Bryn's hands. "More. Please."

Bryn eased up, just to be contrary. And maybe a little to

coax out the mewl of denied pleasure from her lover. She wrapped her arms fully around Amelia, one arm holding her close, and the other drifting down. For the first time their height difference was inconvenient; she could only really brush her fingertips along Amelia's pubic bone, toying with the top of her underwear, dipping beneath the elastic to encounter closely trimmed hair and lingering there to tease.

"Bryn, Bryn . . . Bryn, *please*," Amelia chanted.

"Hmm? Please what?" Was there Pilates for more acrobatic fucking? If only she was confident she could hold both of them up while balanced on one leg. Then she could use her other one to lift Amelia's leg and . . .

Not tonight, anyway. She kissed along Amelia's shoulder, which allowed her to bend both of them just a bit, though she still didn't reach lower. Waiting on Amelia's response, or only on her moans.

"Ame-lia," Bryn sang softly. "Tell me what you wa- ant . . ."

Amelia shuddered, blew out a breath, and said, "You."

Which was all Bryn needed to hear. She shifted them both, guiding Amelia to the bed, and then lying her back. "Gods, look at you. Will you put your hands over your head? I'm getting off on the you-being-exposed thing."

"Me too," Amelia admitted, raising her arms and scooting backwards so her legs were better supported. "Except, do you mind if I take my socks off? They're distracting me."

"Allow me." Bryn ran her hands down Amelia's smooth calves to the tops of her socks, and peeled first one, then the other, off her feet. Amelia had grabbed a pillow to prop up her head and was staring down at her, flushed and focused, her breasts rising and falling quickly with each breath. "Better?"

"Much better. Will you kiss me again?"

"Everywhere," Bryn said reverently, and bent to press her lips to the top of each foot, then the top of each knee. Then, shooting a wicked look upward, she bent first one leg, then the other, and pressed a kiss to the inside of each of Amelia's knees.

"Oh *gods*." Amelia did not look away. She watched as Bryn moved farther up between her legs, kissing her inner thighs, spreading her open just a little more. "Bryn. Gods, Bryn, fuck me, *please*."

"Hmm." Not so fast, though. Bryn slid her hands up over Amelia's belly, using her thumbs to brush over each nipple, then gently squeezed each breast.

"You're a tease. Such a—"

Bryn pinched a nipple and held it there, long enough for Amelia to gasp, and arch, and gulp. Then she let go. "Sorry, what were you saying?"

Amelia grabbed Bryn's arm with two hands and pulled herself up, stealing a hard kiss before breaking away to say, "If you don't touch me, or let me touch you, or taste you, or *something* in the next three minutes, I'm going back to my rooms and getting off without you."

It was so surprising that Bryn laughed out loud. "Noted," she echoed, and pushed Amelia back down, climbing on top of her. "Is this okay? Any physical things I need to watch out for?"

"Only your health if you don't—"

Bryn loved kissing someone in this position, one of her

hands holding theirs pinned down, her body over them, her lips searing against theirs. She used her tongue to seek entrance, and Amelia's surrender was all grace and need, pushing upward, hands writhing, though not trying to break from Bryn's grasp. After they'd kissed each other breathless, Amelia wiggled, using her feet for leverage to thrust upward, though with Bryn's weight on top of her, she didn't manage to get far.

She groaned in frustration and Bryn grinned smugly down at her. "You know, we could do this for hours. I could keep you all tense and wanton, waiting for you to confess all your darkest desires to me . . ."

"Dearest Bryn," Amelia said severely, "you have papers to grade and I have to return to the world that requires me to make a million decisions a day. That would be fun—for a long holiday. But tonight we need to *focus*."

It sounded so much like something Bryn herself would say to her students, and she grinned. "Fair point. I guess I'll just do this, then." She let go of Amelia's wrists, slid down between her legs, and spread her open. "Though one day I'm going to do this when we have more time so I can tell you just how hot it is to see you get this wet for me."

Amelia's lips parted in what might have been the beginning of another protest—or another threat—but Bryn didn't wait, only inhaled the warm, sweet scent of her and applied her tongue to the sort of careful and meticulous exploration that her teenage self could only have imagined.

Teasing Amelia was fun, but so was this sped-up play of pleasure and power. Using her fingers to expose Amelia's clit, then sucking on it with abandon, far too fast, far too much, and listening to Amelia's strangled cry. Lower still, tasting arousal and sweat and *Amelia* as she pressed her tongue into that hot, wet cunt.

"Oh, fuck, oh gods, oh *Bryn*," Amelia said, the words staccato and rhythmic. "Please, please, please—"

Bryn slipped two fingers inside and returned to her first prize, this time flicking at Amelia's clit from the side as she used her fingers to press upward.

"Too fast," Amelia gasped, arching her back, her body opening more, her clit practically on display.

"Hold like that," Bryn said. "Right there, presenting yourself to be fucked." And then she went back in, plunging her fingers deeper and faster, sucking on Amelia's clit as she used her tongue on the underside of it.

Amelia cried out again and held herself up as long as she could, legs shaking as she tried to speak. "Can I— Can I—"

Bryn, whose mouth was busy, tried to nod against her, and Amelia seemed to understand, because this time the climax was unmistakable. Her body seemed to take over, shaking and shattering against Bryn's lips, against her tongue, around her fingers. Her moan lasted for a long, incredible exhale, only to be replaced by panting and whimpering as Bryn slowed down, fingers coming to a stop inside Amelia's body, lips kissing just above her clit. Bryn watched with lidded eyes as Amelia caught her breath, as her hands released fistfuls of bedding.

She slowly, carefully, withdrew her fingers, using her thumb to softly stroke Amelia's thigh, still watching her.

"That was . . ." Amelia licked her lips. "That was fucking

amazing." She looked down. "Are you a sex demon, by any chance?"

"Nah. Just a witch who likes to get a lady off."

"If you say 'aww shucks' right now . . ." Amelia began, in a slightly less threatening tone than she'd managed earlier.

Bryn raised both eyebrows. "Yes?"

Amelia smiled and let her head fall back on the pillow. "I'll think of something. Give me like two minutes and I will gladly do anything you like. Gods, Bryn. That was amazing. Thank you."

"Anything?" Bryn asked innocently, batting her eyelashes.

Not to be drawn in too quickly, Amelia only gazed back at her. "What are you thinking?"

She'd never said it before to any lover, never asked for it. But it would take— Realistically, Bryn didn't think she would last even two minutes once she got started. She was going to need to do laundry after this. She pulled herself up and, with a lot less savoir faire than would have been ideal, shucked off her pajama bottoms then moved into position with her knees on either side of Amelia's hips. Feeling far more vulnerable than she'd expected, she said, "Can you go again? And um . . . how do you feel about overstimulation?"

Amelia's eyes widened. She reached down to put her hands on Bryn's waist. "Show me."

So Bryn did, shifting into position, lowering herself so her clit brushed against Amelia's. Both of them shuddered. "Sensitive?" Bryn asked.

"So, so sensitive."

"It's, um . . ." Bryn began to lightly rub herself against

Amelia. "Just, the idea of coming while you kind of writhe because you're so sensitive it's hard to take . . . um . . . really . . ."

Amelia's fingers curled, nails biting into her. "Do it. Get yourself off." She shifted, parting her legs a little, pushing upward.

The additional stimulation made Bryn's clit even harder. "Tell me if— If it's too much—"

But Amelia wasn't having it. She thrust again and Bryn bent down to kiss her, changing their angle again. The kiss turned into a moan and she could feel how wet she was, how incredibly hard her clit was now, as it brushed against Amelia's.

"Fuck me, Bryn," Amelia said, hands pulling Bryn harder against her. "Do it. Faster."

Bryn simultaneously wanted to orgasm and to fly on the edge of her orgasm forever. But her body had only so much restraint left, and Amelia was kissing her desperately now, her own body in a rhythm of its own.

They moved together, until Bryn shuddered hard, held her breath, and sent all of her awareness down until every nerve ending in her body resonated with arousal and pleasure and something very like joy.

"I'm coming," she gasped into Amelia's ear. "Oh gods—"

The peak held for a breathtaking moment, then crashed down over her, and she rutted against Amelia like a beast, drinking in Amelia's cries as her overstimulated body gave into another orgasm and she pulled herself against Bryn with a wild, savage strength.

They collapsed together in a sweaty heap. Bryn's legs felt

lifeless. Her heart was still racing. Her forehead seemed to steam against Amelia's neck.

"Extraordinary," Amelia was saying somewhere far away. One of her hands was gently brushing over Bryn's side. "Thank you. Thank you, Bryn . . ."

Bryn wanted to push herself upright and check in, and fetch water like a good host, but for the moment she just lay there, her pajama top somehow still on, her cunt pulsing with aftershocks, her mind soothed in a way she couldn't remember it ever being after sex in the past. "Thank you," she whispered.

Amelia tugged her into a more comfortable position, resting Bryn's head on her chest, and kissed her temple. "You're a good lay, you know that, Bryn Delmar?"

Bryn laughed, tired and sated, and closed her eyes. Just for a second.

When she woke up in the middle of the night, Amelia was gone, but a spelled illusion lit the room from the sheets where she'd lain. A sparkling emerald-green heart. Bryn let her fingers brush through it, wondering how she'd slept through Amelia's departure. But she did not wonder for long. With her hand still resting inside the illusion, she fell asleep again.

16

When Bryn finally woke up for real that Saturday morning, she was already having second thoughts. Not about the sex—the sex had been incredible. She'd had no idea that Amelia was also just a little bit kinky, and the discovery had been extraordinary, fantastic, exciting, and *new*. And definitely fun.

Then again, Amelia had left in the middle of the night. What if she regretted it? That was the worst part. Bryn had skipped breakfast at the castle, which she normally did on Saturday mornings. She liked to take a hike around the campus—the kind of hike she had never taken when she was a student there. Partially because there were only limited paths students were allowed to hike, and mostly because the campus just wasn't that interesting to her when she lived there all the time. For a good portion of her school years, she had just been waiting to escape it.

But now, back again, only temporarily, she realized what a gorgeous place Grimoire Academy really was. Acres and acres of land. The parts nearest the castle were more utilitarian—a paddock for the horses and livestock, the extensive gardens, a rather large stable fit for many uses, including medical appointments for all the school's various animals. But beyond that, there were some zebras still living in the wild from when they'd been released there decades ago.

The land was not formally fenced in at the boundaries; it was magically protected by barrier spells that three experts in the field needed two full weeks to maintain each summer. They kept out strangers and kept in the wildlife. Not that, on her walks, Bryn had ever encountered any of these beasts. At least the tigers had been rounded up a long time ago—she didn't fancy meeting one of them. But the local native wildlife was still active. Coyotes, deer, loads and loads of rodents, rabbits, and birds, the occasional skunk family.

Only when she was forty-five minutes into her hike did she realize she hadn't left a note or even texted Amelia. What if she had come by the cottage to talk, or eat, or kiss? She'd have found the cottage empty, and Bryn hadn't even gone to breakfast. What if that was sending the wrong message, making it look like she wasn't interested when she definitely, definitely was?

Not that what they had done had been any kind of big deal, but she shouldn't be out of range. She quickly sent a text simply saying, *Taking a hike, see you later.*

Amelia had sent back a thumbs up. Thumbs up? What the heck did that mean? *Thumbs-up emoji.* But she kept hiking, her thoughts whirling around her. She visualized them, like her thoughts were a series of sparkles surrounding her head—different sizes, different colors, some with spikes, some with gentle curves . . .

The sex had been absolutely spectacular. She'd do it again in a heartbeat. She'd do it again right now if Amelia booty-called her—a concept that should obviously be a verb. She would be back at her cottage faster than she even thought was possible under normal circumstances, leaving a cloud of dust in her wake. But Amelia had texted a thumbs up, which was basically a neutral acknowledgement.

What did it mean? What were they even doing? It was already April. The MSEs were the first week of June. She'd be gone after that, back to her apartment, back to Denver, back to the mountains. A totally different world than this. No more teaching, or grading, or lesson planning. It was strange to think of how recently she'd been looking forward to that release: a clear path forward, no more being bad at her job all the time. Yet now it felt different. Was that only because she and Amelia had fucked? Because that felt like a wildly insubstantial reason to feel less bad at her job.

Plus, this was only sex. Maybe a fling. That's what she could call it. Very brief, very hot, and then very *over*. No doubt that was how Amelia was thinking about it. That was how Bryn had conducted every sexual encounter of her life. No pressure, no big deal.

Except, every time Bryn even thought about Amelia, it felt like the circuit boards all over her body lit up with electricity, like she couldn't wait for the next time they saw each other, even if it was in the corridor and all they could do was smile hello before vanishing into their respective days. But maybe Amelia had a different kind of second thoughts. By the time Bryn got back to the cottage, she'd pictured Amelia there so frequently that she was almost surprised to find it empty. Amelia had only been to visit twice. Bryn had only been at the school for two months. She had no business thinking about it like this was her life. It wasn't. It wouldn't be.

Bryn was not the type of person who ended up with Amelia Hexford. She'd always known that. Amelia would probably marry some super smart hottie who only ever looked artistically disheveled and knew exactly how to navigate conversations with the Governor Schneiders of the world without being so intimidated that sweat pooled in her unmentionables.

Back at the cottage, she set up her paper grading, which she mostly did in Professor Herringbone's study. But the idea of going to the castle right now and possibly having to face Amelia (which might be great or might be devastating), let alone anyone else, was too much to handle. What would Mr Wicks think if he knew that they had— Screw it. Mr Wicks was just some dude; his judgment was irrelevant, though Bryn had to admit she didn't want to be judged—not by the people at the school, not by the board of governors, not by anyone. And certainly not for the feelings she had for Amelia.

She set a timer and diligently graded papers for two hours, at which point she was not quite caught up, but caught up enough to at least feel better about things. She set the timer again and did some lesson planning, though this was slightly less disciplined. Halfway through, she stopped for a snack, and that quickly turned to imagining Amelia there with her, also eating a snack. And that quickly turned to imagining Amelia there, eating a candlelit dinner, sharing a bottle of apple cider. Relaxing in the flickering shadows, her skin, kissing . . .

Before she knew it, Bryn had run out the last of her timer, not lesson planning, but fantasizing. This was absurd. She sent another text to Amelia, hoping to sound casual and not weird. This time the text read, *Thinking about you*, with a smiley face. Not a heart. A heart would potentially be overstepping, but a basic smiley face was as neutral as an emoji could be following the words *thinking about you*. If Amelia thumbs-upped this, well, it would probably be the last text Bryn ever sent, because she'd have to leave the country and change her name.

Instead, nothing. Left on delivered. She finally surrendered to the inevitable and went up to the castle, fearing encountering Amelia in a corridor and having an awkward one-sided conversation. But she didn't. She made it to the kitchens and collected some food for later so that she wouldn't have to leave the cottage again. So much work to be done, she told herself. She needed to start outlining the book that she hoped her publisher would ask her for. The second volume in her series of spell books for the everyday witch. She had a career, and it was definitely not teaching. She was . . . excited to get back to it? To her tables for one at breweries and cafés, to her evenings in a neat, orderly apartment, to refreshing her emails way too often, hoping to hear from her editor that it was time to discuss a second contract.

Any day now, any week now. She felt almost certain her

first book had sold well enough to warrant another, though she had often felt like success in publishing was about the personality of the author, which did not work in her favor. Bryn wasn't really sure she had much of a personality, but she was very good at spells. And the more she'd planned out her next book, the more prepared she'd be when (please let it be *when*) her editor came calling.

She did not see Amelia in the corridors, but she did encounter Piper as she was leaving the castle on her way back to her cottage.

"Oh, nice to see a friendly face," they said. "After the day I've had."

"Bad one?" she asked, thinking about how much she'd sometimes envied the Phys Ed teacher for not needing to grade papers.

Piper linked an arm through hers. "Do you have a week for me to verbally process?" But their voice was light enough and Bryn found that even though she halfway wanted to hide in her cottage for the rest of her existence (or at least until she left the country and changed her name), she didn't mind lingering in the grounds at her friend's side.

"Maybe not a whole week. What's up?"

"So, you know that today was the big governors' tour, right?"

She looked over, frowning. "Governors' tour?"

"Yeah, poor Amelia. She's had it even worse than I did. The governors don't like the PE program, but at least I was only on their hit list for an hour. Actually, it was just under an hour, though it felt like an entire agonizing year. Amelia's been stuck with them since 7 a.m."

"7 a.m.?" Bryn echoed. Why hadn't Amelia told her? They'd stayed awake until— She had no idea when they'd finally gone to sleep.

Piper looked at their watch. "Yeah, I think they should be finishing up soon, though."

It was already four in the afternoon. "That's like a . . . nine-hour day with the governors."

"This is what I'm saying." Piper shuddered so theatrically that the carrier bag in Bryn's hand, laden with food, shuddered too. "So, as I understand it, this is a thing that happens every year, but usually it's just a sort of friendly walk-through, you know, catching everyone up, blah, blah. But this year, it was basically a full inspection."

Bryn glanced around to ensure they were alone. "Because they're trying to find a way to get Amelia to leave?"

"You said it, not me. But it sure felt like we were being investigated for crimes or something. I halfway thought they were going to call out a forensics team—or dismiss me on the spot."

"It went that badly?" Bryn asked sympathetically.

"It was all right. The governors, of course, don't buy into the program at all, but when you start with that as your basic premise, then it's actually pretty easy to let it go. I knew I wasn't going to impress them, but a few of them were tolerably engaged in the idea that moving the body is good for minds and magic." They rolled their eyes.

"As if we don't literally know that's true," Bryn said.

"I know, but Amelia and I talked about it beforehand, and we decided that continually saying we have studies to prove the concept wasn't going to make a difference. So I

181

laid off all of the, you know—" they hooked their fingers in sarcastic air quotes "—'scientific evidence' and just talked about how the kids seemed to really enjoy the program."

Bryn reflected on how the enjoyment of students actually seemed to be working against some of the things she was doing when she talked to the governors. But no point in bringing it up.

"But I'm free now," they said, then nodded at her load of food. "What are you doing?"

"Oh, gathering supplies. I think I might do a work-in day tomorrow, try to lesson plan for the next—well, until the MSEs."

"At least I'm spared that trial," they said. "How's it going? I mean, after the cheating scandal."

It hadn't really been a scandal, but that's what she and Piper were calling it, just for fun. They'd done it once around Amelia, who had winced, so they hadn't done it again.

"Well . . ." A long silence drew out, filled only with the sound of their steps on the gravel and birdsong all around.

"That good, huh?" Piper asked, when it was clear that Bryn really didn't know what to say.

"Yeah, pretty much." She glanced over, assessing whether after the day they'd had, they would be interested in entertaining what was probably a ridiculous idea. "I was thinking. What if we set up some kind of mentoring system, or a group-work scenario? What if we get the kids who are more or less up on things to teach the kids who aren't?"

"I don't know how effective that would be." It wasn't the most positive response, but they sounded thoughtful.

"I don't mean teach formally. I just mean . . ." She struggled to find the words. "I was reading about the use of group-work activities."

"I mean, vomit, but okay." They grinned to show they didn't mean it.

"And you're into team sports!"

Piper opened their mouth as if to argue, then shrugged. "Fair play, so to speak. So team studenting?"

"Maybe. Hear me out. Teaching helps cement concepts, right?"

They nodded. "Yeah, I'll grant you that."

"Right. Teaching a skill is known to help you remember that skill for longer than just learning it from someone else. If we can do this across the board, most of our students will have opportunities both to teach things and to learn things from their classmates."

"Okay, but if you're already struggling in one thing, how does being taught it by another student help you?"

She shook her head. "I don't know exactly yet, except I think maybe, in smaller groups, there might be less pressure, and they'll be able to solidify their gains a little bit more."

Piper didn't look fully convinced, but they did look intrigued.

"I like the idea a lot and it doesn't feel like I have much to lose," Bryn admitted as they turned towards her cottage. "I mean, at this rate, I can't teach them everything they need to learn before the MSEs, unless I could open their brains and download all of it directly."

"Have you done another practice test?" they asked.

She sighed. "Once. The results were so depressing, to

183

me as well as the kids, that I vowed I wouldn't do it again. They don't need the mindfuck of it."

"I get that."

She realized suddenly, almost at her door, that she hadn't cleaned up. Clothes were probably still strewn about. She'd tossed the comforter over her bed, but not really made it. What other evidence was there from last night? Burned-down candles. Things she didn't have time to consider. Did it still smell like sex? There was no way she could invite Piper inside.

She cleared her throat. "Back to work, I guess. I'll see you around."

Piper blinked. "What, you're not gonna ask me in to share some of your snacks?"

"Um, not right now. Maybe tomorrow." *Don't blush, don't blush, do not blush.*

This time, Piper looked at her more cannily. "You're hiding something."

"I am *not*. What would I be hiding?" She could feel the blood in her cheeks and willed them to cool down.

"Hmm." Piper raised a single eyebrow, arching it expertly. "I don't know yet, but I think I'll find out at some point. Maybe Amelia knows."

Bryn should have been able to keep her expression totally blank, except at the mention of Amelia's name, she looked away, and then, realizing she'd done it, she looked back. She had no idea what her face looked like, but she'd been thinking about it way too long for it to be natural.

"Oh, my gods," Piper said. "Amelia knows. Are you— Is something going on?" They waved a hand between Bryn and the empty air beside her, where apparently phantom-Amelia stood. "It *is*!" they said delightedly. "Oh, my—"

Bryn used the hand not holding a sack of food to lightly shove Piper down the path. "Time to go."

"Are you getting ready to see Amelia?" they teased, though they did keep their voice down.

"No, no, I'm not. No." That third "no" sounded confident and assured. The first two sounded like guilty denials. Dammit.

"Are you hoping to see Amelia later?"

This time, her mouth fell open in what she felt certain was an emoji-worthy *O* of surprise. Piper laughed, turned their back, and started to walk away, looking over their shoulder only once to say, "Good luck," then cackling as they left.

Bryn escaped inside and shut the door, feeling like her face was probably steaming, but also, obscurely, reassured. Piper was acting like anyone whose friends might or might not be hooking up: amused and unconcerned. Had she ever had a friend in this role before, or just read about it in books? Sometimes she felt like she'd been so apart from people her whole life that she'd missed out on a lot of "normal" activities. The memory of Piper's good-natured cackles made her smile, until she caught sight of her bed and the memory of Amelia, naked and open, made her blush.

She distracted herself by putting the food away, then pulling it out again, then telling herself that she needed to calm the hell down and putting it away for good. She did manage to make the bed and clear up from last night, including putting fresh candles in the candle holders, even though it felt a little bit like jinxing the whole situation.

Finally, as dusk was falling over the grounds, Bryn decided to take the bull (or the headmistress) by the horns and go to see Amelia herself. Her message was still on delivered. She spent twenty minutes drafting, revising, and finalizing a two-sentence note she could leave in case Amelia wasn't back in her rooms. Who knew what the governors' tour included? Did they stay for a meal? Was Amelia in the refectory with the other professors right now, wishing she had a bottle of wine instead of sparkling grape juice? Was Bryn making an absolute fool of herself and overthinking literally everything?

Even if it had been a one-off, it had been a *fantastic* one-off, she reminded herself. She had a ton of snacks for lesson planning in the morning. She and Amelia would go back to Professional Mode. Everything would be fine. Probably better, actually. Less chance of heartbreak that way.

She gathered her note, her Sapphic Pride hoodie, and her wand. It was no big deal. Just sex. A fling. A one-off. What was the difference? A month or two? Bryn could handle disappointment.

She pulled open her front door, bracing against the chill . . .

To find Amelia standing there.

17

"Oh, hi," Amelia said, clearly shocked to see Bryn about to step outside.

"I was just going up to the castle to—" Bryn held up her hand. "Leave you a note. I guess you've saved me the trouble."

"Oh, good," Amelia said. They stood there awkwardly. "Sorry, this is on me. I had an all-day thing, and I kept meaning to text you, and then I would compose a text, and it would seem so long and like I was mad about last night, which I'm totally not, and then I just didn't— I didn't want to say the wrong thing, so I didn't say anything, and saying nothing is almost always the wrong thing in this kind of situation, and I apologize."

Apparently, Bryn wasn't the only one overthinking everything. The fact was obscurely comforting. "I saw Piper earlier," Bryn said. "They told me a little bit about how your day must have been. I had no idea."

"No, I know. I'm sorry. I meant to tell you about it, but then we kind of— Well, we did more interesting things instead. And at that point, I really didn't want to spoil it by saying, 'By the way, I have to spend all of tomorrow with seven old husks who think I'm worthless.'"

Bryn realized that as much as she wanted a repeat of last night, if Amelia was willing, Amelia probably needed something different right now. She stepped back and waved her arm. "Please come inside. I did procure some food from the kitchen, if you're hungry."

"I'm famished, but also not. Like, I'm not even sure I could eat right now. It was really stressful."

"I can only imagine, and even then, probably not. Do you want to tell me about it?"

"Only if you have the capacity to hear me whine. I try not to. I am obviously so grateful for all of the opportunities that have come my way. But I will say, it's a lot of work." Amelia grimaced in apparent annoyance. "I don't mean being headmistress, which of course is a lot of work, but Professor Herringbone prepared me for that part. What she didn't know she needed to prepare me for was what would happen once she was no longer here, and I was trying to be the headmistress without her . . ." She trailed off, searching for a word.

"Backup?" Bryn suggested.

"Backup is actually exactly it. That's what it feels like."

They spoke for a while—or Amelia spoke, and Bryn listened. She thought that as much as she respected and admired Amelia in Headmistress Mode, she could listen to the real Amelia—more vulnerable, more forthright—talk forever. She laid out a thin blanket over the rug, and set out some of the food, all easy stuff that didn't require much in the way of dishes. Amelia began by picking at things, but then, as her story gained momentum and, Bryn suspected, as she stopped thinking so hard because she was processing out loud, it seemed easier for her to eat.

Bryn made sure to keep the water glasses topped up, and the apples and cheese sliced. Amelia liked making cheese and crackers and fruits into these cute little sandwiches that crumpled the second she bit into them. It would have driven Bryn bonkers, but Amelia seemed to enjoy the assembly ritual and patiently picked up the crumbs as they fell.

"I'm sorry," she said eventually, sitting back with a satisfied pat to her stomach. "Apparently, I did need to eat."

"The caloric expenditure of that type of anxiety is probably pretty wild," Bryn said.

"I'm sure it must be. I felt like I was sweating gallons and gallons. They wanted to see everything." Amelia paused thoughtfully. "To be honest, I suspect all of them were using some kind of buoying spells. Some of them are in their eighties and they never flagged."

"Potions?" Bryn suggested.

Amelia grinned. "Maybe that's what accounts for Mr Wicks always having the energy to pursue rule-breakers in the corridors."

Bryn smiled as well. "'You, there! Absolutely no running in the castle!'"

"'This is a *safety* issue, young lady!'" Amelia quoted, though she didn't seem mad about it. She picked up the second-to-last apple slice and ate it.

"Are you okay, though?" Bryn asked. "Today sounds really awful."

"It was. I mean, I don't want to mince words. It was really hard. And at the end of it—and I think this is the worst part—it feels as though, if possible, they like me even less. For the job, not my sparkling personality."

"Cheers to your sparkling personality, though," Bryn said, and lifted her glass.

With a slightly softened expression, Amelia clinked hers against it and took a sip. "Thank you. I really will stop complaining soon, I swear. It's just that every time the governors meet, I'm expecting them to fire me with their next proclamation."

Bryn nodded. "Piper said they thought the same today, like the governors might just decide to chop the whole program."

"They can't without my agreement, technically, though I completely sympathize with the sentiment. How was Piper? The governors visited all the other classrooms during normal school hours, but wanted a special look at the new department."

"They were fine, I think. Worried about you, stuck with the governors all day."

"Boy, was I. But not now." Amelia stretched back, propping herself up with her hands. "I'm sorry I left in the middle of the night. I shouldn't have. Then I didn't want to go poking through your stuff to find paper and a pen, and I didn't want to wake you." She offered a rueful headshake. "Though, I admit, I made more noise than I needed to while getting ready, just in case you woke up spontaneously, and I could give you a proper kiss goodbye."

Bryn, who had resigned herself—and had felt somewhat

relieved—to avoid this conversation tonight, now straightened up. "Oh, um, well, you left a heart. So, I saw that. I can't believe I slept through you leaving. I didn't know I was that deep a sleeper."

"To be fair to you," Amelia said mischievously, "you did work out quite hard."

Bryn laughed. "No regrets on that front." She steeled herself. "But I wanted to tell you, I don't have any demands. This can totally be a one-off. It was great, but, you know, I don't want things to be weird between us, and I completely understand if you're not interested."

"Oh." Amelia blinked. "Do you mean *you're* not interested? Because that's also completely okay. I also would understand if you wanted it to be a one-off. I know you're not here that long."

For a moment they stared at each other in mutual bewilderment, playing emotional chicken. Someone was going to have to take the risk. Or—and part of Bryn's mind was attracted to this idea— no one took a risk, and they left it at that. One-off, done and dusted.

Then she remembered the sensation of snuggling up under her duvet, the heat and tiredness and scent of Amelia in the air . . .

Both of them started speaking simultaneously. Bryn said, "I," and Amelia said, "We." And then they stopped again, and laughed a little bit weakly.

"You first," Amelia said.

"Oh, okay." Bryn had planned a lot of different things to say, none of which sprung to mind, nor seemed to fit the context of this specific scenario. "Well, maybe it's just a fling, you know, but I could do it longer than one night, if you wanted to. I am only here temporarily, but not *that* temporarily."

"A fling," Amelia said slowly. "Okay, and what does that look like?"

Bryn, somewhat desperately, searched her face for some hint of how she felt, but damn, Amelia was so good at not showing what she didn't want to show. Maybe you couldn't be that popular in school if you didn't have that skill. She took a deep breath and braced for emotional honesty, incoming. "I think it looks like we spend as much time together as we want to, and we do whatever we want to do in that time. And when you inevitably hire a real teacher to take over my job, and I go back to Denver, then it'll just be over, and we'll both move on." Bryn sat back after speaking, expecting to feel . . . better than she did. It had sounded like a sensible, practical idea when she'd come up with it, when she had thought about it as an alternative to getting too serious, or serious in a way that wasn't justified by who they were and where they were in their lives. But now— Now it sounded weak, like hedging a bet. Or worse, like salting a mine. Like maybe there was nothing here at all, and she was just inviting Amelia to pretend with her.

Amelia seemed to be looking at her as if trying to see her with X-ray vision. There were, of course, truth spells. They didn't really work as truth spells, though. They worked more as spells that initiated a period of lax internal censorship, inviting the subject (or target, in some cases) to be a little loose with their reality. But Bryn didn't think either of them wanted that right now. In fact, she thought both of them were hanging on to practicality with all their might.

"A fling," Amelia said. "Yes, okay. I like that. A summer fling, except we're doing it in the spring. Right. Perfect."

It was the most reasonable thing. They agreed. There was no need to push it. No need to try for anything else. This was the obvious, best solution. Sensible adult women making a sensible adult decision.

So why did it feel so hollow?

Bryn reached for a piece of chocolate. Amelia intercepted her hand and brought it to her lips. Pressed the lightest kiss to her palm, her eyes entirely on Bryn's.

"The thing is," Amelia said softly, breath dusting over Bryn's skin. "I want more than a fling. Last night was incredible, and I want to keep doing it for as long as we can. Even forever, if we want. I don't want to plan for it to stop if it's not . . . necessary. You know what I mean?"

No. No! We're being logical. Rational. We are not saying things like "forever" because that would be ludicrous. Bryn swallowed hard, her heart suddenly galloping in her chest. "I'm supposed to go back to Denver." Maybe Amelia was going to offer her a longer-term position so they could stay together?

Amelia nodded. "You are. But we could make long distance work, couldn't we?"

Of course Amelia didn't want to hire her permanently. Foolish thing to imagine. She was patently *bad* at teaching, and anyway, she'd need to go to school to gain some credentials before she could get a permanent job. Teaching was not Bryn's life; she had to go back to her apartment, her un-begun book two, her fledgling career. Yet she stared at their joined hands, feeling Amelia's gaze like an ember smoldering on her skin. It was terrifying. There was no way it could work out, surely. Long distance never worked out.

But the alternative was . . . what, just giving up? Bryn did not consider herself a person who gave up. "I don't know why this scares me so much," she confessed.

"If it's not what you want—"

But Bryn interjected before Amelia could misunderstand. "Of course it's what I want. *You're* what I want. This is what I want. And I know it. But it's scary to imagine it failing."

Amelia squeezed her hand and said, using the words Bryn had said to her the night before, "Look at me."

So Bryn did. And in Amelia's face, creased with exhaustion after her day, her eyes slightly bagged due to lack of sleep, there was so much that she already loved there. And *love* was the only word for it. She could dither if she wanted to, but she knew her own emotions. She knew what this was, even though she'd never felt it before. This was why it scared her so much; love was not a thing she could control, and it clearly wasn't waiting for the situation to be logical, or rational, or reasonable.

She leaned up on her other arm and kissed Amelia. "I know it's too early to say this, by a lot, but I love you. And no matter what happens, I want you to know that."

Amelia, apparently not that tired after all, tackled her backwards, laughing. "Oh gods, I can't believe you said it first. I love you too. It's just . . . You were so cute when we were younger, and I wanted to hug you when you looked

194

lonely, but I didn't know if you'd welcome it—if you'd ever asked me out I would have said yes, but I was too shy to ask you. And now you're back here, and so am I, and it just feels like we have to take the chance. Don't we?"

Bryn shook her head. "No, we're choosing to." And then she pulled Amelia down on top of her.

And for a while, they only kissed, communicating with lips and questing hands, nerve endings, skin, the brush of eyelashes, the flutter of breath.

Love, Bryn thought in a stunned, heavy haze. That was real.

18

Having never been in love before, Bryn had no idea if she was doing it right. What she did know was that this feeling brightened every part of every day. Like being in love was a layer of clouds and she walked on them everywhere.

When Amelia was there, when Amelia wasn't there, when she was thinking about her, when she wasn't thinking about her, her baseline buoyancy as she went through the world had increased to a level that made everything seem more vivid. Not that she wasn't capable of frustration or impatience or slightly wanting to throttle Luke because he was out of his seat for the fourth time in one period— but she was just happier. Maybe like she was breathing a higher concentration of oxygen than usual and it was going straight into her system. It made everything look sharper and brighter, more colorful. In short, she'd never felt better. And a huge part of that was Amelia.

Obviously, they could not be seen in public being lovey-dovey, but in private all bets were off and somehow they managed to cobble together far more private time than she would have thought possible. Part of it was that both of them enjoyed the challenge of their respective jobs. It wasn't uncommon for Amelia to come down to Bryn's classroom after the end of the school day and do her own work in the study as Bryn graded papers. Once Piper caught on to this, they started showing up too, after specifically asking if they were "interrupting anything". But Bryn had assured them they were not.

No sexy times in the castle, or at least not in the school rooms. She also hadn't gone to Amelia's bedroom for more than a brief look as Amelia gathered a change of clothes; aside from occasionally kissing, it just felt weird to be intimate in the castle. And while Amelia didn't feel bad walking in from the cottage in the morning, Bryn was pretty sure that leaving Amelia's rooms in the castle would feel like an actual walk of shame, even if she wasn't ashamed.

So things progressed. A young staff member, a somewhat mild, hard-to-read woman from a vampire background (not that she was a vampire, but she had been adopted into a vampire family), had also been hired by Amelia for the year. Her role was to be house warden to the students who lived on campus, like Circe. Her name was Andi and she spoke with a very slight Scandinavian accent, though Bryn didn't know her well enough yet to ask where she was from.

Andi was also only twenty-three, but she had a reputation amongst the boarding students for being un-push-aroundable, though all of them seemed to like her a great deal and treated her like something of an older sister or young-ish aunt.

Bryn had noticed that Amelia's hires had been universally

young—a lot younger than the average age of the teachers at the school when she had been a student there. Piper had been the one who brought Andi in, and while Bryn suspected there might be some sense of romantic attraction there, it was clearly in a fledgling stage, if it existed at all. (And Amelia wasn't ready to comment either way, though she agreed that there was *some* potential.)

Having Andi around was nice, because she was always happy to talk about the kids and strategize ideas to improve the school for everyone. The four of them got together a couple of times a week to do their various work and have some interesting conversations. Andi had a lot of thoughts about Circe, who, she reported, was an excellent resident of the dormitories: she always picked up after herself, worked with other students whenever there was a group cleanup, and offered emotional support, without words, to her friends and roommates.

"We still don't know why she doesn't speak?" Bryn asked. Everyone shook their heads.

"I've decided," said Andi, "not to question it. If she had any physical or mental disability, I wouldn't ask why. I wouldn't troubleshoot. I would just accept that's who she is. So I'm trying to do that with the speaking thing as well, though honestly it would be nice sometimes if she could tell me things. But when she needs to, she writes a note. So there's no real reason for it to be an issue, and clearly it's not."

"Do we know anything about her family?" Amelia asked. "Professor Herringbone did mention to me that they are pretty far away."

"Alaska," Andi confirmed.

Piper whistled. "Isn't the witchy community up there supposed to be pretty insular?"

"Yes," Amelia said. "Consistent with most geographically isolated witching communities."

Bryn realized she'd never really considered the issues faced by isolated witches. Sure, she'd been the weird one in her family, but she'd always lived in a town with witchy stores, and a big witchy school on the hill.

"It's just Circe and her parents and grandparents, I think, though they're non-magical," Andi explained. "She does get letters from them, actual letters, in the mail. Circe is my only resident who gets paper mail consistently, and it seems to make her happy." She smiled with genuine fondness. "She keeps her letters in a folder hanging on her wall. It's really quite sweet. I think she could be a leader, or at least that's how she functions in the dorms."

"Interesting," Amelia said. "You know, because she doesn't speak, I hadn't really thought about that, which I guess shows a flaw in my logic, but I'll keep it in mind, Andi. Thank you."

The after-school club also moved on. The kids had bewitched the spell items they'd bought at the magic shop in town, to various degrees of success, and they were mostly pleased. Luke, still charmed by Bryn's dolphin trick, had bewitched his little bunny rabbit toy to twitch an ear. The first time he'd made it work, he'd gasped, and the rest of them had applauded. Circe had picked out a glitter globe with a magically changing skyline (Tokyo, Moscow, Dubai), which she had diagrammed out at a fourth-year skill level, and then designed a spell so that the cityscape would change with a flick of her wand—a piece of magic that Bryn suspected even Circe didn't know how sophisticated it was. And Violet, ever practical, had debated for a long time before finally settling on a pair of magical gloves that were bewitched to get warm, and then they tried to add a spell layer that also bathed the wearer's skin in aloe.

It hadn't worked. It hadn't worked at all. They'd gotten the gloves to do *something*, though only Bryn could see that shimmer of magic at work. To Violet's extreme frustration, Bryn could not look at it and describe exactly what it was doing or how to force the magic to deliver the results they wanted. But Bryn had pointed out that even though it hadn't worked, it had been powerful, *very* powerful for a second-year student. Which, at last, had seemed to reassure Violet.

The club meetings had gone from being something they did because the headmistress forced them to, to something they tolerated without having to be forced into, to (Bryn thought) something they actually enjoyed. The three kids got along and had formed their own sort of found family in the last couple of months.

Violet continued to be at times overconfident, but always confident; Circe continued to support her friends however she could; and Luke continued to bounce off walls and provide an awful lot of oddly insightful redirection when the moment called for it.

As it did after Violet had heard some disappointing news from back home. Apparently, their two closest friends had gotten in what they called a "cataclysmic fight" and now weren't speaking. It sounded like the kind of thing that happened with teenagers all the time and would eventually pass, but clearly Violet didn't think so.

Luke tried some of his normal antics to distract her, and when that didn't work, he sat down next to her and said, "So what does that look like for you when you go home over the summer?"

"I don't know," she said. "Usually we spend all of our time together, and now if they're not talking to each other . . ." She slumped in uncharacteristic defeat. "I know no one's died, but it actually kind of makes me want to cry all the time thinking about it."

"So don't think about it," Luke suggested.

"That's not going to change how I feel."

After a moment he nodded. "Okay, why don't we roleplay? You be your friends and I'll be you, since you would only react like you would, but I would definitely not react like you would."

After a little bit of cajoling, Violet went along with the idea. And Bryn had to admit it was both funny and actually pretty interesting. Sometimes Luke went for laughs, because he was Luke and he loved going for laughs, but other times he said things like, "How did you feel when she said that?" or "What did you think when that happened?" Bryn was genuinely impressed with both of them. Violet even hugged him once they were done with their roleplay and said, "That was super silly, but anyway, thanks, Luke."

It shouldn't really have made her cry, but Bryn found

she had to turn away to hide the tears in her eyes. It wasn't sad; it was lovely.

Her master plan for group work in her classrooms was met with a great deal of resistance. The younger kids went along with it because first-years went along with a lot of things. It was so overwhelming just being in witchy school, Bryn remembered this quite well, that for them, being told what to do was a relief.

Everyone else . . . Well, maybe it wasn't that strange that Grimoire Academy—a traditional sort of place founded on traditionalist principles and upheld by a traditionalist board of governors—had in its very marrow resistance to change. At the end of the first week, she was frustrated, tired, and a little bit hopeless.

"I don't know," she said to Amelia that afternoon. They'd stopped at Amelia's office for her to pick up a few things before retiring to the cottage until dinner. "It's just, I don't know how to get them engaged, keep them interested. It's such fascinating material. How are spells formed? Why do we teach the basics the way we do? What even makes them qualify as basics? Who made these decisions? Who is trying to interrupt these decisions? What should we be thinking about going forward? What would they want to teach the next generation that is different from what they've been taught?" She sighed. "How do they find this stuff boring?"

Amelia smiled, drew her closer, and kissed her. "I really love your passion. It's super hot."

"Ew, I'm talking about the kids." But the protest was only playful; Bryn wasn't exactly going to argue with anything Amelia loved about her.

"No," Amelia said, "you're talking about teaching, which is one of my passions. So I'm allowed to find it hot."

Bryn let herself be towed in. "Okay, I will accept this argument."

"Good. But it's Friday night, Bryn. You need some time off."

It was too early to think about time off. They had six weeks before the exams. She was too overwhelmed to take time off. "Yeah, but what if it doesn't work? What if they all fail their MSEs? You need them to pass."

"It would be nice if they passed," Amelia acknowledged wryly. "But if they don't pass, the world will continue on. The sun will rise."

It was bravely said, but it didn't fool Bryn for a second. "Amelia, you love this place. I want you to be able to stay here."

Amelia leaned in and rested her head on Bryn's shoulder. "I do love this place. I would be devastated if I had to leave it. But nothing will be helped by you collapsing in exhaustion from trying to save the world. That is, by the way, totally a teacher trait, FYI."

"I'm no one's teacher," Bryn protested.

"I beg to differ," Amelia said. "Anyway, I had a different idea."

"Did you now?"

"I did." Amelia lowered her voice. "It's a secret."

The hint of play at the end of a hard week won an anticipatory wriggle from Bryn, who said, "Oh, a secret idea. That's even more exciting."

Amelia, with a twinkle in her eye, said, "You have no

idea what's in store for you." She leaned in closer and added, "It's going to be super sexy, just so you know what to expect."

Bryn felt heat surge through her, starting somewhere below the belt and moving outward from there. "You're quite cocky tonight," she said, grinning.

"Oh, I am," Amelia said. "But it's time for you to go home and do your Pilates and whatever else needs to be done. And then I'll let you know when I'm ready for you."

"Ready for me? What do you mean?" Were they going out somewhere? Bryn was so tired, she feared she'd fall asleep the second they got in the car, but she could hardly say so if Amelia had planned something special.

Amelia pressed a finger to her lips. "Just let me do this for you. Let me surprise you. This one time. Go along with it."

Bryn found herself a little bit choked up. Amelia was amazing. She was so smart, she felt things so deeply. She was so good at teaching, at being headmistress, at talking to the students and the staff. Gods, Bryn wanted to rip her clothes off and take her right there in her office. But no, tonight was Amelia's.

She shivered pleasantly and wondered what that meant.

19

Bryn did a short Pilates video, showered, groomed, and put on fresh, cute clothes, still totally unsure what to expect. Were they going out somewhere? But if so, what was Amelia getting ready for?

Or maybe this was the night they overcame their reticence to banging in the castle. She was here for it, if Amelia was. Bryn could see how Amelia might want her to feel just as at home there as they both did at the cottage.

Sometime after she was fully ready to go, and sitting expectantly on her only chair, she got a text from Amelia.

Be there to pick you up shortly. Sorry it's taken so long.

Pick me up? She had considered the idea that maybe Amelia would tell her to meet at the car, or even somewhere on the property, and take a walk. Though she couldn't imagine them getting up to any hanky-panky out in the open. Not unless they had plenty of time to magically shield the area they would be in. And even then, she couldn't imagine it. The idea of someone walking by, even if that person was totally oblivious, was a total boner-killer. She put on her shoes and then fidgeted until the knock came at the cottage door. Bryn opened it, feeling absurdly nervous, like this was a first date with a serious contender—feeling, in fact, more nervous than she'd felt on any actual first date.

Amelia stood there, looking beautiful, as usual. She had also taken a shower, Bryn thought, noticing her hair still damp and combed back. Her pale skin flushed, which could have been due to the sudden spring chill in the evening air, or . . . other things. Whatever it was, Bryn found it delightful.

"Hi," she said. "Um, are you coming in, or am I going out? I'm not sure what to expect, sorry."

"No, I'm sorry. I meant to be ready so much sooner than this." Amelia held out a hand. "I'm taking you somewhere. Not anywhere fancy, don't get your expectations up, but I think you'll like it."

Bryn took a breath, not entirely sure why this felt like more than whatever they'd done in the past. Maybe it was down to how much effort Amelia had put into it, or just the natural progression of a relationship both of them were serious about. She placed her hand in Amelia's and said, "My lady."

Amelia grinned. "My lady." She led them out.

They did not go into the castle. At first, Bryn wasn't sure where they were going at all. Around the far side of the main building—away from the gardens, away from Bryn's cottage—along a path she supposed she'd known was there but had never taken. Once they rounded the corner and she saw the steps leading down, she remembered.

"Oh gods, are we going to the grotto? I don't have a bathing suit."

208

Amelia smirked. "Do you need a bathing suit? It's just the two of us."

"I mean, naked in the grotto?" Bryn realized she was blinking at Amelia with her mouth open as they stood at the top of the steps.

"We can go back for one if you want one," Amelia said. "I am totally fine with that. I wasn't planning to wear one myself. And obviously I've done roughly a million locking charms and sound barriers and blocks for all the windows. I think I've thought of everything, but you might contribute as well and then we'll be doubly sure."

Bryn took this in, nodding slowly. "I'm sure you've thought of everything." She glanced downward, at the stone steps leaning to a nondescript gray door that she suspected was much, much heavier than it looked. Oak, no doubt. Probably oak from this very land. "Okay," she said. "Let's do this."

Amelia laughed a little nervously. "I don't know why my heart just started pounding. And I mean, I'm not going to ask you to marry me, just in case you were worried I was about to spring something like that on you."

"Should I have been?" The idea hadn't occurred to Bryn, and obviously there was no way, but it was delicious to see Amelia slightly wrong-footed and flushed at the notion.

"No, no, obviously not," Amelia said quickly.

But the fact that she'd even brought it up made Bryn lean in and kiss her. "Okay, so you aren't going to propose. Check. But I'm still not totally sure what we *are* doing? I mean, the grotto, obviously, but . . ."

They linked hands and went down the steps together. Amelia waved her wand, presumably to unlock whatever magical lock she'd put in place, and pushed open the door. A light mist, which rolled into the darkening air outside. Bryn sucked in a delighted breath at what lay beyond, only distantly aware of the door closing behind her and the sound of mechanical locks re-engaging.

The grotto looked like some human imagining of fairyland. Lights twinkled everywhere, but not too many: the space still looked shadowy and mysterious, but in a way that was inviting instead of forbidding. Bryn realized that whatever charms Amelia had done to those high windows, they were good, because she hadn't even sensed all of this light from outside.

"Oh gods," she said, her own voice sounding shaky.

Amelia, beside her, asked, "Do you like it?"

There were candles glowing in all the stone alcoves at various intervals along the walls. There were even candelabras scattered around, on the built-in benches and on the narrow windowsills. Only as she walked farther into the large, echoing room did she see more. The twinkly lights inside the pool cast the warmest, most intriguing glow. Steam rose from the surface of the pool. Along the top, more candles floated, lit and flickering, their light skating across the water. Bryn had always imagined this room would feel cold and damp from all that stonework and the constant presence of water, but it didn't feel dank at all. It felt warm and cozy, not nearly as humid as she would have thought.

Were there dehumidifier spells? Was that a thing? And if not, could she invent it? She put the thought aside and continued to look around.

Laid out on what appeared to be a thick blanket was a

picnic, with two candelabras set up at a corner each casting light down on a spread of cheeses and fruits, breads, olives. It was beautiful. Bryn felt strange tears prickle at her eyes and turned to Amelia, not even trying to hide them. "I can't believe you did all this for me."

"Of course I did," Amelia said, "I love you." And then she shrugged the robe she was wearing off her shoulders. And she was beautifully, gloriously naked beneath it, only wearing her shoes.

"Oh my," Bryn murmured, stepping forward for a long kiss, the kind of kiss she felt all the way to her toes. "You are a miracle, Amelia Hexford."

"I am a woman in love," Amelia said, correcting her. She blew out a breath. "Not to ruin the mood, but I was kind of counting on you going around and topping up my spells with yours, if that's okay."

"Oh, sure," Bryn said, though she didn't move away. "Sure, of course, I would like that too. I just . . ." Her hands brushed very lightly down Amelia's back, who shivered. "It's hard to focus with you, you know . . . all naked and gorgeous."

Amelia stooped and put the robe back on, which made sense, though it did inspire Bryn to lean forward and whisper, "I'm going to be the one to take that off later. Just so you know. I'm really looking forward to it."

Amelia kissed her fervently. "That better be a promise. Now go do magic. Can I watch? Do you mind?"

"Oh, not at all. Be my guest."

As Bryn walked the perimeter of the grotto, she could sense Amelia's magic. Not everyone was sensitive to such

211

things, but Bryn certainly always had been, and it was uncanny how Amelia's magic affected her. They cast slightly different versions of the same spells for the most part—barriers preventing all sounds and lights from escaping the room—with their own personal twists. That was just how magic worked: every person's magic had a slightly different tone, a slightly different cadence, just as voices did. She'd known that, and she'd sensed it herself.

But she had never done this before, never specifically intertwined her magic with someone else's, reaching out to fold and twist them together. There were stories of witches back in the persecution days combining spells to strengthen them, but Bryn had never been sure if that referred to blending their energies or merely layering them.

Now she realized the scope of power available to two witches who wished to connect along their magic, and it was shockingly intimate. She wondered if Amelia felt it too; if she, watching nearby, could sense this somehow. Bryn was almost afraid to ask, as if discovering that Amelia didn't see it, couldn't sense it, would be disappointing. But when she glanced over, Amelia's eyes were not on her. They were on the twisting patterns of spellfire all around them.

"You see it," Bryn said softly.

Amelia, not taking her eyes from the sight, nodded. "It's beautiful."

"It's us," Bryn said. She continued working, her wand a conductor's baton, playing through the energies of the room, tightening the spells until they were in their own little world, buffered on all sides by magic. It became, after a few minutes, not just more comfortable, but more effective. She realized

212

while pulling on the last shimmering threads that she was deeply, profoundly aroused by the process. Combining their magic intensified everything she felt—for Amelia, for their relationship, for the future. She was sweating lightly by the time she finished, and she turned to Amelia, who embraced her, pressing their bodies together, breathing in sync.

"That's the hottest thing I've ever seen," Amelia murmured.

"Me too. I've never done that before."

Amelia shook her head. "They did not teach us this in school."

Bryn laughed and leaned back, just far enough to catch Amelia's eyes. "I'm not sure we should pitch this one to the governors quite yet. Magical sex ed?"

"Bite your tongue."

"I'd rather bite other things."

Amelia snorted. "This is really going to screw me up if we ever have to do magic in public. I'm just going to be watching your hands and thinking of all the other things you're so good at with those fingers."

A complication Bryn hadn't thought about before; would she ever be able to sense Amelia's energy without on some level finding it arousing? "I suppose we'll cross that bridge when we come to it," she said. "Though this is really shifting the nature of some of the books I'd planned to write. We can't be the only people who've ever experienced this?"

"No. But . . ." Amelia looked gold-dusted in the candlelight. "I've never heard of it anyway, not like this."

"No." It was hard to focus on anything but sex at that moment. Bryn forced herself to look at Amelia's eyes, not just her lips. "What do you have in mind for us first? Refreshments?"

Amelia assumed a mock-stern expression. "We can't eat before swimming. We'll get a cramp."

"Oh, will we? I suppose that means we'll have to swim first and then rest long enough after eating to swim again later." Bryn tucked her wand back into her jeans, wishing that she had worn something a bit more appropriate. No matter. She slid her hands inside Amelia's robe, settling them on her bare hips. "So, what do you have planned for us next? Cannonballs?"

"In the grotto?" Amelia laughed. "Absolutely not. I don't trust the floating candles to stay upright."

"Clearly, I need to design a non-tipping spell," Bryn said. This time she did look down, biting her lip at the sight of the skin now exposed between the sides of the gown: Amelia's breasts and belly beneath the flickering light, only shadows below.

"What did you say before?" Amelia murmured, licking her lips. "About undressing me?"

"Yeah, that." Bryn pulled her closer, not shedding the robe quite yet, pressing her clothed body against Amelia's naked one. "Ask me for it."

Amelia's eyelids fluttered. "Will you undress me, Bryn? I want to be naked for you."

No sexier words had ever been spoken in the history of speech, Bryn felt absolutely certain. Still, she played the moment out, kissed Amelia again softly, hands running up her sides beneath the robe. "You want to be vulnerable for me? Exposed and open and mine?"

Amelia blew out a breath, and on that exhalation was the slightest hint of *Yes*. Still, Bryn did not hurry her moves. She was careful, gentle, slow, drawing out the moment as long as she could, pausing to drag a fingernail along the underside of one breast, to brush a thumb in the hollow of Amelia's clavicle, to duck her head and trail kisses up Amelia's throat to her lips again. Only then did she push the robe off Amelia's shoulders, allowing it to drop at their feet.

"You are so beautiful," she said, drawing Amelia in against her again. They kissed for a while, standing like that, Amelia's arms wrapped around Bryn's body, and Bryn's hands never stopping their exploration of Amelia's bare skin. It was intoxicating to have access to Amelia like this, to soothe away the gooseflesh on her arms, to drag fingernails down her spine. "Can you get addicted to someone else's skin?" she asked finally, moving her head slightly away so they could look at each other.

"We'll find out," Amelia replied shakily.

Bryn, having considered this with some detached part of her brain, sighed. "There's really no sexy way for me to get naked right now, so I'm just gonna take all my clothes off and we're just gonna pretend it's totally not awkward."

Amelia smiled. "You're never awkward."

"Correction, I am always awkward. You're just so used to it, it doesn't strike you as awkward."

After a moment, Amelia nodded. "That seems fair." She never looked away as Bryn undressed, leaving her clothes folded neatly and then folding Amelia's robe on top of them. Amelia led her to the gradual entrance of the pool, where

215

the water was just slightly warmer than body temperature. Amelia kissed her and said, "There's actually a cold-water pool just over there, which I didn't know existed the first time I came here. It's freezing, though."

"We'll have to do that later," Bryn told her, and drew her forward until they were both submerged in water to their chins, staring at each other, light reflecting everywhere around them.

The water felt exceptionally buoyant, so much so that Bryn even tasted it just to see if it was somehow salt instead of fresh water. But it wasn't. It was just something about the grotto, something about a room infused with magic, sex, and love.

"I feel like I have twice as many nerve endings as usual," she confessed. The water allowed them to be at eye level. She could look directly across at Amelia and see an answering recognition.

"That's how I feel as well. I might orgasm the second you touch me, FYI . . . It feels so good to be here with you."

Bryn leaned in, kissed Amelia's cheek, then the other, then her forehead. Only then did she kiss her lips, and the crackle of sensation seemed to burst through her body, unlike anything she'd ever felt from a kiss. They held each other as if in a steadying movement, surrounded by warm, welcoming water. It was almost too much, as if the volume and intensity of emotion was more than Bryn could handle.

But then she felt Amelia's hands on her back beneath the level of the water. She put her own arms over Amelia's shoulders, and they embraced. Of course, she'd meant them to be having sex by now, but this felt vital, even necessary.

They could have sex—well, not any time, but plenty of times. Whatever this was, whatever they had somehow stumbled into building on this particular night, it felt precious and rare. And she knew, without any evidence, that she would never feel like this with anyone else, anywhere else.

She wanted to put words to it, wanted to find some way to communicate to Amelia how meaningful this moment was to her, not just because it was Amelia, but because there was something between them.

"I feel as though this is the most complete version of myself that I have ever been." She searched Amelia's eyes, hoping so much that she would not be confused by this statement, that she wouldn't doubt it or analyze it. It was such a silly thing to feel, but Bryn couldn't deny it, and she wanted very much to know that Amelia felt it as well.

Amelia shifted forward, pressing her lips to Bryn's lips, her forehead to Bryn's forehead, allowing only enough space between them to whisper, "I feel like we *are* magic right now, magic in the form of two people in love."

And if she'd needed confirmation that they had stumbled into something very, very real, that was it.

"Exactly," Bryn murmured and kissed Amelia again.

20

Bryn almost couldn't believe this was her life. She got up every morning in a beautiful place. If she took a five-minute walk, she could see the ocean spool out into forever (unless there was fog). She could take deep lungfuls of fresh, clean air. It smelled like home.

Each morning she would take the short walk to the castle and return to the classroom in which she had spent so many good hours as a teenager. That also smelled like home. Now that she knew her students better and was beginning to build the slightest teaching skills, she didn't dread every new class period, but relished the challenge of it. She actually enjoyed her work. Sure, it was still frustrating at times; she needed to keep her anti-cheating spells active, and the kids were improving steadily but not nearly fast enough to take the MSEs in three weeks. But things felt good.

In the afternoons, she would sometimes grade papers on her own, sometimes with just Amelia, or just Piper, and sometimes they would gather along with Andi and enjoy themselves. They had even taken to meeting up in the refectory, working until it was time for dinner.

When other professors saw this, they sometimes arrived to do the same. Bryn hadn't realized she would even enjoy such a thing—surely she had always preferred to be alone?—but it was genuinely communal and lovely. Parallel play for adults. Even Mr Wicks would sometimes join them, though she suspected he did so purely out of curiosity.

Bryn felt full in the best of ways. The work was intellectually challenging and also sometimes emotionally challenging. But then there was Amelia, and their relationship filled her cup to the brim, overflowing. If she needed to vent, she could. If Amelia needed to vent, she could too, and sometimes they did. But it was strange how having that space somehow made her need it less. Not never, but less, as if the comfort wasn't in venting, but in knowing it was safe to do so. And they just had so much fun. She felt like she had never laughed more in her life.

She placed a super-secret order to her favorite sex-toy company, one which offered "charm-ready products" in discrete packaging . . . though even so, she'd had it delivered to her mom's house instead of the school. Why take the chance?

When her sister Luna had sent her a picture of the package and offered to bring it to the store, if she didn't want to go by the house, Bryn said yes. It gave them a chance to catch up, and it gave Luna a chance to ask incredibly personal questions about the nature of Bryn's relationship with Amelia, which actually Bryn couldn't help wanting to answer. She *wanted* to share this thing that meant so much to her with her sister, whom she increasingly felt like she didn't know nearly well enough. There was only a five-year age gap, but five years had always seemed like a very long time. Now that they were both technically adults, it seemed like much less.

She returned to the campus with her package in a bag, and even thinking about using it with Amelia, or perhaps on Amelia, or even deep, deep *inside* Amelia, made Bryn shiver. Her body immediately flowed into a state of arousal that made her wonder if she should be carrying a change of clothes. That always seemed so melodramatic, and yet in that moment, it was just hot. *Yes, I am so turned on by the woman I'm in love with that I am soaking through my underwear.* How something so impractical could be sexy, she didn't know.

They had a date planned for the following evening, which was a Friday. It was always so nice to plan a date for a weekend night. She had skipped dinner to hang out with Luna, getting takeaway from the place down the street from the spell shop, and even that had felt good. She'd texted Amelia that she wouldn't be there, that she was hanging out with her sister, and Amelia had texted back heart emojis and said, *Have fun. Tell her hi for me.* How lucky could Bryn be? She was with a woman who delighted in the things that pleased her.

Still riding a high, both of anticipation for what she was planning to do with her new toy and for the pleasant feeling of having spent so much time with her younger sister, she got back to the cottage and settled in, sated, warm, and happy. Amelia was prepping for an early meeting in the morning and wouldn't be coming down, but that was okay. Bryn had gotten comfortable enough that she was far less worried that she would wake up and all of this would be a dream. Amelia Hexford was no longer her schoolgirl crush, but her girlfriend. At least, she was pretty sure. They hadn't talked about it. They should have talked about it. They *would* talk about it.

She found herself playing with the idea of using the word *partner* instead, but it still felt too soon. She was in this for the long haul, but also, whoa, that was a commitment word. She wasn't quite ready for a commitment word yet. They'd talk about that too. *Girlfriend* felt juvenile, but then, they didn't need to define their relationship right now. They didn't need to define it ever.

As she was tidying her cottage for the evening, she logged on to her computer one more time, just for the normal things: shut down all the open programs, close all the tabs in her browser that she'd been using throughout the day. This was a task that she had genuinely designed a spell for, but it was finicky. Any spell that interacted with technology was a little finicky, and she rather liked the mechanical resolution of doing it the old-fashioned way, clearing the decks so she could start fresh tomorrow.

And that's when it happened. She had a handful of new emails, most of which would be either spam (no spell to prevent spam yet) or things she'd subscribed to: offers, notifications of sales at her favorite online spell-supply shop. Except one. One email immediately caught her eye. It was from her editor. The subject line read: *I know this is last minute, but . . .*

Bryn sank into her chair. She hadn't bothered to sit down when closing down her computer because it usually only took a second to shut down for the night, but now she read the email once, then twice, then she drank some water, refreshed the page, and read it a third time, just to make sure she wasn't imagining the whole thing.

All the bright lights in her life that had seemed so vivid just minutes ago dimmed. The publisher wanted a second book. This was the email she had been waiting for since before her first book had even launched, except it was the last email she wanted to receive *right now*. Because they wanted the book immediately. She stared at the dates, willing them to be different. Mid-June. Who demanded a book to be written in a month? Except, she had told the editor she was already working on it, which hadn't been a total lie. It had just been maybe more aspirational than realistic.

There was no way she could get a book together by mid-June, the week after MSEs. July, sure, she could do it by then. August would be even better. But . . . there was no earthly or indeed magical way she could get her book written while teaching every day and prepping students for their exams.

The email was very clear: offer contingent upon stated deadline. Another book had dropped out of the calendar, and her editor had thought of her, assuming she was already much further along than she was with the writing. The editor even signed off with a celebratory confetti emoji.

Bryn stared at it and wanted to cry.

21

She couldn't sleep that night.

Why? Why now? Of all times. Why now? Why did this have to happen at the very moment when she was happy?

Except . . . wasn't this what she wanted? Wasn't this everything she'd always wanted? She hadn't been a girl who fantasized about being a princess, or about marrying a princess. She hadn't thought of her future as one in which she would ever settle down with anyone, let alone Amelia Hexford. She just wanted to be happy and write books, two things that had felt inherently related. This was what she was meant to do: create spells, refine them, perfect them, share them with people. She loved doing that. She loved hearing that someone had used her spells or found that they did something new and exciting, that they helped. She probably had fan mail stacking up at her apartment, expressing just those sentiments. Sure, not boxes and boxes, but a few notes here and there, which the publisher would send in a plump envelope.

But now? Now, when her group work was just beginning

to pay off and it seemed like there might be a chance her students could pass their MSEs; when she was beginning to think that she had made a difference. How could this be the moment it all derailed? How could getting an offer for a second book suddenly feel like it was screwing everything up? This was impossible. She had no idea what to do.

Of *course* she wanted to write the book. But like this? And what if she said no? If she said, "I'd love to, maybe in two months"? Everyone knew how fickle publishing was, and *magical* publishing was, if anything, even more fickle. The spell book that people wanted today was not the same as the spell book they would want in six months or a year. Magical publishing went fast. If you missed your opportunity, there was no guarantee you would ever get another one. Her editor had mentioned the momentum of the first book, and how now was the time to hit the market with book two, while people were still excited, while the name Bryn Delmar was still on the lips of folks buying books.

She understood all that. But how could she trade the world that she, until this email, had just been settling into? It was as if her life had split into two very different paths. How could she choose between them? How could she even begin to choose between them? It made no sense.

Yet here she was. It was Friday, a school day. She had read the email from her editor at least a dozen more times throughout the night, pulling it up on her phone, looking it over, her mind beginning to trip over the familiar phrases in an effort to uncover some new meaning, some less fraught conclusion. She felt sick and exhausted and devastated.

She wanted a career, yes. She knew she wasn't a good

teacher, and that even improving wouldn't make her a good teacher. It would just make her less of a terrible teacher. But here was where Amelia was. And Piper, Andi, even Mr Wicks—the tentative beginnings of, if not family, at least a sense of home that was about both place and people. A sense of home she felt she'd been chasing her entire life, ever since some early, indefinable moment when she knew she was not like her mother, that she would never be like her mother, and would never be as independent as sirens were supposed to be. She wanted a family around her—not children of her own, but deep friendships, intricate loves.

She suddenly wished she had thought to ask Luna about this. Luna, who was a siren, but who was also social and active. Did Luna struggle with these things? Or did she have no desires beyond chatting and partying? And, wow, didn't that seem like an enviable state right about now? Wouldn't that make everything easier? Then she'd just need to say, "I'm sorry, Amelia, this offer has come up. I have been waiting for a long time. And as much as I hate to leave you in the lurch, this is my future calling." It would feel bad, but at least she would be sure. Instead, all she had was uncertainty. It felt like being asked to choose between limbs. "Would you like this future in which you have the career you always dreamed of, but you will be alone? Or this future in which you will be with a beautiful, smart, funny, amazing woman, but you will never have the career you've always dreamed of?"

When the students in her first class asked her if she was feeling ill, she realized she needed to be a better actor. She had skipped breakfast, and she did, in fact, feel quite ill.

But she had to get it together. If Amelia knew about this . . . Bryn didn't even know how Amelia would feel. She did know that she didn't want to say, "I'm leaving you so I can write a book." And she also didn't want to say, "I have the opportunity to write a book and I'm turning it down." Neither of those things felt like they could possibly be real.

For the first time since they'd gotten together, she wished it was a school night. She regretted buying a fancy dildo and having it shipped express, after telling Amelia she had a surprise waiting for her. Because Bryn couldn't begin to think about sex right now. It seemed like the part of herself that understood arousal had gone permanently underground.

And of course, despite Bryn's vow to be a good actor, Amelia saw it instantly. She stepped into the cottage that night, wearing a sheer sort of robe over her regular clothes, and Bryn knew without asking that she would go into the bathroom, take everything off, and put the robe back on, just so that Bryn could take it from her, so that Bryn could reveal her. All of her desire to put on a brave face, to not let Amelia in on her turmoil, dissolved in that instant, because she knew that moment wasn't going to happen tonight.

"What is it?" Amelia said immediately. "What is it? What's wrong? Is Luna okay?"

Even that hurt. "She's fine," Bryn said, trying to keep the emotion from her voice. "She's completely fine. Everything is . . . Everything is . . ." Her voice faltered. She couldn't say it. Nothing felt fine.

"Darling, what is it?" Amelia said, taking her hands. "What's wrong?"

She didn't think she could lie now, even if she wanted to. And, ultimately, she didn't want to lie to Amelia. Not even about this. "I got an email from my editor."

Amelia's face became momentarily excited. "Wait, a good one? You've been waiting for so long! What did it say? Does she want another book? Why do you look so upset? Did she email you to tell you she doesn't want another book?"

This last out—an out that Bryn hadn't even considered—almost tempted her away from the truth. Could she pretend her editor had said a definitive no? But then would she spend the rest of their relationship thinking that if she hadn't lied in that moment, she would be a successful author? A real one? With a career? That she'd thrown it all away for one night? Or one person?

She shook her head mutely, not sure she could speak. And then she opened her computer, found the email, and let Amelia read it. Watching Amelia's face was one of the hardest things Bryn had ever done, because she saw the excitement, the joy, the shared thrill of success—this confirmation that she was good at the things she loved, that people wanted to hear more from her, that her book was selling, and selling well enough to justify another book. And then the moment when Amelia saw the deadline, and her face didn't fall but went still. Her animated features grew blank, wiped away completely.

"Oh," she said, her eyes finding Bryn's. "Is it usually that fast?"

"No, never. I mean, I guess I've only done this once, but last time I had months."

"I see." Amelia read the rest of the email, then read it again, much as Bryn had done. "She says she thinks you've been working on the book. Have you been?"

"I meant to. It's not . . ." If she had been working on the book as much as she had promised herself she would, would it be nearly done by now? Would this whole thing be moot? It would all be there on her computer and she could take a few hours, read over it, send it off. She thought of all of those days sitting in cafés and breweries, getting distracted by the internet, or looking at photographs or nebulous research. All of the notes she had taken with no clear understanding of how or where they would fit in. What did she really have for book two right now? A collection of maybe-spells that she hadn't finalized yet? A much longer list of ideas that hadn't even coalesced into actual spells. Her first book had been original work, spells she'd either invented herself or modified so fundamentally that they had transformed from their initial use into something far more complex. She remembered the work it had taken to perfect those spells, the hours and days of testing. This was not something she could throw together.

And she'd loved it, at the time. Working a day job to pay the bills had instilled a desperate need for something more, and writing the book had been everything to her. So why, why did she feel so gutted now that she had the opportunity to do it again?

"No," she finally admitted. "I really haven't."

"Well, you've been busy teaching, I guess."

But Bryn knew this excuse was too good. She hadn't earned it. "Even before this, I was just screwing around.

I don't know why. I wanted it so bad that I could have written the whole book by now if I'd only focused. I could have written two more books by now if I'd been doing that instead of refreshing my inbox."

"But you haven't written the whole book," Amelia clarified, eyes bleak.

Bryn shook her head again, unable to speak, feeling disappointment seeping through her cells.

Amelia took one breath, and then another, even slower, breath. And then she said, "Well, um, I guess I will come up with a schedule of how I can take over some of your classes, and Piper can too. I can probably combine a few of the first-year classes for the last weeks of school so we can get the kids through the end of the year. And you . . . You need to write your book, right?" There was the slightest edge of question in her voice, the tiniest hint of hope that even now it might not be true.

That was the moment. Bryn could feel how encouraging Amelia was trying to be, and also she could feel how much Amelia wanted her to say no. She said, "I don't have to . . ." letting the sentence trail off. If only Amelia would insist. If only Amelia would remind her of everything they had, everything they were building. If Amelia had said, "I'm in love with you, please don't go," Bryn would have kissed her and told her that it was taken care of, that if this editor refused to extend the deadline, she was out. She'd wait for the next opening, and if one never came, so be it.

She would stay at the school. She'd have Amelia. She'd have this moment.

But this was always meant to be temporary. If she said

231

no to the book, then when school ended in June, she would have nothing at all. If she said yes to the book . . . at least she would have a book. A possible future. She swallowed. "I don't want to leave you in the lurch right before exams."

For a long second, they stared at each other, and then Amelia said, "We'll get through it. Don't worry about the school. This is what you've been waiting for. Bryn, this is your dream, and I'm so happy for you. It's going to be such a good book. It's going to sell even better than the first book, which was a great book." There were tears in her eyes.

Bryn could feel tears in her own. "Right," she said.

"Good." Amelia squeezed her hands and then released them. "It's good. You . . . You didn't want to be a teacher anyway, you know? So this is good. And I have no idea if I could get the governors to hire you permanently, and who needs that kind of stress, right? This just saves us both the trouble."

The words bubbled up inside of Bryn as if they were a geyser on the edge of blowing—she could stop this even now, just by saying, *Amelia, you are what I want. This, with you. This is what I want.* But she choked the words back painfully. "Right," she said again.

"Okay, then. Well, I better leave you to it." Amelia stepped away. "I am . . . I need to plan. And it's Friday, so I have the whole weekend, and . . . and that gives you . . . time to figure out your travel. So I guess I'll go." She stumbled over her feet as she walked backwards towards the door.

Bryn wanted to call out to her, but then Amelia was opening the door and disappearing into the night, and Bryn couldn't muster what words she would even say. Maybe this was an out for Amelia as well. How awkward would it be if your girlfriend wanted to keep teaching but was terrible at it, and you didn't know how to tell her? Maybe that's what this was. An opportunity for both of them to do the thing that would have felt almost impossible to do otherwise. Amelia could hire a real teacher—someone the governors wouldn't question and who actually knew how to get the kids to pass their MSEs—and Bryn could move on with her life.

She had never intended to come back to Grimoire Academy. She never intended to see Amelia Hexford again. Her life was planned. She would write books. Spell books, yes, but she also wanted to dive deeper into history and spell language and the magical sciences. This was the first step on the way to doing all of that.

So why was she crying so hard, alone, in her cottage right now? Alone with her *discreetly shipped* parcel, and her computer with its devastating email still on the screen. Through a sheen of tears, Bryn hit reply and said of course she could meet the deadline, and thank you so much for the offer.

She sent the email, curled up on her bed, and cried into her pillow, feeling somehow more alone than she'd ever been in her life.

22

The logistics of packing up her life at the school and moving back to Denver were almost too easy, as if her presence at Grimoire Academy hadn't even made a ripple. It had always been temporary, and maybe this was further proof that she was doing the right thing, since it took next to nothing to pack her stuff and make her travel arrangements. By the time she went to bed on Friday, still feeling weary and tear-stained, she had her flight booked for Monday afternoon. She even had a car booked to take her to the airport.

Amongst the things she'd intended to do but had failed to complete was the boxing and shipment of Professor Herringbone's library, so she had texted Piper to ask them if they could help her with at least the stuff she'd already packed up, shipping it once she was back in Denver, so she knew she'd be around to receive the boxes. She didn't have anyone she could ask to go to her apartment and get them, or whose address she could use. She'd known Piper for barely a handful of months and already felt more comfortable with them than she did with anyone in Denver, including the people she'd had sex with, and even the couple of witches she'd networked with in her time there. It had never felt like home, but maybe that's because she'd never committed to it—and she would once she was back. Now that she had some idea what it felt like to be part of a community, maybe it would be easier to do that in Denver? Surely, it couldn't get any harder.

Piper had, predictably, said yes, of course they'd help, and immediately showed up at her cottage where, despite promising herself she wouldn't, she wept into their arms.

"Oh honey," they said. "Why are you leaving at all if it upsets you this much?" And so she explained far more than she was comfortable explaining, about her insecurities, about her dream to be a prolific author, about all the things she'd planned, and about Amelia. She didn't go into great detail, but she went into enough detail that Piper held her close and let her cry on their shoulder until she was thoroughly cried out.

"It's none of my business," they said at last, "but I think you're judging her wrong. I don't think she's trying to get rid of you."

But Bryn didn't want to hear it. "Of course she is. And it makes sense, I don't hold it against her. She has a whole school to maintain, and I'm a weak link. I would get rid of me too." Piper opened their mouth to speak, but she shook her head. "No, I know I am. You don't have to spare my feelings. I get it. So, ultimately, this is best for both of us, and definitely best for the students, who deserve a teacher who knows what they're doing."

"Bryn—" Piper tried again.

"No, it's decided. I have non-refundable plane tickets. And once I'm back there, you can send me everything I need, and that'll be that. I'll never have to come here again."

Piper sat back, hesitated, then nodded. "All right, if that's what you want to do, okay. For the record, I think you're wrong on a lot of levels, but you are an adult, and you're allowed to be wrong." They hugged her tightly, undermining what might have been a contentious statement. "So, what do we do now?"

They spent much of the day together. Bryn had the impression that Piper didn't think she should be alone. With a pang of guilt, she wondered who Amelia was with right now. Who comforted the headmistress when she needed comfort? Did anyone? Did she even need to ask?

She got Piper up to speed on where her classes were, how her group projects were going, who to look out for, and who needed extra help with the MSEs. And then, feeling her heart break again, she realized she was abandoning the after-school club. That was almost as painful as leaving Amelia. She'd worked so hard to gain their trust, and they'd taken a chance on her. She knew they had stood up for her when other students tried to get around her rules or acted like she didn't know what she was doing. Hell, Violet had stood up for her to the governors. The after-school club had been there for her, and now she was not going to be there for them.

As much as she told herself that this was just life— sometimes people changed plans, and disappointment was something everyone had to live with—she still felt sick about leaving them. It wasn't like she was their parent. She had no more obligation to them than any regular teacher.

So why did it feel like she was committing a crime? She sent a message to Amelia, asking if she could have leave to meet with the after-school club during their first period, before the car arrived to take Bryn away. Amelia said, *Of course*, and that she would gladly arrange it, since she was the one who would be teaching Bryn's classes that day anyway.

Bryn wondered if Amelia had spent the whole weekend making a schedule, reviewing the curriculum for the various year levels, drafting a job listing for Professor Herringbone's position. The professor had been at Grimoire Academy for thirty-seven years. What would that feel like? Looking back on your life's work and seeing not just a single year of students, but *generations* of students? Interacting with so many families, so many other professors—and then there was the part of her work that Bryn hadn't truly appreciated until recently; the professor had been internationally known for her expertise in spell craft and analysis. What a body of work she'd left. Bryn could only aspire to a fraction of that impact, even if she wrote ten books, or twenty.

She got her emotions under control and sent Amelia a thank-you message that went through many drafts of varying lengths before she settled, simply, on: *Thank you.* Full stop, end of story, sent.

On Monday morning, the kids were excited to be pulled out of their class, though mystified by Bryn's appearance in the library, which had been the first place they'd ever met with her. They thought it might be another field trip, with Luke saying, "Are we going back to the spell shop?" and Violet elbowing him and saying, "I told you, that would be wasteful. We must be going somewhere new." Circe, though, only gazed at Bryn with dark, perplexed eyes, already seeing that this was not another field trip. She immediately let her hair fall into her face, obscuring the rest of her emotions.

And then Bryn explained why they'd been pulled out of class. The jocularity and silliness died utterly. When she told them she was leaving, they responded in specific, individual ways.

Violet was so mad that they couldn't even get a sentence out. They stumbled over their words, finally settling on, "I hate you, you know. I really do. I can't believe you're abandoning us like this." Then they stormed out.

Luke only shook his head. "I don't understand. Why is this other job more important than we are? You can't just wait a couple of weeks? I don't get it."

Bryn struggled not to cry. The kids did not need to see her cry. She couldn't lay that on them. "I'm sorry," she said. "That's just how it worked out. I couldn't predict the timing, and I didn't think it would be this fast."

His frown only deepened. "Okay. Well, um . . ." He scratched the back of his head. She didn't know if it was her mind playing tricks on her, but she swore he looked older than he had in February, when they'd first met—more like the man he would eventually become, than the boy he had been. "All right, well, um, it was really nice having you as our teacher." He glanced at Circe, who did not nod or shake her head. "Right. Okay. I better get to class. Um, bye, Professor Delmar."

"Bye, Luke," she said. "Bye, Circe." The words were physically painful, knifing into her stomach and twisting there.

Circe got up too, her eyes dry, her brow furrowed. She, of course, said nothing, but she looked back at Bryn once as they left the library together, and in that look, Bryn thought she saw all of the disappointment that could exist in one fifteen-year-old.

* * *

She had fantasized that stepping into her apartment after three months away would actually feel like coming home. That she would set down her bags and feel a sense of relief. No more teaching, no more being profoundly bad at the things she was trying to do every day. Now she could get back to her real work, the work she was meant for. Once again, most of her interactions would revolve around ordering coffee or thanking people for delivering it. No more communal meals. No more stressful interactions with the governors. No more sensing that Mr Wicks was judging her, even when he was trying to help. Or maybe that was especially when he was trying to help.

No more heated looks from Amelia. No more anticipatory messages or hands brushing as they ate dinner, knowing that later they would be able to do so much more. No more low-voiced teasing. No more mingling their magic until the heightened sense of power seemed to permeate her every cell . . .

She shut all of those thoughts down. Denver. This was her apartment, her home. She could use her favorite mug again, which she'd missed. Her food had been left to go bad because, again, she didn't even know a neighbor well enough to leave a key with, let alone to ask for the favor of throwing away the milk in her fridge. But that only took half an hour to take care of, if a little longer than that for the smell to dissipate.

She opened all the windows and turned on the fans, let the musty air out. She looked out at the view and enjoyed the city. She *liked* Denver, she reminded herself. It wasn't a lie. Denver had felt like a safe haven away from the sea, away from her family and everything she'd known. A place to start fresh.

It was why she had come to Denver. She didn't want to be in some urban area that smelled only of diesel and smog, but she hadn't wanted to be on the coast either, and Denver had been the perfect place. So why did it now feel like it was a million light years away from where she wanted to be? She couldn't help missing rolling green fields and the scent of the sea in the air.

That first night, back in her bed, fresh sheets pulled on, pillows newly fluffed, she couldn't help crying a little, because she missed her tiny cottage, and the arms that she wanted around her.

23

Bryn didn't remember ever feeling lonely before, or at least never processing it as loneliness. Sure, when she was a kid, when she was the only witch she knew, when she was still trying to be somehow what her mother wanted, even though she suspected she couldn't be . . . Maybe that had been loneliness. But as an adult, she thought she was just a loner, not lonely. There was a difference. She didn't want to get tangled up in romance.

Once left to her own choices, she'd landed in a city that had a very sparse population of witches, which now, looking back, she wondered about. It hadn't been intentional; she hadn't looked at a witchy heatmap and picked the coolest possible place to live. She'd wanted somewhere more urban than Grimoire (but less urban than a big city); less coastal than Grimoire (but not without a strong sense of the natural world around her). Perhaps she hadn't realized what it would be like to be so far away from a sense of witchy community, or maybe she'd forgotten what it felt like to be so firmly rooted in a place where no one knew her context. The adjustment had not gone well, though she couldn't rule out the notion that mostly it was down to how bad Bryn was at peopling in general.

After all, the few other witches she knew in Denver had great lives. They were friends with all kinds of people. They were happy. Those who wanted partners had them. Some of them had families, children, extended networks of connection. While Bryn had none of that, she told herself this was not a problem for now. *Now* was suddenly very straightforward, in contrast to the last few months.

Problem: the book.

Solution: write the book. That was all she needed to do.

It took two days to sort out all of her notes: some of them had been written a year ago, but most of them had been written over six months ago, before she had become so inured to the idea that there would be no second book that it was hard to focus on writing it. She didn't even have a skeletal outline to send her editor, who seemed to email her every few hours, asking in a slightly different way if the structure was ready yet. The editor was clearly not pleased that Bryn had so little to share. But she'd pull it off. After all, this was no more than another school report, and she had been good at those. She was excited about the work, at least when she was working on it.

But after the third day of finding a new café to work at, the old ones all having been tainted by her failure to achieve anything in them before, she went home early and sat down on her tiny couch. It wasn't working. She needed to make it work. She didn't have a choice. She had thrown everything away to write this book, everything she cared about. The kids, the school, Amelia. The looming MSEs that she wanted to ask for updates about, roughly as often as her editor asked for updates about the book. She had failed the kids. She knew that now. It was so much clearer from far away. Failed them not by being a lousy, untrained teacher, but by abandoning them. Violet's intense, factual *I hate you, you know* seemed to echo in the chambers of her heart.

The worst part—one of the worst parts—was that she had no one she could turn to now. She'd given that up too, without even fully acknowledging she'd had it. Only, looking back, it was clear that for a brief moment, she'd had a support network. Now even messaging Piper, who readily replied the second they had a moment, felt cheap. They didn't have a ton of free moments, because they were picking up the slack she'd left in her wake.

Thinking about Amelia hurt most of all. If she could have stopped herself from thinking about her, she would have. It was the first time she'd ever understood the temptation of having memories removed altogether. Then she wouldn't have to think about anything. Any woman with a haircut even close to Amelia's made her do a double take, fingers tingling with the desire to stroke Amelia's neck, through the short hair there. Any glimpse of a flowy dress, a pale ankle. Any scent of jasmine that she happened across made her think of Amelia and long for her with a desire so intense that it took her breath away.

Even though she'd never been in love before, she'd felt so certain of it—most of the time. So clear on what it was to be in tune with Amelia, so seduced by the way energy and magic crackled between them. But now? How was she meant to cope with this deep, hollow place inside her? Like she had lost some part of herself she'd only just gotten to know. Was this what being heartbroken felt like? Because this was awful. The siren way of not becoming entangled made so much more sense now than it ever had before. Why would you risk this? Why would anyone do this to themselves willingly?

She even longed to call her mom and ask if this was why she was always so cold. Did she stay detached from people because she couldn't handle emotions? Couldn't handle being tangled up with other people's emotions? But she suspected her mom would have nothing to do with such a conversation. She did, however, call Luna, having completely forgotten to tell her she was leaving California.

And with the unerring instincts of a sister, Luna said, "But what about Amelia?"

"What about her?" Bryn replied, like she had no idea what Luna was asking.

"Don't do that," her sister said. "Don't act like you don't know what I'm talking about. I saw the way she looked at you and I saw the way you looked when you talked about her. What are you doing, Bryn?"

"I'm pursuing my career."

"Are you? Or are you running away from something?"

"I'm not running away from Amelia."

"Okay, then why haven't you told me about how hard a long-distance relationship is, or how much you miss her, or when you plan to travel back to see her? Why haven't you told me when to keep an evening free so we can go to dinner? The obvious thing to do would be planning your next trip."

"We're not doing that."

The silence that followed this was very loud.

"No offense, big sister, but I think you fucked this one up."

Hearing those words—words that Bryn feared, somewhere deep inside, were true—pissed her off. "We weren't even together that long. You don't know what you're talking about. You're just a romantic eighteen-year-old kid. You don't know anything about love."

Luna choked on something that might have been a laugh, though it sounded anguished. "You don't know anything about *me*."

Bryn realized she was right. She knew about little bits of Luna's life, but they'd never been close. They'd been specifically encouraged to remain distant. Until recently, when it had felt like maybe they would someday attain the status of not just sisters, but friends.

"You're a siren," she said. "Don't sirens inherently not care about other people?"

"Not all sirens are Mom, you know." Luna's voice sounded tired beyond her usual happy self. "Anyway, I hope your book goes well. I should go get ready for work." Before Bryn could follow up on this, Luna was gone.

Feeling more bereft than she felt the situation warranted, Bryn waved her wand at her phone to disconnect the call. She stared at her phone and thought about all of the things it symbolized: connections to other people, the ability to have conversations even when far away. What would happen if she called Amelia right now? Left a message, saying, "I've been thinking about you."

Except Amelia had pushed her away. Amelia hadn't fought for her. Hadn't fought for *them*. If Amelia wanted her back, she could reach out just as easily as Bryn could. And she hadn't. Which meant she didn't want Bryn back—a thought that should have been a relief, but in the end just made her feel gutted and heartbroken all over again.

She'd been in Denver long enough to know which restaurants she liked and which streets to avoid during busy times of day, but not long enough to have anyone to tell that she was back. Not long enough for anyone who knew her to even notice she'd been gone.

And that thought brought her back to loneliness. If she didn't go to breakfast at the castle, someone would ask how she was doing, or if she needed anything sent down. If she didn't check in with Mr Wicks, he would check in with her. Maybe he wasn't exactly supportive, or not supportive in the way she imagined Professor Herringbone would have been, but she knew she was on his radar. He was invested. She missed Andi telling funny stories about things the kids got up to in the dorms, as well as talking teaching and strategy with Piper.

And in the middle of the night, when she couldn't sleep, when the insomnia was very bad, she thought about Amelia. About their separate strands of magic twining around each other, filling the space between them, making every hair on her body stand up, waking up every cell. The way she thought she'd never feel anything like that in her life, and then she did. A gift, she'd told Amelia the night they'd made magic and love in the grotto.

A gift she had thrown away.

It was very, very hard to get back to sleep on those nights.

24

Despite everything else, Bryn wanted to write her book. She had dreamed about this forever. No, it wasn't ideal. The timing was bad. And maybe in her heart of hearts, she wished she hadn't made the decision she'd made. Maybe if she was very, very honest with herself, she wished the email had never come and she was still teaching, even badly, still meeting up with her fellow teachers after school, still looking forward to Amelia—the scent of her, the feel of her, her lips.

But she'd made her decision, and Amelia had made hers. All of the fantasies, all of the alternate universes, all of the wishing in the world didn't change that. The best Bryn could do was follow through. She found an out-of-the-way brewery she hadn't been to before and set up at a table in a corner. She tried their non-alcoholic brew and didn't love it, but they made a pretty good chai latte, so she went with chai after that. She'd brought a backpack full of paperwork and notebooks, and her laptop—everything that contained all the spells that she wanted to try, techniques, little quirks she thought might improve their efficacy or duration. She'd brought everything she could think of, thankful that she had a car, because lugging her biggest backpack on the bus would have been a nightmare.

Today was the day. Before she left the brewery, she vowed to have a plan and an outline for the book that she could send her editor.

She'd been back in Denver for only four days, and it already felt like a trap she had willingly walked into, locked up behind her, and thrown away the key. But that wasn't the book's fault. Wasn't writing a spell book sort of like teaching anyway? With more students and less feedback, and no Lukes to annoy her and cause her to take a deep breath before saying, "Luke, please return to your seat," and no Violets to go from rage to excitement to brilliance in the span of forty-five seconds. And no Circe to look to for a nod or a head shake or a moment of quiet kindness.

Before Bryn even realized she was doing it, she'd stopped outlining her book and somehow begun outlining a whole new curriculum for spellcasting and magic class, for an educational plan that didn't separate everything into subjects, but crossed over, integrating the world for students the way the world would be integrated for them when they were no longer students. She wrote faster and faster, her fingers flying across the keys. She thought about the after-school club kids, their spell objects: Luke's bunny, Circe's glitter globe, and Violet's practical gloves. They hadn't stopped to consider what subject each attempt belonged to; they'd come up with their ideas and then pursued those ideas with trust and dedication.

On impulse, she opened the share menu and added Piper to the document, without comment, without even sending a message or an email.

Writing a book was a little bit like teaching, yes, but teaching was better, even though she wasn't nearly as good at it. Even though it would probably take years before she felt like she'd reached basic proficiency. But the rewards, on a good day, were astronomical. And even on a bad day, hearing from her fellow teachers that she wasn't the only one who'd struggled, that even Mr Wicks had needed a mentor when he had first started teaching, made up for it. Or perhaps not *made up for it* exactly, but gave her the strength to keep trying. There was so much depth to teaching, so many different levels of challenge and interaction and opportunity. She missed the intellectual part nearly as much as she missed the people, which was ironic given how much she'd struggled in the beginning.

Hell, maybe teaching was what Bryn had really wanted to do all along, and she'd picked writing books as a way to do that without having to confront her specific difficulties with people. It felt weird that she hadn't known that before. She'd never even considered it. When she left Grimoire Academy, she hadn't ever wanted to go back into the classroom. But from the second she returned to campus, even before she saw Amelia, she'd felt something there.

She sat back in her chair at the table she'd commandeered in the darkest corner of a little-utilized brewery in Denver, Colorado, and realized that this sudden insight was only half of her problem. Maybe not even half. She could pursue teaching at any time, now or later. She could write the book. She could choose not to. But if she was being nakedly honest with herself, the biggest regret wasn't about feeling like she'd betrayed the kids, or her career, or even about whether or not she could learn something new at the ripe old age of twenty-three.

It was about Amelia, and whether they could find their way back to each other after Amelia had told her she could go, and she had gone. It wasn't strictly a betrayal, but when they'd had the chance to fight for whatever they felt for each other, both of them had turned away. Both of them had chickened out.

The realization left her breathless and aching. She wanted to say she was sorry; she wanted to say she had figured it out now, and she needed a quick do-over so she could make everything right. She could set things back on the correct track, the one she'd been afraid to take, the one she'd seen as having only two potential outcomes: complete failure (of their relationship, of her teaching, of her writing) or complete success (they lived happily ever after, she was the best possible teacher, and she had a satisfying career writing spell books as well). Bryn preferred the world to sort itself neatly into boxes, each one with a guarantee scribbled on the side so she didn't need to worry about uncertainty.

She could almost hear Piper's voice saying, *That's not how it works, honey.*

When she got home that evening, she organized all of her notes and files, and sorted and stacked the boxes of Professor Herringbone's books that had arrived earlier that day. She pulled out the ones she thought would be most helpful, and put away those she would read when she had time. She hadn't done any big grocery shopping since returning to Denver, maybe because she hadn't known how long she would stay, or maybe because she'd become used to stopping at the school kitchens for anything she liked, and was too lazy to cook again. She acknowledged, ruefully, that this was probably the most likely explanation. She'd never enjoyed cooking anyway.

She looked at her calendar, where *MSE WEEK* was still blocked off. It was Friday. The kids had one more week to prep for exams. Bryn forced her fingers to stop beating a frantic drumroll on the table.

It didn't matter now, not really. Her return wouldn't suddenly drill the notion of proper spell syntax into their heads. Arguably, her absence hadn't made much of a difference either. Yet, exams were not just about skills, but also about confidence. Especially magical exams, where the caster's will factored in so heavily.

Mouth dry, Bryn opened a text to Amelia and began typing. Then she deleted what she'd written. She tried again, attempting different tones. Casual: *Hey, do you still need a teacher?* Casual but self-deprecating: *Hey, do you still need a totally unqualified teacher?* Super way-too-serious: *When we said, "I love you", I meant it with all my heart. Can I come back?*

She deleted every single one of them and instead of typing another one, she did what she always did when she didn't know which way to go. She got out a notebook and began to write. When she thought about Amelia, her heart grew. Her capacity for feeling grew, until it was almost more than she could encompass. She tried to think of any other sensation in her life that had even come close, but there was nothing. This was like petting a kitten to the millionth power. It was

253

also the best sex she'd ever had, even before they touched each other. She didn't know how that was possible, and she wouldn't have believed it without proof, but she had experienced it now more than once. The anticipation of having sex with Amelia was hotter than actually having sex with other people, but she had no guarantee that Amelia felt even a fraction of the same way.

The more she thought about it, *really* thought about it, the more she realized that she was looking for a guarantee that trying again was the right thing, that it would result in success. She was trying to go into the experiment already knowing the outcome, which was folly, if nothing else, not to mention completely unscientific. She acknowledged that wanting a guarantee was natural, but refusing to take action without it . . . Well, if she didn't act, she would fail, no matter what. There was no future with Amelia if she opted out of choosing. As scared as she was of rejection and loss and the deep emptiness of heartbreak, which would inevitably be the result of Amelia not wanting to try again, Bryn knew she had to give it one more shot. She might be a bad teacher, and Amelia might be better off without her in so many ways, but she hadn't said that.

She hadn't said, "Bryn, I want you to leave." She'd said, "Bryn, this is your dream." And it had been.

But, too late and too far away, Bryn realized she had different dreams now. These dreams required no less dedication and commitment than writing books had, so she could do no less than take a chance on them.

She didn't text Amelia. She looked up flights out of Denver and bought a one-way ticket home.

25

It had only been one week since she'd left the school, but summer had come early and it felt so much warmer now. Bryn had the driver drop her off in the front circular drive—the same place she'd pulled up in her rental car that first night. But far from being deserted, this time there were many other cars lining each side of the drive, halfway down to the road below. She couldn't think of what would account for it. Nothing had been planned, in any case, which meant this must be . . . a spontaneous event?

When the school had its usual open house days, inviting folks from the community, parents of the children, and alumni, they used an improvised parking lot down at the bottom of the hill and ferried people up in shuttles. This was something else. She'd never seen so many cars this close to the castle. It was surreal when compared to her first time returning, just her and the sunset and the palm trees swaying in the wind.

She said goodbye to the driver and went through the gates. It was midday, on a weekend, and the place felt oddly empty; if it wasn't for all the cars, making it clear that a lot of extra people were present on campus, it would have been spooky. Bryn went up the broad steps and through the wide front doors. A magically sparkling sign read MEETING, with an arrow pointing down the broad main corridor. What meeting could they be having in the middle of a Sunday afternoon? She followed the arrow, though she could tell, merely by guesstimating the volume of people who must be here, exactly where it would lead.

The Grand Hall was not commonly used for big school events, rather than classes. It was a beautiful room: three gorgeous glass domes overhead, where crystals dangled at the top to catch the light and reflect it everywhere. Wood paneling down the sides, except where there were stained glass windows and French doors, now standing open to let in fresh air. The Great Hall was beautiful at every time of day, in every weather—even in the rain, because any light from outside would refract through the wet glass.

Today, the room was as full as Bryn had ever seen it. The students in their official school robes were all sitting down at the front, and although it was the weekend, it seemed like all of them were present. The professors, also in formalwear, sat on two rows to either side of the students. She could see Mr Wicks and Piper, and Andi also sitting with the staff, but it was Amelia to whom her eyes were drawn and locked.

Amelia stood tall, her shoulders back, her chin raised. She stood before the governors, who were arrayed in a semicircle on the left side of the stage. Amelia was the only one on the right side. The visual could not be more obvious:

the school governors versus the headmistress. Bryn, who knew how to sneak into most of the rooms at the school, slipped inside and stood under an archway at the back. The magically amplified voices were clear and carried to every corner.

Governor Schneider, standing in the center of the group of governors with three others on either side, seemed to be mid-scold when Bryn entered, referring to "this public debacle" and "pursuing your idealistic agenda in a manner unsuited to an institution of tradition and excellence, such as Grimoire Academy".

"You have manipulated the student body of this school, Headmistress," Governor Schneider said. She waved a hand at the rather large crowd. "You have manipulated all of their families as well. Do not think that we will be scared into taking any action we do not believe is what's best for the academy. You cannot intimidate the governors of this school, Ms Hexford."

Bryn's heart was racing, and her hands, which she had stuffed into her pockets to keep them from obviously clenching into fists, were clammy with anxiety. She wanted to scream. She wanted to rescue Amelia from the dragons she was facing down. But as the silence lengthened, she realized Amelia did not need rescuing.

"That's *Headmistress* Hexford, Governor Schneider," Amelia said, her voice low and mild.

"Not for long," one of the other governors said, and Governor Blake of cursed memory smiled.

Amelia nodded. "I see that you have reached a decision. I'm sure it will come as no surprise to anyone here that I want what's best for Grimoire Academy as well. Not so very long ago, as the governors are so fond of pointing out, I was a student here myself. The years I spent here at the academy changed my life. I encountered ideas I never would have encountered otherwise. I met people I wouldn't have met. I had the opportunity to practice magic with some of the best witches this world has to offer, some of whom are here with us today." She gestured to the professors, a few of whom nodded. She then added, "And others we are so, so unfortunate to have lost. I recognize that making me headmistress was never your intention, Governor Schneider. I can see now that you were in an incredibly awkward position when our former headmistress, Professor Herringbone, insisted that you do so."

Madame Schneider cleared her throat as if uncomfortable at the reminder. There was a ripple in the audience, as if other people hadn't known this detail.

"I know that I am young and inexperienced, and that my ideas are not shared by the majority of the governors, and in fact often not shared by the majority of my professors. But something Professor Herringbone said to us when we were still students has always guided me. She told us that ideas aren't wrong. They're just ideas. Even when we disagree, even when we think they're misguided, we learn something if we pursue them."

"Ms Hexford," said Governor Blake gruffly, "you cannot argue that pursuing your ideas at the cost of these students, whose parents have settled them here with all trust, makes you a worthy headmistress."

Bryn trembled with withheld rage. Not that wanting

to punch stuffy old men in the face was a new sensation, exactly, but she was definitely closer to following through with it than she ever had been before. Was this the kind of idea that Professor Herringbone had been talking about? She remembered that lecture, and she remembered the challenges to it. The professor smiling and saying, "If it harms none, do what you will. That's more than a platitude; for some of us, it is a valuable life principle." Her anger ebbed as Amelia smiled.

"It is with no disrespect that I must tell all of you—the governors, the professors, the students, and our families— that my experiments will not always work out the way I would wish them to, but they will always be better than doing the same thing over and over and over in a rapidly changing world. Our students will not be prepared if we do not prepare them. Do we wish them to leave Grimoire Academy, pursue their lives, their careers, their university courses, and be behind the other magical children their age?"

"I hardly think that's what we are doing," said Governor Schneider, though her voice had changed timbre a little. It wasn't less arrogant, but there was a quality to it that Bryn thought was slightly less assured.

"Governor, your argument to me has been that the way we do things here has worked for over a hundred years, and therefore it will work for another hundred years, and I must tell you that I think that is a grave disservice to our students." Amelia put out a hand, palm up, towards the audience. "A lot of people here also think that. I have a standing offer to return to the school where I trained."

"A *demon* school," scoffed Blake.

"Yes, a demon school where I learned things I would not have learned here or at any other witch school. I trust that I brought them ideas they wouldn't have learned from other demons. That is the nature of an integrated life. Should I decide to leave Grimoire Academy—" the emphasis on *decide* was slight, but Bryn could see the governors had clocked it "—many of these students will go with me, and without its students, Grimoire Academy collapses."

"If you are seeking to threaten us, Ms Hexford—"

"I'm not threatening you. I wouldn't. There's no need. I'm merely explaining the consequences of one particular action. Should I choose to leave this academy because I feel it is backwards and petrified and unwilling to accept that its students are already outpacing it—that modernity is here whether we like it or not—I have already extracted an agreement that witches can attend my training school as students."

A murmur of shock rippled through the audience, but Bryn felt herself grin. Witches at a demon school. What was next? Vampires? Fairies? Sirens? She imagined Luna dancing through the halls of Grimoire Academy on her way to class. It was preposterous, and also somehow extraordinary. She wished she was sitting beside Piper and could take their hand and squeeze it, because she knew they were just as delighted by the idea as she was. She didn't even know for sure that Amelia was serious, but the thought of it was enough.

"It is the governors, Ms Hexford, who decide upon the headmistress of this institution," said Madame Schneider.

Someone in the audience called, "It's we who decide where our children go to school!" Another person cried, "Hear, hear." A few people raised their hands and shook them side to side to show their agreement.

"I will not be blackmailed," Schneider snarled. One of the other governors put a hand on her arm. She shook it off. "Do not attempt to force me into the decision that you want, Ms Hexford."

A throat cleared. A professor stood. "It's *Headmistress*. Governor."

Bryn knew that voice very well. She knew it in that exact *I will give you one more chance to straighten up* tone. Mr Wicks, on his feet, nodded to the governors. "Governor Schneider, you and I were colleagues for a very long time. All I ask is that you maintain the respect the headmistress deserves while you are here in front of our students. If we do not respect the office of headmistress, how can we expect them to do so? How can we expect them to respect us?"

At this, the students, as if released from all obedience by their sternest professor's words, cheered. One of them called, "Headmistress," and others took up the cry. Bryn didn't even have to look to know it was Luke, with Violet right beside him, chanting with all their classmates, and Circe on her feet with them. "Head-mis-tress, head-mis-tress, head-mis-tress."

It wasn't over. It wasn't going to be that easy. But through a sheen of emotional tears, Bryn saw the governors retreat, leaving only Amelia by herself on the stage. Bryn saw the moment when Amelia found her at the back of the room. Even though there were a few hundred people between them, and even through the chaos of chanting students, their eyes found each other. Amelia knew her in every stance and every mood, and probably would have known her magic anywhere, as Bryn would have known Amelia's.

The headmistress coughed, the amplification for the first time working against her, and winced as the students shuffled and took their seats again. "I thank you all for coming here today. It is so important that we embrace what it means to be a community of witches and non-witches, of magical people and non-magical people, of parents and families, children, siblings, aunts and uncles and grandparents, and community members from the town, who care about the future of this school and the students here. Whatever happens with the governors, whoever is headmistress next year, I want all of you to know that we value you very much and that we love our students with all our hearts."

This time it was Violet dragging Luke to his feet and Circe on her other side. They clapped. Other students stood and clapped with them. And then, as if in a wave, everyone in the room was on their feet.

Bryn clapped until her hands hurt with the force of it, tears streaming down her face.

26

It was Piper who found her first. As much as she'd wanted to run up to the front through the crowd, everyone parting in front of her, jump on the stage, swing Amelia around in her arms and kiss her—obviously, she couldn't do that. Didn't even know if that would be welcome. All she could do was slowly make her way forward.

It was harder than she'd anticipated it would be. The students who had family in attendance were with them. They were introducing their friends and meeting their friends' loved ones. She saw at a distance that Luke was introducing Violet and Circe to his family, with wide smiles. She was too far away to wave or say hello herself, but just close enough to hear Luke say, "They're in the club with me, you know, for the weirdos."

"We are not weirdos," Violet said and hit his arm.

He laughed. "Like I said." Luke's family laughed too.

But then Bryn was farther away, passing through, avoiding clumps of people. When her students saw her, they exclaimed happily and introduced her: "This is Professor

Delmar, Mom, Dad, Grandmother," and, "I love her class. We get to do new spells, Mom, she's teaching us how to make our own."

She smiled and shook hands and her smile grew even wider. And as glorious as it was to meet her students' families, she always had one eye seeking out Amelia. Yet, because Amelia was also walking through the crowd, also being stopped at every step to meet a new family, they weren't getting any closer to each other. And then suddenly Piper was beside her.

"Oh, Dad, this is Professor Alexander! They teach PE."

"PE," said the dad with raised eyebrows. "I didn't realize that was part of the curriculum here."

Piper, pink-cheeked, laughed. "Well, it hasn't always been, but we're trying."

The dad nodded and turned to the woman beside him. "Why don't we tell them how Mariana's mother was nearly an Olympian? Weren't you, dear?"

Mariana's mother shook her head. "Don't tell that story again, it bores people."

"Surely, it doesn't!" With the blissful obliviousness of someone in love, he told the story again. Non-magical, Mariana's mother had been on the swim team all through high school, then at university. She'd competed in every meet she qualified for and missed the Olympic team only because of a badly timed injury, though Mariana's father claimed that since they'd met shortly thereafter, maybe it hadn't been the *worst* outcome after all.

Piper and Bryn nodded and laughed in the right spots and congratulated Mariana's mom, who added that she'd been exhausted from all those years of competition and considered it something of a blessing to have an excuse to step back. Piper took the opportunity to ask her if she had any tips for teaching athletics to students who might not always be interested. She laughed and said, "Even when I was training every day, swimming more than I was sleeping, there were days I didn't feel like it. But I never regretted getting in the pool after I was there."

"That's good," Piper said. "Thanks, I'm gonna use that. Excuse us." They took Bryn's arm and led her away.

"Do you think that's true?" Bryn whispered. "That she doesn't miss it?"

"I don't know if it was true at the time, but it's obviously true now. Maybe that counts."

Bryn nodded. "I grant that argument."

Piper squeezed her arm and said, "I'm so glad you're home."

And maybe it was all the emotions of the day—being back at the school, seeing Amelia defend her position with so much fire and so much passion—but she felt herself tear up. "I'm glad I'm home, too. I hope other people will be too."

Then they were pulled aside by another student. They met more parents. They met younger siblings who hoped to attend Grimoire Academy someday. ("You'll love PE, Julio, *and* there are horses!") They heard a mix of compliments and complaints, because people would complain. But Bryn realized that she'd had impeccable timing, maybe for the first time in her life. She wouldn't have wanted to miss this moment for anything, and certainly not for all the publishing contracts in the world.

Sometime later, when she looked around again, she couldn't find Amelia anywhere. She did, however, see Mr Wicks standing with an older gentleman whose hand he was holding and shaking like he'd forgotten to let go. He caught her eye and smiled, gesturing her and Piper over.

"Now, I bet you youngsters don't know who this is," he said jovially. "This is the headmistress who was here when I was a boy."

She and Piper blinked at each other. Mr Wicks had gone to Grimoire Academy? "You went to school here?" Piper asked.

"I did indeed. Graduated and everything."

The older man leaned forward. "It was a near thing, but we all felt so sorry for him. He tried very hard, even though he was always a bit daft."

Far from upsetting Mr Wicks, this made him laugh. "I struggled a bit when I was a student, but I think I turned out all right, didn't I, Headmistress?"

The man chuckled. "You did indeed, Professor, you did indeed. Devon tells me that our current headmistress is surprisingly good for being so young. In my day, you couldn't be a headmistress unless you were, oh, at least fifty."

"She's very good, sir," Piper said.

"Very, very good," Bryn added, feeling foolish, but also wanting to say something.

Mr Wicks reached out to clasp her arm for a second. "Are you back with us, Professor Delmar?"

"I hope to be, though, obviously, I still need training."

"Training can be achieved. You only need to commit to it."

Bryn inhaled, exhaled, and said, "I'm committed, Mr Wicks. I didn't realize how much I wanted to be a teacher until I left."

He grinned. "You will make a great one."

People began to leave. Bryn did eventually meet Luke's family, who were taking both Violet and Circe out to dinner, after the necessary permissions had been sought and granted. Piper had been rounded up with a cadre of professors to direct traffic and cast quick magical spells to ensure that everyone got out of the logjam of cars safely. The kitchens, seemingly caught up in the energy of the day, had provided a buffet spread of delicious foods for those lingering: pasta with various sauces, samosas, multiple curries, spanakopita, mouth-watering tamales second only to Bryn's mom's tamales, and a selection of desserts that made her want to spend the rest of the evening in the Grand Hall.

Somehow, in all the activity, Bryn still hadn't seen Amelia. The group eating dinner was a mix of current and retired professors, alumni—none whom she immediately recognized—plus donors and stakeholders in the school. After only snacking on a tamale as she wandered in search of Amelia, Bryn set her plate down and went looking farther afield. She roamed the halls, vaguely going in the direction of Amelia's rooms, while listening for any voices she might hear, any hints. Just as she was about to round the corridor where Amelia's office was located, she heard what she'd been subconsciously waiting for: the grating and distinct tones of Madame Schneider.

"Are you wishing for the entire board of governors to resign?"

"No, Governor Schneider. I am wishing for the board of governors to give this school a little bit of time to grow and change, just like we give our students."

Bryn bit her tongue and went still in the shadows at the end of the corridor.

"You can have one more year," Schneider said, as if giving into what she felt was a distasteful and unnecessary demand.

"I'm afraid I must insist on the usual five-year contract," Amelia replied. "I did some research, Governor Schneider. I could not find a single case of a headmistress being put on a one-year contract. I am serious about this role, and Professor Herringbone was serious when she insisted I have it."

"You are not as experienced as our previous head-mistresses."

"And yet you hired me for the role anyway, so I insist on being granted the same opportunity to succeed as any of my predecessors." After the slightest pause, Amelia added, "We can count this year as the first year of my contract, if that helps."

Bryn bit down hard on her tongue to keep from gasping at Amelia's audacity, or laughing at the sour-lemon tone in Schneider's voice. "I will bring it to the board," she said grudgingly. "But I make no promises."

"I don't ask for any."

Then the governor turned and began walking straight towards Bryn, who knew with the instincts of a former student that there was nowhere to hide, no silent way to escape the stairwell without being seen (or revealing herself through running steps). So instead of hiding, she walked forward, rounded the corner, raised a hand to Amelia, and smiled. As if surprised, though she didn't imagine anyone was fooled, she said in a cheerful voice, "Oh, hello, Governor Schneider."

"And you," Schneider said. "We only allow *teachers* at this school, not overblown authors of popular books." Her words were clipped, angry, and oddly defiant, as if she was the one who had something to lose.

"I've signed up for my first-term courses already. They start over the summer," Bryn said sweetly. "I very much look forward to learning more about teaching." Her eyes drifted to Amelia's. "I am so lucky that Headmistress Hexford gave me the chance to realize this is where I belong, and teaching is what I should be doing."

Governor Schneider's eyes narrowed, as if she suspected some kind of a joke. But instead of speaking, she brushed past Bryn and went down the stairs, leaving the two women standing alone in the corridor.

Bryn approached, but didn't stand too close. Didn't kiss Amelia with her whole body, as she so dearly wished to. She said, "Congratulations. I mean, about keeping your job. And the school. Um . . ."

Amelia blinked at her. "Did you really sign up for a teaching course, or were you just winding Schneider up?"

"Oh yeah, I did it. On the plane on my way here. Not—not that I expect you to rehire me. I wouldn't presume like that, but I want to teach again, even if not here. I, uh, figured that out. Finally."

"But you're an author. You want to write books."

"I still want to do that, but not as much as I want to do this, Amelia." And now Bryn did step forward. "Not as much as I want to be with you."

Amelia's cheeks were flushed and her eyes searched Bryn's. "I would never ask you to choose between me and your dream."

"You don't understand." Bryn took a breath. "Amelia, you *are* my dream. You are so much more than a dream to me. A dream is nebulous, and you are real. And if you will have me back, I want to be yours."

Amelia opened her mouth, tried to speak, closed it, and swallowed, and then she pulled Bryn against her, hard, and kissed her, as if the repressed emotions of the day made her feral, made her need and desire and passion all combine into one kiss. "I thought you'd left forever," she said. "I'm so glad you're back."

"Does that mean yes?" Bryn asked breathlessly. "Will you give me another chance? Not as a teacher—well, yes, as a teacher, too, but I meant—"

"*Yes*, Bryn, now would you just—"

They fell into each other, hands gripping tightly, both of them breathing hard as they kissed. There would be more to talk about later, but in that moment, they did not need words. They needed only the language of touch— but they were in the corridor, so when they heard steps coming up the stairs, they sprung apart like naughty children.

But it was only Piper, who clearly wasn't fooled. "You guys have to come down to dinner. It's amazing. It's delicious. It's incredible. Come on, chop-chop. Can't hide up here all night—" they winked "—even if you might want to."

Amelia and Bryn, as if in one rehearsed movement, smacked Piper on each arm.

"Hey!" they cried, but they were laughing. Then all three of them laughed as they trooped back to the Grand Hall for dinner, talking, and enjoying being home.

27

The emotionally mature thing to do would have been to sit down like adults and discuss their relationship and their future.

The emotionally mature thing would have been to start with talking, resolve all of their issues with cool heads and, only after having done so, progress to the physical extension of emotion that Bryn felt certain both of them were waiting for.

But there was a dinner to be had first—an occasion so celebratory that Bryn couldn't help grinning. Her muscles were sore from it. Mr Wicks had approached the two of them as they ate scrumptious little cheesecakes for dessert, admitting that he'd imagined the governors proclaiming him headmistress in front of everyone, and sharing the speech he'd have given to turn down the job.

"I'm afraid I rather fancied myself the hero of the day, deferring to you and stepping back so you could succeed," he said, shaking his head slightly.

"So I wasn't paranoid," Amelia asked. "They really did want you to replace me."

Mr Wicks reached out and patted her arm. "Indeed. But you didn't need a hero, Amelia. You *were* the hero."

"I . . ." She trailed off, flustered, staring up at him, her bulletproof Headmistress Mode derailed by his candidness. "What if I'm really not ready, though?"

"Oh, if you think you're ready, you're almost certainly the wrong choice." He leaned in and lowered his voice, so only they could hear it. "There will be a learning curve. I know you know that, but it bears repeating. You've been good at almost everything you tried for most of your life, Amelia. This will take longer, and some of it will be harder, but I'm here. I will back you. I will always tell you when I disagree with you, but even this old dog can learn some new tricks."

Amelia had tears in her eyes when she thanked him. Bryn had tears in her eyes when she pulled Amelia into a tight hug and whispered, "Even Mr Wicks thinks you're a good headmistress."

Celebratory though dinner had been, it had also been exhausting. Some families had chosen to stay. A few who'd come from far away were even spending the night in Grimoire. A flurry of administrative tasks followed— people signing off on their children going with them or with other students, Andi soliciting permission for children whose parents were not there, the final chaotic crunch of departing cars.

Bryn helped as much as everyone else did, making phone calls, organizing rides, acquiring signatures, entering them into the school's fledgling computer system. Amelia explained how that had been a big change in Professor Herringbone's time, from the paper ledgers that had been used even while Amelia and Bryn were still at school. It was staggering. Relying exclusively on paper ledgers was one tradition even Governor Schneider had not fought to maintain.

After-dessert refreshments (in the form of beverages and fruit) had been a much smaller affair, and they had been taken out into the back gardens.

This gave Bryn the opportunity, finally, to approach Circe. "I know you were angry at me for leaving, and you were right to be angry. I'm sorry I left at such a crummy time, but I'm back now. For good."

Circe looked at her for a long moment, solemn-faced, nodded, and then her face split in a grin, and she hugged Bryn tightly for a second before running off. It was one of the nicest hugs Bryn thought she had ever had.

She spent much of the evening talking to people, eating, laughing, enjoying updates about what had been happening in the week she'd been gone: who had gotten up to what, who had been caught cheating again, this time plagiarizing a well-loved spell book for a school paper. Mr Wicks had told that story, even though no one in his class had been involved. "They think they've invented everything," he proclaimed. "Students always do."

The laugh the teachers had shared at this—including Bryn herself—felt like community, like the kind of found family she hadn't known she needed. If she had been looking for any confirmation that this was the correct move for her, she found it in that moment. She didn't want to be on the outside when the teachers talked about their classes, about their papers, about their students, troubleshooting behaviors, sharing both challenges and triumphs. Bryn wanted to be part of that too, and she was.

Still, she intended to talk to Amelia, to Discuss Things. To have The Talk. It was important to both of them, she knew, not to start anything on unstable ground; communication was the foundation of any relationship they would have. Yet when they finally went back to Bryn's cottage, which she had missed more than she thought possible, kissing came first, before words, before logic. Kissing as its own language, just like magic, a form of communication that required a great deal of trust in order for it to be effective.

And kissing inevitably led to other things. Not immediately into the kind of sex fest she might have dreamed about while she was gone, but something else again. The cottage was warm and comfortable. This time, Amelia lit the candles, and Bryn doused the lights.

"We should talk," Bryn said. "Right?" They were looking at each other, standing, hands linked.

Amelia stood on tiptoes to look her in the eyes. "We will, but would it be so bad if we chose an alternative way to reconnect?" She kissed Bryn and then tugged her towards the bed. They removed each other's clothes in the flickering light, fingers lingering, touches prolonged, until both of them were naked. Bryn felt hungry for touch, drawing Amelia down over herself, reaching up to kiss every bit of skin she could reach.

Sometime later, when the sweat was drying and both of them were catching their breaths, Amelia lay her head on Bryn's chest and they did actually talk. Amelia's fingers traced lines along Bryn's skin while she spoke.

"I didn't want to hold you back. I knew that writing the book was so important to you, and I thought that if you stayed, you'd only be staying for me. I never, ever want you to pick me over your career or the things that you want to do. So that's why I told you to go. I didn't *want* you to leave. I just didn't want you to stay out of a sense of obligation to me, or the school, or anything else."

"I thought maybe you were relieved to have an excuse to get rid of me," Bryn admitted, her voice softer than she expected it to be. She realized only in hearing the words how hurt she'd felt, how vulnerable. How starkly painful that belief had been.

"*No.*" Amelia's hand went flat over Bryn's navel. "Never. I would never push you away."

"Never?" Bryn asked, raising an eyebrow even though Amelia could not see it.

"Well," Amelia said, "I might accidentally push you away, but I wouldn't use the school or teaching to do it. I don't think you understand how hard teaching is, even for people who always wanted to do it. It's hard for everyone."

After a moment, Bryn said, "I think I need to be gentler with myself. About teaching, but probably also about anything that's hard. Anything that doesn't come as quickly to me as I'd like. As much as I have wanted to write this book, I haven't done it, Amelia. I had all the time in the world, and I still didn't write it. What does that mean? Am

I not meant to be a writer? Is that just some dumb childish fantasy I took way too far?"

Amelia lifted her head and looked around, cupping Bryn's cheek with one hand. "You're already a writer. I don't think that all the best books were written easily or quickly, or without a great deal of work. A lot of them were probably incredibly difficult. That doesn't mean they weren't worth writing. Probably a lot like relationships." Her thumb brushed over Bryn's lips. "Just because things get hard doesn't mean they're not worth fighting for. Bryn Delmar, you're worth fighting for."

Bryn blinked, tears standing in her eyes. "Everything in me told me to stay with you, to be where you were. But I worried that I would lose my chance to write books and . . ."

"You'd regret it?" Amelia finished for her.

"Maybe. I mean, I didn't think of it exactly like that, but maybe that was a big part of it."

Amelia lay her head back down, sighing. "I'm glad you went."

"Wait, what?" Bryn's heart sped up again, and the irrational fear that somehow Amelia was dumping her surged forward until she took a slow breath and fought it back. Amelia was not dumping her. She absolutely knew that.

"Think about it, though." Amelia's fingers began to trace over her side again, soothingly. "If you had stayed, neither of us would be completely sure that it hadn't cost you the future you wanted. Now we both know that you've chosen this for the right reasons. Not just because of me."

"Although," Bryn teased, "the sex is really, really good. I might have come back just for the orgasms."

Amelia laughed. "I know, but no sex is worth throwing your life away."

"No." Bryn craned her neck forward to kiss Amelia's head. "This isn't that at all. This is establishing a life I never even realized I wanted until now. And that feels like a gift."

"It is. It's a gift we give each other."

"So what happens now?" Bryn asked. "Do I still have a job? Can you even actually hire me?" While she wanted to teach, and would go back to school to train for it regardless of what happened, she did desperately want to be able to stay in the cottage, and follow the after-school club through the rest of their schooling, and steal the occasional night with Amelia in the grotto . . .

"I have been thinking about our human resources here at the school," Amelia mused. "As happy as I am to be headmistress, I don't think the way Professor Herringbone went about it was right." Bryn began to protest, but Amelia fully sat up. "I don't mean that I wasn't a good choice. I just mean that if you have to force people to accept someone in a role this important, it sets that person up to always be insecure about their place. How will I ever know if I could have gotten hired otherwise? I probably couldn't have. And I'm not going to throw away this opportunity, but I want to set future headmistresses and teachers up for more. So anyway, I think we need a committee for hiring, and I asked Mr Wicks to be in charge of it."

Bryn blinked at her. "Mr Wicks? You're not worried he's just going to hire a bunch of fuddy-duddy old crones?"

"I don't think so. And more than that, considering the way he has been with you and with Piper, I think I can trust him to be a good mentor for new teachers. Even if we disagree on a lot of things, that's the most important aspect of the job. I don't want to only work with people who agree with me."

Bryn nodded. "That's fair. I did feel like he was supportive. But does this mean I have to apply to Mr Wicks for my job?"

Amelia grinned. "Mr Wicks and his hiring committee, yes. But I think you'll probably get it." Then she lay down again, and they linked hands.

"It's been a long day," Bryn said, only beginning to realize how tired she really was.

"And it's a school night," Amelia added.

They fell asleep soon after, letting the candles gutter themselves into little pools of wax, the light dimming until only the occasional glimmer of magic shone in the dark.

28

The run-up to the MSEs was intense and exhausting. Having only experienced it once from the student side of things, Bryn hadn't realized all the effort and time that teachers put into prepping for exams. Even though it seemed like Amelia had won her job fair and square from the governors (who had capitulated and granted her a four-year contract beginning the following term), Bryn knew she wanted to be able to throw the exam results back at them as if to say, "Even by your standards, I deserve my job."

Bryn wasn't sure at what point all of the professors realized this was a thing. She didn't think Amelia had been telling people, but it was more than obvious that all members of staff understood at least that exam performance would be evaluated by the governors. They might have been forced to give in, but weren't going to do it gracefully, and certainly not if it appeared that Amelia's work wasn't paying off for the students (and the school's financial bottom line).

Bryn's work hours grew longer and longer in the next

week. Some of the students who lived in town had applied for temporary residence in the dormitories—enough of them so that Amelia had hired another resident advisor, a job for which Luna had applied (without telling Bryn) and Mr Wicks had hired her (also without telling Bryn). Although she liked working at the spell shop, she only worked two shifts a week. She wanted more, and when she'd heard from some folks who were buying potion ingredients that the school was hiring, she'd applied. When Bryn asked Amelia how the whole thing went down without her knowing about it, Amelia pointed out that Mr Wicks was the head of the human resources committee, and they needed someone responsible who could move on site immediately. The owner of the spell shop—an Academy graduate, naturally—gave Luna a brilliant reference.

At first Bryn was annoyed, thinking her sister had gone behind her back, but Luna hadn't even mentioned they were related. "No one made the connection, as far as I know," Amelia said, "and I didn't want to put you in a weird position by asking you what you thought. Plus, we didn't get that many applicants. Surprisingly, not a ton of people want to temporarily live with a group of teenagers. Luna is perfect for it. She's already graduated, and she didn't go to school here, but she understands the pressure they're under, and she knows enough about witches and spellcasting to not be completely done under by them."

All of which was true. And after Bryn got over herself, she admitted it was kind of fun knowing Luna was around. Both of them were busy, but they did get to see each other at mealtimes, which was something that hadn't happened in years. Not since Luna was too young to be a pleasant eating companion.

Faster than Bryn was expecting, the MSEs were upon them. On the Monday morning of exam week, Bryn thought she was going to fall apart long before Friday afternoon arrived. Mr Wicks took the seat next to her at breakfast and leaned over to say, "The first time is always the worst."

"Am I that transparent?" she asked.

He smiled. "Yes, but I remember it. The exams are not a measure of how well we teach. Remember that. Whatever happens, your impact on the students goes much deeper than any exam can ever show."

She thought about that for a long moment before saying, "I think that might make it worse."

Mr Wicks laughed. "Just, whatever you do, promise me you won't watch the practicums," he said, and offered a theatrical shudder. "Really, the practicums are agony."

Since this kind of melodramatic language was uncharacteristic for him, she said noncommittally, "Um."

He only shook his head. "Really, I snuck in my first year, and seeing them all so nervous, stumbling over things I knew they could do . . . It's not worth it, Bryn. Whatever else you do, don't do that."

Bryn, who had been planning to do exactly that, nodded. "Okay, I'll try to resist."

Resisting was harder than she'd anticipated, and she still had all of her other classes to teach. It wasn't as if exam week was a week off for everyone else. They all had to go about their business and pretend that each day was the same as any other day of the year. It was much harder than

283

she expected. She confessed to Piper later that she thought she'd had it bad as a student, but this was way, way worse.

"I know," they said. "My subject doesn't even have an exam session, and I'm so nervous for them."

Of all of them, Amelia was pretending the most effectively. People kept telling her that she looked so serene, that she clearly wasn't troubled by the exams at all. Some of the professors even grumbled that she wasn't taking the exams seriously, which Bryn knew for a fact was not true. By midday Wednesday, Amelia had sought out Bryn's office and hidden there for the last two classes with her nose in the considerable stack of Professor Herringbone's books that Bryn had brought back with her from Denver.

Bryn had been pleased, happy to offer whatever calmness she could, but of course Amelia had not been relaxing. She'd been studying. She burst out of the study the second classes were over for the day. There were still three students in Bryn's classroom, but Amelia had two books in her arms and a third on top of them, open. "I think I figured out your scaling issue," she said to Bryn, then smiled and waved at the first-years, who looked back over their shoulders at her.

"My scaling issue?" Bryn asked.

"Yes, you know, for the pressure washing, remember?"

It took a moment, but Bryn did remember. "Oh right, spell scaling. It's not just the pressure washing, though. I think it could have applications—"

"It can," Amelia interrupted, then bit her lip. "Sorry, sorry, but look." She passed the book over to Bryn, who began reading the text until Amelia pointed at the professor's scrawl in the margins.

It was a simple yet elegant solution. Bryn had been focused on trying multipliers on the spells, expanding their scope by essentially repeating the spell for as long as it needed to be repeated. There were a couple of problems, such as not knowing how to stop the spell from repeating endlessly, and how to limit the physical space the spell applied to in a way that could be duplicated for other spells in other environments. She could, of course, simply craft a spell for the exact area of the courtyard that needed to be washed, but then it would only work for that space in those dimensions, and only if she cast it from roughly the same spot. What Amelia had discovered was a note in the professor's distinctive handwriting that amounted to something much simpler, something so obvious that Bryn couldn't really believe she hadn't figured it out herself.

She looked up at Amelia. "Boundaries," she said. "We have to set the boundaries."

"Exactly," Amelia agreed, eyes alight.

And that's what they did for the next two days. Bryn taught her classes and Amelia did the many, many things the headmistress was expected to do all day, and in the evenings they practiced this new form of scaling magic. It didn't work perfectly the first few times. It took the entire evening on Wednesday for them just to figure out how to effectively cast their boundary spells. Bryn resented the fact that she actually needed to draw them out by walking the perimeter of the area with her wand, which seemed like cheating. When she said this to Amelia, Amelia only laughed, reminding her about all of the things they'd had to do when they were younger in order to ensure that spells worked. The precise enunciation of words, the exact syntax of each spell, the wand motions that had not come naturally, and which had to be modified to do different things.

"Remember when it was all confusing?" she asked. "And you know how now it's not? I bet this is the same. Give it a couple of weeks and you'll be flicking your fingers in the general direction and the magic will know what to do."

Bryn wasn't so sure of that, but Amelia's confidence in her made her feel warm and fuzzy anyway.

The last day of exams dawned rainy and warm. The humidity was stifling. Every openable window in the castle was open, and every door was propped. She felt bad for her students taking exams because the exam rooms, in order to prevent cheating, were kept tightly shut.

"It must be like taking exams in a swamp," Piper murmured.

Indeed, when the students finally emerged, many of them were sweating, not only from the anxiety, but also from the somewhat rainforest-like conditions of the hall.

The traditional end-of-exams meal, to which all the students who had already taken their MSEs were invited, commenced in the afternoon and went on until evening. Amelia had brought in pillows and blankets and set up a nest area, which she called the chill-out zone. Piper leaned over to Bryn and murmured, "Worst rave ever." Bryn laughed. When Amelia saw them laughing, she came over.

Piper gestured to the chill-out zone. "Nice touch."

Students were already gathering in small groups, some of them pulling blankets over their shoulders, two or three at a time, others gripping pillows, holding them to their bellies, as if clinging to life rafts. Even aside from the theatrics, Bryn was pleased to see that the second-years looked shell-shocked and weary, but also proud. Every magical child enrolled in magical school had to take the MSEs. There were different exams for different types of people, but everyone took them. Bryn could see Luna describing her own siren MSEs to a group of fourth-years who were only one year younger than her, waving her hands around, illustrating some siren feat that, Bryn realized, she knew nothing about. Amelia's idea of integrating all of the magical kids was a good one. Wouldn't it be better if they all knew the challenges the other ones faced, even if they weren't facing them themselves?

Amelia looked at her phone, touched the screen, and then her eyes raced across it. "No cheating," she reported with an exhalation of relief. "No cheating incidences reported. No behavioral incidences reported. Everyone took their exams and, as far as the proctors are concerned, did as well as they could."

"Nothing on fire?" Piper asked. "That actually happened at my school, not the year I was taking MSEs, but two years later, when I was still at school."

"No fires," Amelia said, "or at least none that have been reported to me." She put away her phone and took another deep breath. "Of course, we don't know their scores yet, but whatever happens, I think we did well."

Piper and Bryn traded a look, and Bryn suspected they were thinking the same thing. They had done well, yes. The students had made it through. The school was still standing.

But there would be so many more problems to deal with if the students had not passed their exams.

She looked around, told herself there was nothing she could do about it now, and focused on the celebration. There were only a few days left of school and she had been teaching for four whole months now, and it was what she wanted to do for the rest of her life. Knowing that, if nothing else, was a triumph.

29

Grimoire Academy's spring term ended on the Wednesday following the end of exams, and the last week was always fuzzy academically, more about pulling everything and everyone together than it was about teaching (or learning) in the traditional sense. It was a week of short days, half periods where the students spent most of their time making portfolios of their work for the year or giving presentations about things they'd especially enjoyed. Sometimes the professors could be convinced to let them watch movies. Snacks were rife, and this year Amelia had announced that any professor who wished to allow phone usage in class could do so. Mr Wicks, of course, chose not to, but Bryn let the kids have their phones.

Spirited debates were had. Students who didn't always participate did so because there was no pressure. There were no grades assigned for the work done that week. No participation points credited or deducted. Some of Bryn's painstakingly put together groups even elected to do presentations. She used the afternoons to finish grading and entering her grades—and one other thing, something she didn't tell Amelia about until she needed her sign-off on it.

"Emergency teaching credential?" Amelia asked when Bryn showed her.

"It means you—or, I mean, the hiring committee—can really hire me now, not on a temporary basis. You can hire me on a permanent basis, as long as I am pursuing my studies and getting my final teaching credential. And I am."

Amelia, of course, called in Mr Wicks, who was the head of the hiring committee, and presented the application to him instead. Bryn held her breath, wondering if at this last moment he would morph into the uncompromising curmudgeon she'd always assumed him to be when she'd been his student. But he smiled and signed it. When he handed it back to her, he shook her hand and said, "Welcome, officially, to Grimoire Academy, Professor Delmar. I look forward to seeing your development as a teacher." And then he, not Amelia, sent a letter to every professor and staff member of the school to welcome her to their ranks.

She didn't think this gesture should be so powerful, when she'd already been teaching there and they already knew her, but maybe that's what made their response even more impactful. They all seemed genuinely happy, like these were people who thought she could be a teacher alongside them. She hadn't been prepared for the emotions of it.

Graduation was held at dusk, and nearly every

student, professor, and staff member gathered in the courtyard to wish the graduates well. Even though she'd only been their teacher for half the year, Bryn felt like she had personally ushered these students through their schooling. She was so proud of them and so excited by their achievements.

In the traditional way of witchy school graduations, each student marked their passing through the school halls by adding their particular spellfire to the grand cauldron in the middle of the courtyard—a cauldron which had seen thousands upon thousands of witches graduate over the years. As the magical flames grew, some of them sparkled, some of them ignited in rainbow colors or neon or burning indigo. A few particularly daring ones even managed to give off the impression of fiery birds flying away, turning into smoke.

As a student, Bryn had appreciated the spectacle of the thing; as a professor, she knew that no fewer than seven witches had their wands out just in case something didn't quite come off correctly. But this year, all the students' magic worked. The cauldron crackled and flamed into the night sky, and the graduates of Grimoire Academy were ushered into witchhood at last.

Bryn couldn't help the tears on her face, turning to Amelia and reaching for her, and Amelia grabbed her back. One of their fourth-years called, "Just kiss already!" and everyone laughed.

They did not kiss. Not in front of the students, not in front of their co-workers, not in public, but they did laugh, and they did not drop their hands. It was one of the best nights of Bryn's entire life, and she couldn't believe she got to share it with the woman of her dreams.

* * *

Later—much later—after the celebratory feast and magical fireworks, and the tearful goodbyes, the professors gathered for what was evidently also a school tradition: a relaxed round of drinks and desserts in the smallest and most snug library. Bryn felt suddenly like she'd been initiated into a secret society, and maybe she had been.

The mysterious professors' mixer lasted less than an hour and included a lot of stories about the students who'd just graduated, some of which led to stories about past graduations. A way of the professors marking the end of yet another generation of Grimoire witches.

Amelia caught her eye as they were leaving. "Piper is going back to the dorms to say hi to Andi. There are only four kids over there to be picked up in the morning."

"Oh good." Bryn liked the idea of Piper and Andi locking down the dorms, maybe letting the kids stay up late. Luna, not needed now that most of the kids had gone home, had said goodbye after the feast, making Bryn promise to call before she made any "big life choices". When Amelia had raised an eyebrow, Bryn had admitted mentioning to her sister that she did technically have an apartment in Denver that wasn't being used; the location was good and the rent would be doable, maybe with a little help at first.

As she explained, Bryn was a little worried that it might

sound like she wasn't as committed to teaching as she should be, but Amelia's eyes sparkled.

"You mean Luna would take over your place in Denver? That's brilliant!" Then, since everyone else had left the library, Amelia kissed her. "My girlfriend is so frigging smart."

Bryn's heart leaped as if attempting to jump from her to curl up like a kitten in Amelia's arms. "Oh, are we— I mean I'd love to be— I didn't know if we were—"

"Do you want to be my girlfriend, Bryn?" Amelia asked, leaning in closer.

"Hell yes," Bryn breathed, and closed the distance for another kiss.

"I want to show you something." Amelia grabbed her hand and pulled her out of the library and towards the stairs.

Sometime later (and Bryn wasn't entirely certain she could find her way back through all the old servants' stairs and back halls they'd just traversed), Amelia stopped at a door. She pulled out an ancient-looking brass key and inserted it into the lock, then gestured Bryn in as she closed it again behind them. The motion-charmed lights came up, and Bryn found herself in a narrow passage with a rickety-looking staircase at the end of it, with what appeared to be blankets at the bottom.

"Come on."

"Where are we going?" Bryn asked, willing but also astonished that she didn't already know.

"You'll see," Amelia said. "But you have to grab the pillows."

Bryn did so, leaving Amelia with the fluffy blanket. She followed up the steps, surprised when it resolved at the top to be only a platform to another staircase, which she hadn't noticed going over their heads. They climbed three such wooden staircases, magically lit and creaking, but not dangerously—at least, Bryn didn't think so. Amelia used the same key at the top of the final staircase and opened the door; fresh, warm air blew down into the stairs.

"Are we on the roof?" Bryn asked. "I had no idea there was roof access."

"There is," Amelia said. "Professor Herringbone gave me the key. She said most people, even most of the staff and professors, don't know this exists, making us very special."

Bryn smiled, pulling her in for a kiss. "I already knew you were special, Amelia Hexford."

"Come on," Amelia said. They emerged out onto the roof of the school. It was strangely clear and clean—no evidence of animals, not even bird droppings. Bryn could feel the breeze around them, but it didn't feel the way she would have expected the roof of the castle to feel; it was almost as if they were buffered somehow. She shifted her senses until she could perceive magic, and it was everywhere. At first glance, she could not begin to understand the complex, intricate webs of magic around them. She could see that it had been cast by more than one person at many different times, but that was about all she could tell.

Amelia nudged her with one shoulder, as both of them still had their arms full. "You see it, don't you?"

"It's amazing," Bryn whispered.

"We don't have to worry about being seen or heard either. We're probably too high up anyway, but I once shouted as loud as I could and no one below even looked around. Think of the shielding spells they must have used." She nodded upward. "I never knew this was here."

"I didn't either," Bryn agreed. "I mean, I've looked at the castle, what, hundreds of thousands of times? I never even saw the magic."

Amelia's smile widened. "I know. It's like we're all alone at the top of the world, in a magical bubble."

Bryn couldn't help herself. She gently put the pillows down (instead of dramatically dropping them, as had been her first instinct) and reached for Amelia, pulling her in with a deep kiss. Only the fluffy blanket came between them, which was a little awkward—but not that awkward. "I love you, which I know I've already said, but I feel like I've never expressed how much it means to me that you care about magic and spells, and how they interact with people and with places, and how powerful it can be when you share that with someone else."

Amelia blinked in the slight glow of light emanating from the doorway beside them. "All of that means a lot to me too, Bryn. Thank you for sharing this with me."

Amelia's jasmine scent and the distant sea seemed to fill Bryn's awareness, and she indulgently took deep breaths as if she could drink it all in. She leaned in closer, brushed her cheek against Amelia's, and whispered, "But we are going to have sex, right? Because the blanket, the pillows, the hotness."

Amelia laughed. "Yes, you oaf, get the pillows. I've set something up. Come on."

It had never occurred to Bryn to think about how large the broomstick monument at the top of the castle actually was, but now she could see up close just how big it was.

"How did they do this?" she asked, staring up.

"I don't know, but the magical infusion is really strong," Amelia said, passing her hand along the surface of one of the broomsticks. "It makes you tingle, like . . . I don't know, static electricity."

"Power poles," Bryn suggested. "If you stand in the right place, and they kind of buzz the air around you."

"Yes, like that, but magic. Anyway, given all that, I thought it might be an interesting place to . . ."

"Fuck?" Bryn suggested.

"Heck yes," Amelia said, smiling. "Yes, I thought it would be an interesting place to fuck. Fuck me, Bryn Delmar." She spread the blanket out just under where the two statue broomsticks met, the inverted V of their crossing.

Bryn set the pillows down as well, then drew Amelia to her. "Are you sure no one can see us up here?"

"Yes. Though I don't think I want to be bound to one of the broomsticks, if it's all the same to you."

"Well, that hadn't occurred to me, but now that it has, we should definitely figure out a way to try it. But no, I just want to see my . . . er . . ."

"Girlfriend," Amelia said firmly.

"My girlfriend." Bryn kissed her. "My lover."

"Oh yes. Yes."

Bryn loved to undress Amelia, but she also loved this moment, when Amelia undressed on her own and exposed every part of herself just for Bryn. She lay back on the blanket, and waved a hand upward until the broomsticks were illuminated as if glowing from within, a warm pink light that bathed both of them. Satisfied, she lifted her arms over her head and said, "What do you think?"

Bryn fell upon her—passion, love, a certain amount of sexual desperation, and also something else, something she had never attained with any lover before: a sense of assurance. She could do whatever she liked; Amelia could do whatever she liked as well. They could occupy this space together and take each other to new places, explore new ideas, new worlds, new positions, whatever their imaginations could conceive.

Arousal stirred in Bryn's blood, but all she did for a very long time was kiss Amelia—her lips, her cheeks, over each eye, down her throat. She used lips and tongue and teeth, listening for the sounds of Amelia's breath catching. Whatever magic lay on the broomsticks, on the roof, it held them in place. Everything on the other side of it was less distinct, less real—the only thing in the world was the two of them.

Bryn was still dressed and remained that way until Amelia's hands descended on her buttons, where they paused as Amelia looked up at her. "Yes," Bryn said. So Amelia unbuttoned her; together they managed to get rid of the rest of Bryn's clothes. And this time it was Amelia who guided her down, who laid her out; Amelia, whose lips traced paths everywhere on her body, whose teeth tugging at a nipple gently, far more gently than Bryn had done. It did not take force or effort to provide intense sensation in that moment. Bryn's back arched off the blanket and she mewled. One of Amelia's hands strayed downward, pressing Bryn open, finding her clit, only teasing it as she teased Bryn's nipple with her lips.

"Come on," Bryn said, opening her legs wider in the hopes of inviting those playful fingers to do more than play.

"Hmm?" Amelia asked innocently. "What was that you said?"

"Amelia," Bryn growled.

"This is such a fun game." Amelia had the audacity to lay her head down over Bryn's bare torso, as if watching her own fingers toy with Bryn's body, dancing across her belly and thighs, before finally sliding inside her. "Here?" Amelia asked.

"Faster, harder . . . something. Gods, why are you doing this to me?" Bryn heard the utter demolishment in her own voice and giggled, feeling absurd and needy and like if Amelia did not do *something* very soon, she would fall apart. "I really don't understand why you decided now was a good time to tor—" But before she could plead about being tortured, Amelia slid three fingers inside and Bryn gasped. "More," she whispered.

"Greedy," Amelia said, using her fingers slowly, deeply, spreading them, making Bryn gasp.

"When did you become a sadist?" Bryn demanded.

"I'm not. I'm giving you what you need. Aren't I, Professor?"

Bryn, caught between laughter and edging closer

towards orgasm, managed a rough, "Please, Headmistress." She could see the flush on Amelia's face as their eyes met.

After a moment, fingers still slow, still torturous, Amelia murmured, "Wow, that really does it for me. I'm not okay with this, necessarily, but say it again, please."

"Can I come, Headmistress?" Bryn asked, and though she tried to sound sweet, she only managed a sort of helpless pleading.

Amelia's movements sped up. She lowered her face to gently suck Bryn's clit, and Bryn felt herself begin to tip over the edge. It was too much. It was not enough. It was everything, all at once. She teetered there, bucking up against Amelia, and then finally, Amelia did the thing she needed. Strokes in and out, faster and faster, her lips applying suction, her tongue lapping, and Bryn cried out, her entire body going rigid with pleasure as she climaxed, and climaxed, and held the peak for longer than she even knew was possible, before finally coming down and pulling Amelia over her.

The bespelled broomsticks towered over them, casting the world in shades of pink and gray. They lay together side by side. Bryn pulled one of Amelia's legs over her hip so she could idly explore Amelia's slick cunt with her fingers, drawing out her pleasure far more torturously than she had drawn out Bryn's—even pulling away for seconds, whole seconds, coaxing Amelia slowly towards begging.

It was a struggle. Bryn couldn't help smiling as Amelia bit her lip, determined to be strong, to resist. Tension lined her face and the occasional gasp slipped from her lips. Bryn would touch, slip, roll, and Amelia would look at her with all the trust in the world, until finally her resolve broke. Her fingers dug into the back of Bryn's neck as she dragged Bryn in for a kiss, whispering, "*Please, please.*"

And that was all it took. Amelia didn't like it as hard and deep as Bryn did. What Amelia liked was wide and open. Bryn rolled her gently onto her back and pressed her legs apart, using both of her hands to expose Amelia's clit (which she knew Amelia found hot as hell, vulnerable and terribly arousing), and then went at it until she screamed.

It was glorious, beautiful, and the rush of power, of making someone else feel this good, this abandoned, was everything. Bryn's own body pulsed with the rush of Amelia's orgasm, and if she hadn't been so exhausted, she might have gone again.

Instead, she nuzzled into Amelia's neck and pulled the end of the blanket over both of them so they could lie together and stare up at the stars beyond the broomsticks.

"This is our secret," Bryn said softly. "This place."

"I agree, but . . ." Amelia hesitated. "Is it weird that I'm glad people know about us? I mean, they must—the kids told us to kiss."

"I'm glad too. There are secrets that make things better, and then there are secrets that don't. If we had to pretend to everyone we know that we weren't together, I think that would be hard."

"Plus," Amelia added, "I want everyone to know I'm fucking the famous author, Bryn Delmar."

Bryn laughed. "And I'm fucking the headmistress, which is hot. Hotter, I would argue, if in a different way."

"I guess we're both having sex with someone we admire."

"Damn right." Bryn kissed Amelia under the broomsticks, the stars, the moon, in a bubble of magic and spellfire—something she would be happy to do for the rest of her life.

Acknowledgements

I owe the deepest gratitude to the odd, meandering threads of story and timing that brought me the world of this book. In roughly a weekend, I went from feeling stumped about what project to work on next, to feeling absolutely obsessed with this book and these characters.

A thousand sparkly thanks to Leni Kauffman, who made such a gorgeous, whimsical cover for this book that I freaked out all over everyone about how much I loved it. (Even my *teenager* was impressed. He continues to refer to this as "the one with the really good cover.")

Epic gratitude to Phoebe MacKinlay and Cheyenne Faircloth, who read roughly eighteen drafts of this first chapter (maybe not that many, but then again . . .), and had the very best feedback to help me discover the voice of the book (and the flavor of the world).

From first to last, I have absolutely loved working with Amy Mae Baxter and everyone else at Avon UK— the process has been quick, predictable, and full of laughter!

And my deepest thanks to my agent, Courtney Miller-Callihan at Handspun Literary, who always cheers me on, even when I'm like, "So idk, I think I can prob write this book in like a month and a half. Right?"

Grimoire Academy's castle and grounds were inspired by Hearst Castle in San Simeon, California—a stunning complex financed by the most extreme yellow journalism, but designed by one of the first women in the US to have her own architectural firm, Julia Morgan.

So many people were so incredibly supportive when I said I was writing a witchy romance. The world clearly needs more of them! Hooray for magic and laughter and love!